shadows in the asylum
The Case Files of Dr. Charles Marsh

D.A. Stern

emmis
books

Emmis Books
1700 Madison Road
Cincinnati, Ohio 45206
www.emmisbooks.com

For further information, contact the publisher at:

Emmis Books
1700 Madison Road
Cincinnati, Ohio 45206
www.emmisbooks.com

Library of Congress Cataloging-in-Publication Data

Stern, D. A. (David A.)

Shadows in the asylum : the case files of Dr. Charles Marsh / D.A. Stern.

p. cm.

ISBN-13: 978-1-57860-204-9

ISBN-10: 1-57860-204-1

1. Psychiatric hospital patients--Fiction.

2. Executions and executioners--Fiction.

3. Wisconsin--Fiction. 1. Title.

PS3569.T3884A85 2005

813'.6--dc22

2004061969

Distributed by Publishers Group West
Interior designed by Matthew De Rhodes
Cover designed by Heather Francis
Cover photo by Anna Schuleit
Edited by Jessica Yerega

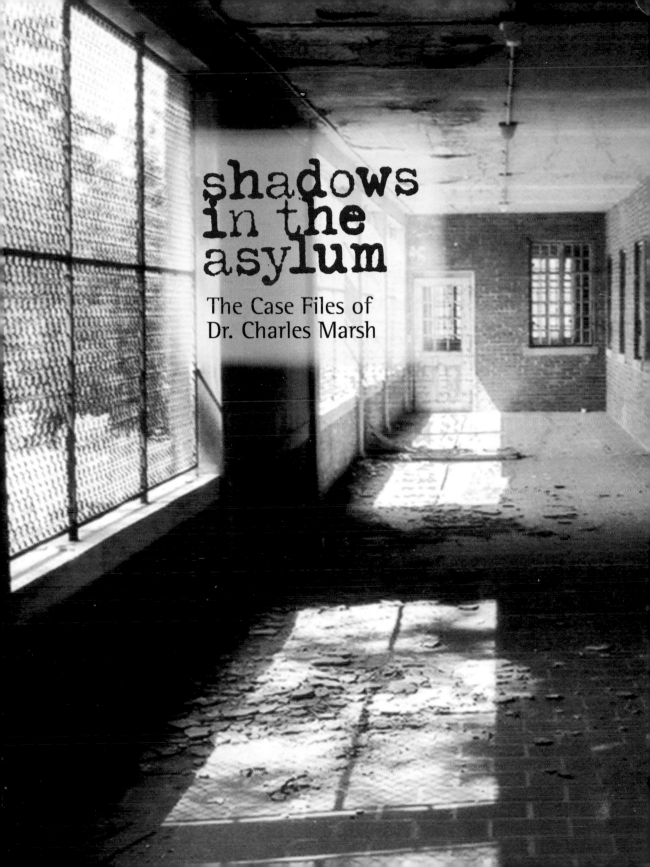

shadows in the asylum

The Case Files of
Dr. Charles Marsh

About the Author

D.A. Stern is the author of several previous works of fiction and nonfiction, including *The Blair Witch Project: A Dossier, Black Dawn, Your Secrets Are My Business* (with Kevin McKeown), and *Enterprise: Daedalus's Children.* A former editor for several well-known New York City publishing houses and a former guitarist for several unknown New York City bands, he currently lives in Northampton, Massachusetts, with his family and two very pointy dogs.

Fear made the gods.

—Scottish Proverb

They called me mad, and I called them mad,
And damn them, they outvoted me.

—Nathaniel Lee

INTRODUCTION

A door creaks. Leaves rustle. And in the dark corners of our mind, something stirs.

Dinosaur bones give birth to the legend of dragons, Vlad the Impaler's horrific crimes to the myth of Dracula ...

Clearly, the human imagination is a wondrous beast.

Where does one draw the line between science and superstition? Between reality and hallucination? Between madman and visionary?

To paraphrase one of our century's most noted storytellers: We submit herein for your consideration the papers of Dr. Charles Marsh—a name no doubt familiar to many of you, thanks to the recent spate of publicity both he and the Kriegmoor Psychiatric Institute have received. The media, of course, has focused on the more ghoulish aspects of Dr. Marsh's affairs; the documents you will find within this volume represent the story behind that story. A potpourri of materials—patient records, historical documents, the doctor's own, fevered scribblings—that comprise an article Marsh was in the process of writing when destiny overtook him. An article that begins with his attempts to cure a single patient's persistent, remarkably vivid hallucinations—and ends in the doctor's unquestioning acceptance of those visions as reality. An article that finds precedent for the "shadows" that tormented young Kari Hansen within the legends of certain Native American tribes, within the writings of philosophers and scientists and musicians, within the ceremonies of the world's most ancient religions. An article in which Marsh purports to provide incontrovertible proof that alongside the everyday reality we experience, there exists another, populated by creatures of angelic and demonic intent.

It is, to be sure, an outrageous claim. To complicate matters, Marsh's arguments are at times hard to follow; events at Kriegmoor rapidly outran his ability to record them lucidly. At a certain point, he began to physically cut and paste his work together in order to accommodate changes in his thinking. Nonetheless, at the very least, we must grant Marsh this: He raises a series of provocative questions, the answers to which modern-day science cannot, as yet, provide.

What you are about to read represents my best efforts at reconstructing the doctor's thought processes. There are gaps in his writing and reasoning, but rather than attempt to bridge those gaps myself, I have provided documents found within his papers that I believe illustrate the point he was attempting to make.

Regarding those documents, I must thank Lucius McCormick, a longtime friend of the doctor's, for providing me exclusive access to Marsh's work during a time when the media at large was clamoring for them as well. Thanks are also due to Red Lion books for permission to reproduce the extracts from Raymond Laszlo's work, Leslie Dunnington for similar graciousness regarding the article by Roy Jennings on "those who came before," Walter McKinnon of the Northern Peninsula Historical Society for his assistance, and Don Dunleavy, who at seventy-one still has more energy than most twenty-year-olds.

As you consider Marsh's arguments—his work, his words, the historical precedents he provides—I ask you to consider the following as well.

We live in an age of renewed faith, of an increasingly shared understanding that when we view the world only through the narrow prism of science, much remains hidden from us. Many would contend that the ancient scriptures that speak to us of higher beings— and alternate realities—are not just superstitious parable, but eyewitness testimony, revelations of a world beyond that occasionally peeks through into our plane of existence. Call it heaven, or hell, or the nth dimension, or what you will.

This, in essence, is Dr. Charles Marsh's contention. These papers, his legacy. View them as a window into his thinking, not an excuse for his actions, which I suspect the doctor himself would now readily grant are largely unforgivable.

On his behalf then, I ask you to open your mind, and considering the following.

D.A. Stern

Las Vegas

July 18, 2005

SHADOWS IN THE ASYLUM

Charles Marsh, M.D., Ph.D.

Jo
2 Fo
deriv

KARI HANSEN

DRAFT MATERIAL: NOT FOR PUBLICATION
ARTICLE TITLE: SHADOWS IN THE ASYLUM
AUTHOR: Charles Marsh, M.D., Ph.D.

PREFATORY NOTE:

Due to the circumstances surrounding the trial of Richard Dale
Lattimore and my role therein, I achieved a certain notoriety,
albeit an unfavorable notoriety, within the community of my peers[1].
A number of them, no doubt, were certain I would never practice
psychiatry again. Even among those I had worked with closely,
who knew the facts of the Lattimore trial and knew of the faulty
information I had relied upon while testifying, probably expected
me to, if not retire completely, then to shun the spotlight, to
find a place to work far from the glare of publicity, and devote
my time to working with patients and atoning for the past. They
will be surprised to see my name in print, attached to what it
is likely to be one of the most controversial papers ever written
in the field, surprised that I would open up my life, my past once
again for public scrutiny. Perhaps some will see this paper as my
attempt to regain professional respectability. I wish to state for
the record that this is most emphatically not the case.

A scientist – and we psychiatrists are indeed scientists,
popular perception to the contrary – is compelled to go where
the facts lead, to reach only the conclusions supported by those
facts, and, as circumstances dictate, to take action as dictated
by those facts, no matter the consequences. Thus it was during the
Lattimore trial; thus it has been here as well.

The facts in this case arise from data gathered during my
work with a series of patients classified as treatment-resistant
schizophrenics, in particular a young female patient who for the
purposes of this article I will designate "K." I shall begin, in
fact, by relating in brief my treatment of "K" upon my appointment
to the staff of the Kriegmoor Psychiatric Hospital[2] in Bayfield,

[handwritten: (NOTE TO SELF: ↓ INSERT PATIENT INFORMATION SUMMARIZE AND REMOVE ALL IDENTIFYING DETAILS)]

1 Lincoln and Cox, "Dr. Charles Marsh and the case against 'future dangerousness.'
Journal of Psychiatric Clinicians, Jan. 2004, pp. 8-14.
2 Formerly the Kriegmoor Lunatic Asylum, from which the title of this article is
derived.

Overlooking the pristine beauty of Lake Superior and the ruggedly scenic Apostle Islands, Kriegmoor Psychiatric Hospital provides private pay residential services for persons with bipolar and psychotic disorders. Offering state-of-the-art medical facilities, experts in all manner of psychiatric care, and a dedicated, experienced nursing staff, Kriegmoor provides an ideal healing environment, specializing in the long-term care of treatment-resistant schizophrenics.

Kriegmoor Psychiatric was founded in 1898 by local industrialist Herman Kriegmoor after his wife fell victim to a crippling mental illness. Now entering its second century of care to the community, Kriegmoor Psychiatric continues to be on the cutting edge of treatment for mental health-related disorders.

Medical Director:
Claire Morris, MD

Superintendent of Nursing:
Althea Blackburn, MEd

CONTINUING CARE PROGRAM

The Continuing Care Program provides long-term residential treatment on hospital grounds. The mission of the program is to provide unique, personalized, comprehensive psychiatric and rehabilitative care. Each resident has an individualized treatment team consisting of a primary care psychiatrist, assisted by the hospital's patient review board, nursing staff, and other qualified psychologists (as needed). Care decisions are made by the primary care psychiatrist in consultation with the director and the patient's family.

Transcripts of all sessions are provided to the review board and the patient's family via in-house recording and software transcription programs.

KRIEGMOOR HOUSE

An exemplar of Kirkbride-style architecture, Kriegmoor House provides residents with a home-like setting in an historic building. There are semi-private and private bedrooms, a common living area with television and VCR, kitchen and dining room where staff and residents prepare and serve meals, a conference room and staff areas. All glass in the building is shatterproof -

continued on back

no sharp objects or potential weapons of any kind are permitted in the living areas.

Residents undergo comprehensive psychiatric assessment upon admission to the program. With their case managers, residents plan individual and group treatment experiences utilizing Kriegmoor's diverse resources. There are house meetings for goal setting, symptom management, medication education and transition. Family meetings, treatment reviews and necessary consultations for psychiatric, medical and neurological concerns are arranged through the program. Once residents accomplish the goals of their treatment, they may transition to community-based homes, to supported apartments or to independent living.

Kriegmoor
Psychiatric
Institute

Red Cliff Parkway
Bayfield, WI 48544

Wisconsin

KRIEGMOOR
PSYCHIATRIC INSTITUTE

Red Cliff Parkway — Bayfield WI 48544

KRIEGMOOR
PSYCHIATRIC INSTITUTE

TO: "staff"<list-admin@kriegmoor-psychiatric.org>

FROM: claire_morris@kriegmoor-psychiatric.org

DATE: 9/8/04

RE: DR. CHARLES MARSH

It gives me great pleasure to announce the appointment of Dr. Charles
Marsh to our resident staff at Kriegmoor. Dr. Marsh, who has spent the
last year on sabbatical, is a graduate of Brown University in Providence,
Rhode Island, where he also received his doctorate. He has extensive
clinical experience, having worked at the Institute for Living at Hartford
for several years, and was also recently affiliated with the State Mental
Health Board in Austin Texas.

Please join me in welcoming Dr. Marsh to Kriegmoor.

MEDLOG 1.2

MEDLOG AUTOMATED TRANSCRIPTION SERVICES
SESSION INFORMATION

CLIENT: KRIEGMOOR PSYCHIATRIC
PATIENT (PT): KARI HANSEN
THERAPIST (TH): DR. CHARLES MARSH
DATE OF SESSION: 9/12/04
SYSTEM PARAMETERS: LANGUAGE DETECT/ENGLISH LINE RETURN DELAY/8 SECONDS
SILENCE THRESHOLD: -5.4 DB FILE FORMAT: MS WORD

SESSION TEXT

1
2 TH: Hello. Are you Kari?
3 TH: Hi, Kari. I'm Dr. Marsh. Can I come in for a minute?
4 TH: I'm just going to sit down right here, okay? Move this tray out of the way
      so we can talk for a minute...there. I take it you didn't care for the meat loaf.
5 TH: I can have them bring you something else if you want - some toast, maybe
      some soup...
6 TH: No? Okay. Well, I'm sorry to get here so late. I've just - I'm new here at
7   Kriegmoor and I've been making rounds all day, saying hi to all the patients
8   here and you, unfortunately, are at the end of the list. Normally I'll be coming
      in the morning to talk to you, but tonight I -
9 PT: Oh my god.
10 TH: Kari?
11
12
13
14 PT: There's one now. Right there - can't you see? On the wall. It must have -
      it followed you in. Oh my god. Help me, somebody please, help me!
15 TH: Kari, there's no one here but you and me. Please take it easy. Kari!
16 TH: Nurse!
17
18
19
20 [TRANSCRIPT ENDS]
21

MEDLOG 1.2

MEDLOG AUTOMATED TRANSCRIPTION SERVICES
SESSION INFORMATION

CLIENT: KRIEGMOOR PSYCHIATRIC
PATIENT (PT): DARRELL COVEY
THERAPIST (TH): DR. CHARLES MARSH
DATE OF SESSION: 9/12/04
SYSTEM PARAMETERS: LANGUAGE DETECT/ENGLISH LINE RETURN DELAY:8 SECONDS
SILENCE THRESHOLD: -5.4 DB FILE FORMAT: MS WORD

SESSION TEXT (CONTINUED)

1 TH: And what do the voices say, Darrell?
2 PT: Why do you keep calling me Darrell?
3 TH: That's your name, isn't it?
4 PT: Is it? Maybe it is. Maybe that's what it's supposed to be. You could be right,
5   I could be wrong.
6 TH: Let's talk about the voices, Darrell.
7 PT: Let's talk about the song.
8 PT: I still can do it, see? I can rhyme with the best of them.
9 TH: That's a very good rhyme Darrell. You're certainly right about that. Now these
10   voices - what do they say?
11 PT: It wasn't my fault. I shouldn't feel bad. But I do - bad and sad sometimes glad
12   sometimes mad a little insane as in loose in the brain.
13 TH: Okay Darrell...
14 PT: Why do you keep calling me Darrell?
15 [Pause]
16 TH: We seem to keep coming back to that, don't we? What would you like me to
17   call you?
18 PT: I don't know. How about the ego that walks like a man? That's what Pete
19   always called me.
20 TH: And who is Pete? Is he one of the voices?
21 PT: Pete? No. He's not a voice.
22 TH: Who is he then?
23 PT: He was my co-pilot.
24 TH: Was.
25 PT: Oh yes. Was. That ship has sailed.
26
27 [TRANSCRIPT ENDS]
28
29
30
31
32

KRIEGMOOR
PSYCHIATRIC INSTITUTE

TO: c_marsh@kriegmoor-psychiatric.org

FROM: claire_morris@kriegmoor-psychiatric.org

DATE: 9/13/04

RE: PATIENT HA-09

I'm sure that wasn't the reception you were hoping for but please doctor
- don't take it personally. She does that - or something like that - to
everyone. Poor girl.

Hardcopy of her file will be on your desk in the morning. To summarize,
patient was admitted 8/29/03; received multiple drug protocols (primary
and atypical anti-psychotics taken singly and in combination) as well as
behavioral therapy, all of which have proven ineffective to date. Mother
has refused ECT as an option.

Don't spend too much time on this one, doctor: HA-09's schizophrenia was
classified as treatment-resistant as of 3/1/04.

KRIEGMOOR
PSYCHIATRIC INSTITUTE

Red Cliff Parkway
Bayfield, WI 48544

HANSEN SOLUTIONS

PATIENT NAME: Kari Hansen
DOB: 4/11/83
S: F
H: 5'5"
W: 124
EYES: Blue
HAIR: Blond
ADMIT DATE: 8/29/03

Adults or children 13 or older must meet the terms and conditions contained in items 1, 2, and 3, and two sub-items contained in 4 through 5.

A child 12 or younger must meet the terms and conditions contained in items 1, 2 and 3, one sub-item in 4, and one sub-item in 5.

Circle the decision made on each item.

(YES) NO 1. Any DSM-IV AXIS I primary diagnosis – with the exception of V-Codes and Adjustment Disorders – accompanied by a detailed description of the symptoms supporting the diagnosis. In lieu of a qualifying Axis I diagnosis, persons over 13 years of age may have an Axis II diagnosis of any Personality Disorder.

(YES) NO 2. Conditions are directly attributable to a mental disorder as the primary need for professional attention. (This does not include placement issues, criminal behavior, or status offenses.) Adjustment Disorders or Substance-Related Disorders may be a secondary Axis I diagnosis, as per reviewer's discretion.

(YES) NO 3. It has been determined by the reviewer that the current disabling symptoms could not have been managed, or have not been manageable, in a less intensive treatment program.

(YES) NO 4. Within the past 48 hours, the behaviors present an imminent life-threatening emergency as evidenced by:

    YES (NO) A. Specifically described suicide attempts, suicide intent, or serious threat by the patient

    YES (NO) B. Specifically described patterns of escalating incidents of self-mutilating behaviors.

    YES (NO) C. Specifically described episodes of unprovoked significant physical aggression and patterns of escalating physical aggression in intensity and duration.

    (YES) NO D. Specifically described episodes of incapacitating depression or psychosis that result in an inability to function or care for basic needs.

(YES) NO 5. Requires secure 24-hour nursing or medical supervision as evidenced by:

    YES (NO) A. Stabilization of Acute psychiatric symptoms.

    YES (NO) B. Needs extensive treatment under physician direction.

    YES (NO) C. Physiological evidence or expectation of withdrawal symptoms which require 24-hour medical supervision.

74
75
76

MEDLOG TRANSCRIPT ... VICES
... ers in Your Business, Partners in Your Patients' Health"
... Duluth MN 08953-0989

HANSEN SOLUTIONS

1309 W. 6th Street
Bayfield Heights WI 48989

August 29, 2003

Accounts Payable Department
The Kriegmoor Psychiatric Institute
Red Cliff Parkway
Bayfield WI 48544

RE: KARI HANSEN

To whom it may concern:

Enclosed please find the completed informational form for your facility. Under separate cover you will be receiving a copy of my daughter's medical records, as well as the diary I had mentioned. I trust you will treat the material therein in strictest confidence.

As per my conversation with the director, Dr. Morris, I understand that as Kriegmoor is a private, for-profit institution, the cost of my daughter's stay there will not be covered by our insurance. With this letter, I agree to be financially responsible for Kari's account. Once you and your staff have finalized my daughter's fee schedule for the first few months, please forward same to me and I would be happy to remit a portion of that sum in good faith.

And as I hope I made clear, I want my daughter under constant supervision. Twenty-four hours a day, seven days a week, until I (and of course, your staff) are convinced she is no longer at risk of harming herself and until whatever sort of drugs she's abused have been throughly cleansed from her system.

Please confirm receipt of this letter with my office.

Cordially,

Ingrid Hansen

Ingrid Hansen

NAME: Kari Hansen
DATE OF BIRTH: 4/11/83
DATES OF ASSESSMENT: 9/2/03, 9/3/03
PAGE 1

Background Information & Reason for Referral

Kari is a twenty-year-old college student involuntarily hospitalized at Kriegmoor after a psychological collapse on August 18, 2003. She has exhibited depressive mood state accompanied by hallucinations and recurrent sleep disorder. Kari's primary care physician, Dr. Walter Shimmelman, directed her to Kriegmoor Psychiatric for long-term in-patient care.

According to Ms. Hansen, Kari's breakdown is attributable to substance abuse which took place while Kari was on a field research program from 6/13/03 to 8/18/03 (date of collapse, above – see accompanying police report). Mother admitted not knowing many details of Kari's everyday life at program. She described daughter as "mostly happy, though given to bouts of depression at times." She further characterized Kari as "very empathetic." No prior history of drug abuse, no prior history of psychological troubles.

Kari is an A student, anthropology major. Her extracurricular activities included writing for the college newspaper and working on the local reservation in the Big Sisters program. She has a few close girlfriends, no regular boyfriend though according to Ms. Hansen her daughter dated frequently. Parents divorced when Kari was six years old, father had infrequent contact with family subsequent to that date. Father deceased 3/93 (suicide) when Kari was ten.

Developmental History

Kari is an only child. Ms. Hansen is now 45, raised Kari as single mom since Kari was six. Ms. Hansen noted no history of mental illness on her side of the family or her husband's. Kari had a broken leg at age 17 in a skiing accident; otherwise, no significant medical history. According to Dr. Shimmelman, she was in excellent physical condition at time of last check-up, 8/12/01.

Behavioral Observations

Evaluations took place early a.m., 9-9:30, on day of admission to Kriegmoor. Kari presented a disheveled appearance, and was generally non-responsive to questioning.

Summary & Recommendations

Kari Hansen, a twenty-year-old Caucasian female, right-handed, was admitted to Kriegmoor 8/29/03

    Diagnostic Impressions
        Axis I: Schizophrenia, Psychotic Disorder (NOS)
            Mixed Episode Occurence
            Depressive Disorder, Recurrent
            Sleep Disorder (NOS)

Axis II: None
    Axis III: None
    Axis IV: None
    Axis V: GAF = 50 (current)

Recommendations are as follows:

1. Due to the current severity and chronicity of Kari's hallucinations, medication is indicated. Care should be taken with the dosage to insure it does not further affect her depressed state.
2. Psychiatric analysis is indicated.

Submitted 9/3/03

MEDLOG AUTOMATED TRANSCRIPTION SERVICES
SESSION INFORMATION

CLIENT: KRIEGMOOR PSYCHIATRIC
PATIENT (PT): KARI HANSEN
THERAPIST (TH): DR. CHARLES MARSH
DATE OF SESSION: 9/16/04
SYSTEM PARAMETERS: LANGUAGE DETECT/ENGLISH LINE RETURN DELAY/8 SECONDS
                   SILENCE THRESHOLD: -5.4 DB FILE FORMAT: MS WORD

SESSION TEXT (CONTINUED)

1 TH: Hello again, Kari. I'm Dr. Marsh. Remember - I was in here the other night?

2 TH: Good. So how are you doing today?

3 TH: This is going to be our regular time together, Kari. Three times a week. We'll
4 talk about the same kinds of things you and Dr. Ferguson talked about, we'll
5 see if we can't figure out ways to make your time here a little easier, okay? But
6 that's for later - today, I thought we'd just get to know each other. How does
7 that sound?

8 TH: Why don't I start? Now, believe it or not, we have a lot in common. I was born
9 right here in Bayfield just like you. But I left as soon as I could - went to school
10 in Rhode Island, then I worked at a place called the Institute for Living in
11 Hartford for - oh, let me think - three years, and then I went all the way across
12 the country again to Texas - to Austin. Friend of mine from school hired me to
13 work with him. Lucius McCormick. I did that for a few years, and then I...I took
14 some time off. And as I was thinking about going back to work,
15 I heard about this job at Kriegmoor - Lucius had recommended me for it, actu-
16 ally - and now here I am, right back where I started. Right in my hometown.

17 TH: So let's talk a little bit about you now, Kari. You've been at Kriegmoor
18 since..let's see, September 2003. Just about a year. According to the records,
19 you were away from home at the time you had a nervous breakdown. Nothing
20 like that had ever happened to you before, had it?

21 PT: No.

22 TH: It must have been frightening. You were - let me see here - you were a student
23 at Cole College, an anthropology major, working on an archaeological dig.

24 PT: Yes.

25 TH: Sounds like a lot of physical labor - a lot of up with the sun, work outside all day
26 kind of thing. That right?

27 PT: I guess.

28 TH: Sounds like a pretty advanced program. Was it hard to get into?

29 PT: I think so. I guess.

30 TH: So you must have been excited to be there.

31 TH: Were you, Kari - excited to be in the program?

32 PT: Yes. Yes, I was very excited.

Two Prentiss Circle
Bayfield, WI 48454

Beadle Hall / Anthropology Department

May 8, 2003

Kari Hansen
1483 4th Street
Bayfield Corners, WI 48454

Dear Kari:

Congratulations! On behalf of the Cole College anthropology department, I'm excited to notify you that you've been chosen to participate in the 2003 Summer Research Project. A group of nine students will accompany myself and Professor Martha Carlson to Lake Superior's Apostle Island chain, where we will continue research begun during last summer's program.

The program runs from June 13th through August 29th, with a break from July 2-5 for the holiday weekend. This is an archaeological dig, with sites ranging all over the island chain. Students are expected to bring their own clothing and sleeping bags: camping equipment, food supplies, and transportation to and from the college campus will be provided. We stress the highly physical nature of this dig; clothing should be minimal and casual. Spending money should be provided, as every Sunday of the dig we will take a ferry back to the town of Bayfield on the mainland. Students are expected to adhere to the college code of conduct; violations will result in immediate dismissal from the program and possible academic sanctions.

Here is a complete list of those chosen to participate.

Tomas Arundsen	Eileen Bart	Laura Drake
Robert Frederickson	Vicki Gayler	Kari Hansen
John Reardon	Jeff Sakowski	Lorna Whitesley

If you have any questions, please don't hesitate to contact me either by phone or e-mail. If for some reason you must decline this invitation, we need to hear from you immediately.

Otherwise, I look forward to seeing you bright and early on the morning of June 13th. A bus will leave promptly at 7:00 a.m. from the circle in front of the administration building to take us to the ferry.

Congratulations again, Kari.

Best,

John Czelusniak
Chair, Anthropology Department

CC COLE COLLEGE

Anthropology Department
Field Research Project

UNCOVERING:
the Copper Culture Indians

Summer 2003 Teams
June 13-August 29, 2003

Supervisors:
Professor John Czelusniak
Assistant Professor Marty Carlson

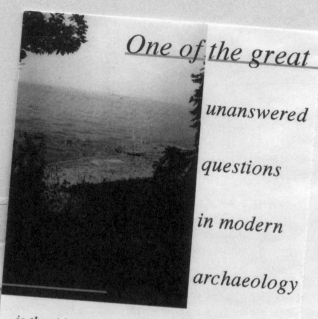

One of the great unanswered questions in modern archaeology

is the riddle of the people known colloquially as the Copper Culture Indians. Named for the tools found at relevant sites, this prehistoric civilization, dated in some instances back to 7000 B.C., apparently possessed sophisticated mining techniques far ahead of their time, and was at the center of an extensive trading network that may have stretched across the globe. Yet at the height of their power and influence, they abruptly disappeared, vanishing from the pages of history completely. What could have caused them to so completely abandon their homes? What evidence of their daily rituals, their gods and religious beliefs, their leaders and their lives remains as yet-undiscovered? Our program will attempt to answer those questions and others.

The most impressive relics
of Copper Culture civilization
have been found on Isle Royale,
in Northern Lake Superior.
We will be conducting digs
at various locations throughout
Wisconsin's Apostle Islands,
near the present-day Red Cliff
Indian Reservation.

Participants in the program will spend a total of eight weeks - two non-consecutive four week periods - working with professors to accomplish the program's goals. A limited number of slots in the program are available, and competition for those slots is always spirited. To apply, please prepare a 5000 word essay enumerating relevant scholastic achievement, prior field research experience, and your particular qualifications for this program. Essays must be submitted to the department chair by March 1; this is a non-flexible date. Students chosen for the program will be notified by mail by May 15.

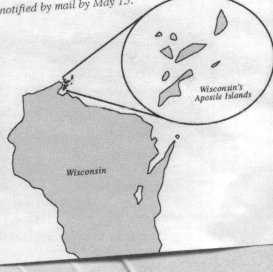

Wisconsin's Apostle Islands

Wisconsin

MEDLOG 1.2

MEDLOG AUTOMATED TRANSCRIPTION SERVICES
SESSION INFORMATION

CLIENT: KRIEGMOOR PSYCHIATRIC
PATIENT (PT): KARI HANSEN
HERAPIST (TH): DR. CHARLES MARSH
DATE OF SESSION: 9/19/04
SYSTEM PARAMETERS: LANGUAGE DETECT/ENGLISH LINE RETURN DELAY/8 SECONDS
SILENCE THRESHOLD: -5.4 DB FILE FORMAT: MS WORD

SESSION TEXT (CONTINUED)

1 TH: so no clues as to what happened to this civilization...why all these people just
2 up and vanished?
3 PT: No.
4 TH: Fascinating. Well...besides the work...I bet you had a lot of fun. Usually when
5 a group of people go away together like that - they become a pretty tight-knit
6 group. Good friends.
7 TH: What do you think about the people you were with that summer? Were they
8 your friends?
9 TH: Kari, I'm looking at your file here, and I see that your mother has instructed us
10 not to permit you any visitors without her written permission. She specifically
11 mentions the people from the dig that summer.
12 PT: I know.
13 TH: How do you feel about that?
14 PT: I don't know.
15 TH: Do you want visitors?
16 PT: My mom doesn't want them to come here, so..
17 TH: It's okay with you.
18 PT: I guess.
19 TH: Kari. Are you and your mom close?
20 PT: Oh yes. Very close.
21 TH: She raised you all by herself.
22 PT: Yes.
23 TH: Since your parents divorced.
24 PT: My dad is dead.
25 TH: Were the two of you close?
26 PT: I didn't see him much.
27 TH: Sounds like you regret that.
28 PT: I guess. I could have been nicer to him. Should have been nicer.
29 TH: Do you think about him a lot?
30 PT: Sometimes. More now than I used to. But my mom and I are really tight. She
31 looks out for me, my mom.
32 TH: Yes. Yes, I can see that she does.

KRIEGMOOR
PSYCHIATRIC INSTITUTE

TO: c_marsh@kriegmoor-psychiatric.org
FROM: ingrid.hansen@hansensolutions.com
DATE: 9/20/04
RE: YOUR E-MAIL

Dear Dr. Marsh:

First of all, I'm sorry we haven't had a chance to formally introduce ourselves yet. My schedule permitting, I do hope to get up there within the next week to see my daughter. I understand from Dr. Morris that you've made some degree of progress in getting her to open up. I want you to know I'm genuinely excited about that and am of course appreciative of your efforts.

In the meantime, though, just so my wishes are perfectly clear, I do not want anyone from the program - anyone, and that includes the professors who were supposed to be supervising my daughter, who I consider complicit in what happened to Kari - visiting her without my express written permission. Which, by the way, I have no intention of granting until I see and speak with my daughter and judge her condition for myself.

Cordially yours,
Ingrid Hansen

P.S. - I hope I don't seem unduly harsh in this matter, doctor, but I only want what's best for my girl. You have her diary: you know what they did to her.

THIS DIARY BELONGS TO:
KARI HANSEN
NORTH HALL, ROOM 1205
COLE COLLEGE
BAYFIELD WI.

PRIVATE AND PERSONAL
REWARD IF FOUND

hate the task. Doesn't matter if it's heinies or Stevens Point beer makes me gag. I don't know why he doesn't get that. Anyway...

Good night journal.

July 6

Back to Stockton Island, back to reality. Fingernails caked with dirt, pb&j sandwiches and more mosquitos than you can shake a shovel at. The first person to invent a bug spray that actually works— I will get down on my knees and kiss their ass for a month

It's about 8 o'clock on our first night back after the break

It was oddly good to get back to camp and see everybody again. I was so sick of them when I left and of course the second I got home

I missed them. This must be what it's like to be on a team - like a football team or whatever - where it's all for one and one for all. You go through something really hard~~and~~ together and it brings you close. Kind of like war I guess.
The camraderie of war.
Of course none of us are likely to die digging for pot shards...

Big excitement today was that Professor C. picked people for the Hermit Island site. Me, Marty (of course) and then

Laura Drake and Johnny Reardon ☺! Well how about that ??! The four of us are heading out there tomorrow.

Did I detect a little frown on Bart's face? Hah Hah...

Good night journal.

July 7

Alice: Hah hah...

Good night journal.

July 7

I'm whipped. Hard getting up at dawn after a few days of sleeping in. Plus we did a lot today. Four of us took the boat over to Hermit and did a preliminary survey of the quarry for Prof. C. Wonder how Marty

TO: c_marsh
FROM: victoria.gayler@sandersonllp.b
DATE: 9/15/04
RE: Kari Hansen

Dear Dr. Marsh:

I got a call from Kari's mom so I was expecting to hear from you. I wish I could remember something that might help you out, but I didn't really seen much of Kari the last two weeks of the dig, so I don't know what I can tell you.

But you could tell her I'm thinking of her, and hoping she gets well soon. I tried to visit last year, but her mom said no visitors. So if that's changed, let me know.

Vicki

feels having to run everything by him when she's the one who found the site in the first place? Not my business I guess. Anyway we spent the day clearing the site and getting pictures for Prof. C. to look at. Came back to Stockton and ate chili. (UGH.)

Laura is farting up a storm and she thinks I don't know. The whole tent REEKS. The way my stomach feels I'll be getting back at her soon though.

Good night journal.

July 8

Big nasty storm today. Did nothing. Could do nothing but sit around and watch the rain and kill mosquitos. Prof. C. gave a lecture in the a.m. on the Stockton site (Jeff snored out loud!) then lunch, sat around some more, killed mosquitos, then

some more, ?... o
dinner, sitting, dead mosquitos...
hanging around talking and
wonder of wonders —— Johnny
actually spoke!!!

We were talking about what
might have happened to the
Copper Culture people and Tomas
~~starts~~ starts droning on about
how all the evidence points to
this and that and blah blah blah
and I'm looking at Vicki and

trying hard not to crack up — the
guy has absolutely no clue about
what a geek he is — and just as
he's saying something about how
it's clear to him that nothing happened
to the Copper Culture people — ~~they~~
just moved everything out and
moved on — it happens: Johnny
opens his mouth and says —
" my grandfather told me
a story."

And all of a sudden — I don't
know whether it was the way
he said it or just the fact
that the great stoneface spoke —
everyone gets really...

about what happened on
Madeleine Island back in the
1600s - all those kids getting
killed - the way Johnny tells
it... it's really creepy;
Enough to keep you up at night.

Just like Johnny...

Damn he's a <u>hottie</u>. And he's not
stupid. So why's he with Eileen
Bart? That girl is a <u>plank</u>. He
could do better. Much better.
Like if he would pay attention to
me once in a while I would
show him how much better...
Like I would... Ahem.

Is it me? Or is it warm in this
tent?

— Good night Journal...
(Good night Johnny)

LOG 1.2

MEDLOG AUTOMATED TR
SESSION INFORMATION

CLIENT: KRIEGMOOR PSYCH
PATIENT (PT): KARI HANSEN
THERAPIST (TH): DR. CHAR
DATE OF SESSION: 9/21/04
SYSTEM PARAMETERS:

SESSION TEXT

1 TH: talk a little a
       dents, okay
2
3 PT: Okay.
4 TH: How abou
5 PT: Johnny.
6 TH: Yes.
7 TH: Were th
8 TH: Kari?
9 PT: No.
10 TH: Why i
11 PT: I don't
12 TH: Did you not want to
13 TH: It seems to me - looking at you
14   friends, and he didn't. Would tha
15 PT: Yes.
16 TH: Did you talk about your feelings for Johnny with anyo
17 PT: No.
18 TH: There was no one on the dig you felt you could confide in?
19 PT: No.
20 TH: I see. Kari - let me ask you something. When Johnny Reardon told you that
21   folktale - the Indian myth - was that the first time you had ever heard a story
22   like that? A story about supernatural creatures that lived here - on the islands?
23 PT: No.
24 TH: No. I didn't think so.
25 TH: No, I didn't think so. Can we talk about some of those other stories?
26 [PAUSE]
27 TH: Kari?
28 PT: Do we have to?
29 TH: I think it's important, yes. I think if we do that, we'll make a start towards under-
30   standing what's happening here.
31 [PAUSE}
32 TH: There's a book I was reading the other day - some oral narratives about -

NORTHERN
PENINSULA
HISTORICAL
SOCIETY

Bayfield Heights
WI 48544

September 19, 2004

Charles Marsh, M.D.
Kriegmoor Psychiatric Hospital
Bayfield Heights, WI

Dr. Marsh:

Here's copies of that stuff we were talking about - can't tell you how many times that summer Kari came in on her day off to look at these things. Guess maybe that should have been a clue to all of us.

Anything else I can do to help, you just let me know.

Walt McKinnon

Walt McKinnon
Director, Northern Peninsula Historic Society

Taken down by hand on 19 March 1871 by Mrs. Claudine D'Passier of Old Fort William, in that same town

I am John Hart, of the Ashinaabe, who was called Strong Heart as a boy. I work for the Iron Lake Canning Company in Bayfield. I was raised on Madeline Island by my grandfather. He had stories of when the island was called La Pointe, and only the Frenchmen lived there. There was a trading post, and one winter, the men who lived there were all killed. My grandfather used to scare me at night by saying they had been murdered by the Wendigo, an evil spirit that was once an Ashinaabe brave. He said this brave was angry at the French for trespassing on our islands, but I have since come to see that it is my grandfather who was angry at the French. I see things differently, for the paleskins have given us much wisdom and trade in miracles. I have ridden the train to Washington DC and New York City, and seen all the lands of this country that my grandfather knew of only in story. I have a wife and two sons and a house on the reservation, and many friends who are good men, who are paleskins.

I thank you for the chance to tell my story.

Taken down by hand on 19 March 1871 by Mrs. Claudine D'Passier of Old Fort William, in that same town

I am Grey Fox, of the Ashinaabe, of the Midewiwin, and I give you nothing. Not my words, not my stories, nor the stories of my people whose land you stole whose braves and women you killed. If I spoke of those things, you would twist them as you twisted the words of the treaties our people signed as you now twist the tales of Kitchiemanidou of Marchemanidou of Windigo to the purposes of your own greedy gods. I give you nothing.

Taken down by hand on 19 March 1871 by Mrs. Claudine D'Passier of Old Fort William, in that same town

My name is Dark Eye, and I am a daughter of the Ashin-aabe, which the saagn'aash [white man] called Chippewa. My father was Green Thunder of the Beaver Band, my mother Thin Deer, who died when I was very young of the smallpox. I had two brothers who died of the same, who I do not remember. We lived then in what is now called the Wisconsin territory [state] of the Americans. I do not remember very many things from when I was a young girl.

As a maiden, I was given in trade to a Frenchman named Charbon, a trader who was much older than I and did not treat me well. I fled to live with the Great Chief Waubojeeg, and spent many years then with him on La Pointe [Madeline] Island. This was our sacred land, which the Midewiwin [medicine men] say we came to from the Saltwater Sea. Those are years whose memory shines bright with me. I have many stories. One I will tell you is of the year the summer did not come. The ice grew so thick we could not find water to fish in. Food was scarce, and many people died. A white man named Pierce came to us at this time. He had been living on Ashuwaguindag Miniss. He said food was scarce for him too but soon we learned a Wendigo had chased him from that island. I felt fear when I heard this for the Wendigo was an evil spirit who ate human flesh. My zhishay [uncle] who was Leaping Frog, told me stories of this spirit when I was young to frighten me. He said the spirit was once a man but he had died of hunger. Now all that was left of him was his shadow, and this shadow was the Wendigo, and was cursed to roam the earth until his hunger was satisfied. The man Pierce begged the Midewiwin to help him. But the Midewiwin said they could do nothing for him. I felt sorrow for this man because I heard his cries of fear at night. But Waubojeeg said he had to leave because the Wendigo might hurt the people. I do not know what became of this man Pierce.

MEDLOG AUTOMATED TRANSCRIPTION SERVICES
SESSION INFORMATION

CLIENT: KRIEGMOOR PSYCHIATRIC
PATIENT (PT): KARI HANSEN
THERAPIST (TH): DR. CHARLES MARSH
DATE OF SESSION: 9/21/04
SYSTEM PARAMETERS: LANGUAGE DETECT/ENGLISH LINE RETURN DELAY/8 SECONDS
SILENCE THRESHOLD: -5.4 DB FILE FORMAT: MS WORD

SESSION TEXT (CONTINUED)

1 TH: went camping myself there once - years and years ago. By the south side of
2 the island, there's a little inlet, a cove...beautiful beach. Friend of mine and I -
3 Brian Swedien. We slept right out there, under the stars. Did you ever go to that
4 beach, Kari?
5 PT: I think so.
6 TH: You want to know something funny? One of Brian's grandmothers- she was
7 Ojibwe. Lived in the Belanger Settlement, by the Red Cliff reservation - you
8 know where that is?
9 PT: Yes.
10 TH: When she heard Brian and I were going camping on Hermit Island...she tried
11 to talk him out of going. She'd grown up hearing so many stories about the
12 place... she was scared for him. And you want to know something else? Brian
13 - he was a little scared too. He wouldn't come out and say it, but the whole time
14 we were there - he wouldn't leave the beach - wouldn't go inland.
15 [PAUSE]
16 TH: What do you think was on his mind, Kari?
17 PT: I don't know.
18 TH: Take a guess.
19 PT: I don't know.
20 [PAUSE]
21 TH: It's interesting, isn't it? Hear enough stories about a place...your imagination
22 starts working overtime, you kind of say to yourself - what if? What if some of
23 those stories are real? What if those things really happened? And then if you go
24 there...
25 TH: Those stories about the Windigo - you read those before the dig started, didn't
26 you Kari?
27 PT: I think so.
28 TH: So were they on your mind a lot while you were on the island?
29 PT: I can't remember.
30 TH: I imagine they must have been, at least a little.
31 [PAUSE]
32 TH: Kari? Please look at me when we're talking.

traces of bauxite (what they make aluminum from) which is highly unusual in this area. But the big thing is the copper — actual fragments of annealized copper, which means there's a good chance we will find artifacts here. So it seems like the quarry was dug right on top of, or right next to, an old Copper Culture site. Very cool.

Goodnight journal. Sleep tight. Sleep late because we have tomor—

July 29
Sucky day. Everybody decided to drive over to Duluth and hang out, but I didn't feel like going so I ended up heading over to the historical society with Marty and Jeff. Some day off. Actually to tell the truth, that part of the day wasn't so bad — we went through a lot of the stuff they have in the archives, found some pictures of the quarry when it was operational, some old surveys suggesting that underneath all the brownstone they mined there was some other stuff — magnetite, copper. We even

some — the stuff — magnetic, copper
naturally. Other things too. We even
found some shots of the house Mr.
Kriegmoor built for his wife on the
island. All cedar — really wild looking.
Cost a fortune and she only slept in it
one night. Jeff said he could show
me where the house used to be if

I wanted. He's ok I guess — I used to
think he was a stoner, but now I think
he's just preoccupied all the time. Always
walking around with his nose buried in
a book. Though he definitely is a stoner
too. Laura said she's gotten high with
him a couple of times already this
summer.

So what sucked was when we were
coming back to the dock — who do we
walk by? Bart and Johnny sitting in
the Burger King sucking face big time.
Marty tries not to notice. Jeff definitely
doesn't notice. But I do, and as soon as
I see them, Bart sees me and smiles.
And then she nudges Johnny and he
smiles, too. Like "Oh there's Kari.
Hi Kari. Have fun at the Historical
Society? Good. You're such a good student
Kari. You're such a good girl..."
Ah, FUCK.
Goodnight t...

JULY 30

Better now.

I woke up vowing not to think of him at all. Of course it's hard not to think about somebody when you're working like five feet away from them all day long, but what happened made it a little easier, what happened being that it was our first real day of digging on Hermit, and I made the big find. Two arrowheads, Marty said they looked old to her, even though of course we have to get them tested, dated back on the mainland. Still, I felt pretty good about that. So did Marty. She was on her cell to C. for like an hour. Talked right through dinner. It was Laura and Johnny's turn to cook, so Jeff and I went for a walk and he showed me where that house that Kriegmoor built used to be. Sure enough, he pulls out a joint and asks

and Johnny and I are

if I want to smoke. I asked if he was an idiot or something — the rules were pretty strict — pretty clear that if you got caught doing anything against the college you're out. Out of the dig — out of the

code your out. Out of the dig
program — and probably suspended, too.
The guy doesn't get it though — he just
lit up anyway. I walked off, left him
standing there cuz I don't even want
to smell a little bit like weed. Marty's
probably a hell of a lot cooler about
things than Prof C., except no sense
pushing it.

Better safe than sorry I say.
     Goodnight Journal

JULY 31

God. I'm a fucking idiot.
Marty takes the boat and heads back
to the mainland with the arrowheads
and we're supposed to keep

working. Which we do — for a
while but then Jeff says let's break
for lunch and Laura and Johnny say
sure and so what am I supposed to
do? Point out that it's only eleven in
the morning and we only finished
breakfast two hours ago? Anyway
we take some sandwiches and
head down to the old quarry, and
after lunch we're just hanging out

head down to the [...]
after lunch we're just hanging out,
and Johnny and I are talking — he
is so easy to talk to — and time is just
flying by, it's like twelve thirty or so,
I think, and I don't want to be the
one to break up the party, but I knew
we had to get back to work, and just
as I'm about to say something, Jeff,
who's been just vegging out, lying
flat out on the beach with this stupid
little bandana tied around his eyes so
he can sleep — he sits up reaches into
his pocket and pulls out a handful

of these little tablets my first thought
is they're advils. They look like advils.

And then Jeff says — Anybody need a
pick me up? And Johnny says Sure and
Laura, who's lying on the sand next
to Jeff — she doesn't say anything —
just holds out her hand and Jeff
puts one of the little tablets in it
and she pops it right into her mouth
and smiles and of course by now I know
they're not Advils, but I have no idea
what they are

what they are. ...., ... i have no idea

So now I say we do have to get back
to work and Jeff tells me to relax a
little and then Johnny grabs two.
He takes one and pops it right in his
mouth and then he holds the other
one out in his hand and says —
Try it.
And for what seems like it has to

be-like ten minutes I'm just
standing there like an idiot.
I don't know what to say. I'm
certainly not going to take whatever
this is — no freakin way — except
that Johnny is just standing there
smiling and of course I don't want to
come off like a total idiot loser so
the words that come out of my
mouth are not "No thanks" but
instead I say What is it?

X — Jeff says and I guess the fact
that I have no idea what that means
shows on my face because Johnny
just keeps smiling and says it's
.... of course I've heard

on my face because Johnny
just keeps smiling and says it's
ecstasy and of course I've heard
of ecstasy even though I've never
taken it. That's the drug they use
all the time at raves, isn't it? I
say. And Johnny nods and holds
the other pill out again.

It's cool, he says. Take

I take it.

And right away - not five minutes later,
not ten minutes later - but right away
I know this is a bad idea. My heart
starts hammering so hard in my chest
it feels like it's going to pop right
through, and all of a sudden I'm
sweating like mad. I thought I was
going to die or have to go to the
hospital or something. Meanwhile
Johnny just keeps smiling and Laura
and Jeff are sitting up on the beach
just talking and laughing about
something. I have no idea what
because I couldn't even concentrat
to listen to them. I had to
Right on the

beata ... enough to listen to them. I ne... lie down right there. Right on the ground, right next to those huge stones, these old stones that they'd

stacked up like a hundred years ago and never bothered to move after Kriegmoor shut down the quarry because his wife went crazy. And I start looking at the stones — one stacked on top of the other, and they make a pattern, and then that pattern keeps going, stone after stone, stone, stone, stone stacked up all the way to the sky and I blink and the stones are all gone and I see a cloud, this one cloud and it starts again — the same sort of pattern repeating. the clouds start multiplying across the sky. At first they're these big white clouds but then they start getting darker, grey clouds then rain clouds and then they're pitch black and all at once the whole sky is pitch black, just one big sheet of black except somehow this other pattern is starting. It takes me

a while to figure it out, but then I
see it's like the black is moving - shifting
around like a puddle of oil - like it's
alive + the sky is alive with all these
splotches of black they're like shadows

Right then I realized I was screaming.

I looked up and the others are all standing
around me looking down and Jeff kneels
down next to me and asks if I'm all right.
I said yes - but you know what? I
couldn't really work for the rest of the
day. Everytime I looked in the same
place for too long, the patterns started
up all over again.

So I don't think I'm all right at all.

August 1

I felt sick all day. Disoriented -
I don't know how to describe it.
It was like - you know when you go
away on vacation for a long time
and you come back to your own house,

on vacation for a long time
and you come back to your own house,
and you walk in the door, and
everything seems strange to you?
Like it's all exactly the same but
still... it doesn't seem right somehow.
Not right at all... Not right at all.
Like everything you're looking at
is fake and there's something
hidden behind it and if you could
just find the curtain to lift up you'd
see... what? I don't know.
Nothing good I bet.
Jesus Christ - listen to me.
It's not even seven o'clock, but I
am going to sleep. Goodnight journal,
please let me be better in the morning.

AUGUST 2
Oh fuck.. I really really fucked up.
There is something wrong with me. I
can't — it was so hard to concentrate
today, so hard to work. Marty pulled
me aside and asked if I was all right,
I said I was fine — just thinking
about stuff. No big deal I said. Hah.
No big deal. I'm just losing my mind,
that's all.

that's all.

I was lying in the tent last night, trying to fall asleep last night, and I got that same feeling, like nothing was real and if I looked too long at any one place... it was like the world was melting away and I could see... behind it? That's not exactly right, but it's the best I can come up with, and that's when it happened. I stared at the tent wall, at this dark spot on the fabric and

then the spot got bigger and bigger and I could see things in it. The same splotches of black, the outlines of thing — I don't know. Shapes coming towards me, moving really, really fast — coming toward me and going away again. Like shadows...

Right. Sure they were.

AUGUST 3

Tried to talk to Johnny but he was all "just relax it'll pass. So you

all "just relax it'll pass. So you
had a bad reaction, don't worry."
Thanks a lot friend. He's a plank, too.
Him and Bart — they deserve eachother.
Jeff, at least he talked to me for a
few minutes. He said he'd never
heard of anybody having this

kind of thing happen to them before.
Hallucinations — yes, he's had them,
but they went away after a few
hours. He's kind of freaked out, too.
Made me feel better, in a weird kind
of misery loves company way.
Goodnight journal.

August 4

Brain damage. Writing this in town
at the Broiler. We had the day off
again and I went to the historical
society and borrowed Walt's computer
to go on the internet. I looked it up —
they said you take MDMA — that's the
drug ecstacy is made from — take it
for four days and there's brain damage
you can find six to seven years later.
well guess what? I don't think I
have to wait.

AUGUST 5

Is any of this happening — really happening? I don't know if I should be laughing or crying. I couldn't sleep and I was sitting by the fire and Jeff came out. We talked for a while and I was so tired I started crying and somehow he and I ended up in his sleeping bag and we started having sex and I was looking over his shoulder and looking at the tent wall and then all at once The

FRANK LESLIE'S
ILLUSTRATED
NEWSPAPER

NEW YORK—FOR THE WEEK ENDING MARCH 15, 1872.
PRICE 10 CENTS

and looking at the tent wall and then all at once They were there again right behind the wall the shapes the shadows whatever you want to call them. Coming straight at me like now that I saw them they could see me and I couldn't help it — I screamed. And Jeff was like "shh quiet" and smiling — he thought I felt good and he put his hand over

my mouth and I'm shaking my head but he didn't get it and so I bit him, bit his hand and he screams and lets go and the whole time I could see it — right over his shoulder — coming nearer and nearer.

And then one of them came through the wall. It came right through the tent wall and it was in the tent with us, I swear on a stack of Bibles. A shadow. First had no shape and then it flowed into the shape of a man. A shadow shaped like a man, just like Pierce wrote about.

God — what is wrong with me?

KRIEGMOOR
PSYCHIATRIC INSTITUTE

TO: c_marsh@kriegmoor-psychiatric.org

FROM: wmckinnon@jetmail.com

DATE: September 22, 2004

RE: YOUR QUESTION

Sorry I missed your call this afternoon, doctor. You asked if the name Pierce meant anything to me, well it sure does, Pierce is the Hermit, the one the island's named after. We have a whole lot of material on him up on our website now, if you want to take a look.

Hope this hel...

Walt McKi...

– People –

The Hermi...
Hermit Isl...

Pierce Letter ...

Pierce Letter ...

Pierce Letter # ...

Pierce Letter # ...

NORTHERN PENINSULA HISTORICAL SOCIETY

Search

| – People – | Places | Historic Events | Exhibits | Library | Visitor Guide |

– click here for a map –

The Hermit of Hermit Island

Pierce Letter #1

Pierce Letter #2

Pierce Letter #3

Pierce Letter #4

Pierce Letter #5

Misc. Pierce Letters

"THE HERMIT OF HERMIT ISLAND"

Some of the more colorful stories associated with the Apostle Islands concern a man we know only as Pierce who, according to local legend, Hermit Island was named for. The tales surrounding his life are legion, and vary wildly in circumstance. In some, he is a backwoods adventurer, honored and respected by the local tribes; in others, a heartless fur trader, who exploits the natives hunger for "shiny trinkets and alcohol," and caused the 'terrible death' of his own wife and infant son.

Tales of his passing are even more fanciful - Pierce was found "dead in his cabin, where he had undoubtedly been murdered...evidently by parties in search of his wealth." "Not exactly," according to another tale; he went mad, a victim of his own, self-imposed solitude, driven "to violent delusions...[as] misshapen monsters appeared against the mud-lined walls of his lonely cabin he forced his trembling old body to go after them until life wrenched from it in a final, violent convulsion" (see Pierce's obituary here).

For years though, there was no evidence beyond the local folklore to confirm Pierce's existence. Then in 1986, a man named Alex Phillips of Silver Springs Maryland was cleaning out the attic of his house when he came across a box of old letters . Among these letters were several addressed to his great-great-great grandmother, Constance Salish of Baltimore, mailed from the trading post at Rice Village, Wisconsin, and signed by a man named Pierce. Are these documents, at last, proof of the hermit's existence? While historians continue to debate their authenticity, one thing remains certain: they provide a chilling record of one man's descent into madness.

We invite you to read the text of the letters here, and to visit our museum in Bayfield, where the originals are currently on display.

Thank you to Amanda Blackwell of the Women's Auxiliary for transcribing these letters.

The Hermit of
Hermit Island

This letter was postmarked April 3, 1792, from the Rice Village Trading Post to Baltimore.

My dear cousin Constance:

I have come to town on business, so I am writing you a letter while I am here. Though I fere (sic) my letters are not what they were once. It was a long, cold winter, and I do not have much to sell, and the british is (sic) cheap devils. It will be hard to buy the gran (sic) I need because they paid me so cheap for the pelts I had. But it is good to be out in the sun and off the island for a time. How is are your husband and young William? I hope they find the city to their likeing (sic). I would be glad to hear news of you and them. There is much talk here of how little turtle and his tribes won the day in battle fighting washington in the Ohioo (sic). I fere (sic) no good to come of these fights though. My heart I must confess is with the people here but they is are too few to win in the end. We shall see. Write if you can.

Your cousin

William Pierce

The Hermit of
Hermit Island

This letter was postmarked June 16, presumably of the same year (1792), and again mailed from the Rice Village Trading Post to Baltimore.

Cousin:

Thank you for yor (sic) kind words about Laura. You will I am glad to here (sic) she remans (sic) alive in your mind as she does min (sic). Cousin I am in a bad way or I would not writ (sic) to ask you this. I have need of some money for a short while as I could not buy gran (sic) enough as I wrote you because of the northwest fur British. Just enouf (sic) for the supplys (sic) I need for trapping. If you pay the northwest man in yor (sic) town a letter of credit can be sent for me here. 2 pounds for supplys (sic) I would pay the loan next spring. Writ (sic) if you can do this. I thank you.

Your cousin

William Pierce

The Hermit of
Hermit Island

Pierce Letter #1

Pierce Letter #2

Pierce Letter #3

Pierce Letter #4

Pierce Letter #5

Misc. Pierce Letters

This letter was postmarked November 8. Because of the historical references contained herein, the letter is dated to fall of the following year (1793).

Cousin:

Things are gone from bad to worse for me, I fere (sic) to say. The crops I planted have failt (sic) and there are no furs to be caught now in the season. I have found some work as a barrel maker for Mr. Jacobson who has one of the shipping companees (sic) here. He is a hard man though and a miser who pays little for my laybor (sic). I am happy to have made a friend, Mr. Denis Latellier. He is an older man, a Frenchman who lives on La Pointe. Mr. Denis speaks fair English and we have spent many a companonable (sic) hour together. He has also given me an acks (sic) he no longer uses, much better than my old acks (sic) for making of the barrels. He has good licker (sic) too, which warms both body and soul. I shall need what of it he gives me as winter draws near. It is scarce November and already the lake is part ice.
Write if you can, cousin. Your letters are a source of comfort to me.

The Hermit of
Hermit Island

Pierce Letter #1

Pierce Letter #2

Pierce Letter #3

Pierce Letter #4

Pierce Letter #5

Misc. Pierce Letters

Only one page of this letter survives. The envelope it was sent in is missing as well. Despite the lack of a signature, the handwriting leaves no doubt that it too was written by the same man as the others, presumably Pierce. Because of the historical references contained herein, the letter is dated to early December, 1793.

...said my work was good but that he did not want to have licker (sic) around the Indians so that is why I was fired. Mr. Denis spoke with him but to no avail. I will find more work cousin do not fear, but I will wait till spring, till the lake can be safelee (sic) crosst (sic). In the meanwile (sic), I will pass the winter here on the island. I have much of Mr. Denis's licker (sic) to keep me companee (sic) though truth to tell I grow somewhat tired of the man and his badjering (sic). He says I am a fool to spend the winter alone here and then tells me stories of some French traders on La Pointe who were cruellee (sic) murdered and none found there (sic) bodies til spring. I think he means to friten (sic) me or perhaps he grows tired of giving me his licker (sic). I joke of course.

This letter was postmarked December 17, and was most likely written mere days after the preceding one.

Cousin:

I have never been so cold in all my life.

The Indians say this is to be the coldest winter in fifty years and I believe them. I had gumed (sic) the insids (sic) of my cabin with mud and sap and still the wind comes through. I wish now I had aksepted (sic) Mr. Denis offer of a place for the winter. I was at his house at the settlement and though I would have to worked choppt (sic) wood and such to earn my keep the house is sealt (sic) tite (sic) and warm with a fire and then there is his licker (sic) and as well companionship.

I am sure you say to yourself now William Pierce in need of companionship you never thought you would hear such a thing. I have my reasons cousin. Please do write if you can.

Your cousin

William Pierce

NORTHERN
PENINSULA
HISTORICAL

The box that held Pierce's correspondence suffered severe water damage at some point. The final few letters, located at the top of that stack of correspondence, bore the brunt of that damage. Despite heroic efforts by local and nationally-renowned archivists, we were unable to rescue any of those last few letters in their entirety.

We present here extracts from them, in what we believe to be the correct historical order.

UNDATED LETTER #1

...there are the Chippewa stories, those stories are old stories, from before the British, before the French, before even the Chippewa themselfs (sic). The stories speak of these same things and describe them in these same ways. You will say it is the drink. Perhaps you are right. There is one good affect (sic) I go to sleep with the Lord's prayer on my lips.

Your cousin,

William Pierce

UNDATED LETTER #2

the British action in the Indees (sic) reaches even here. None care for them, all wish them gone, the Northwest fur man has remaned (sic) hidden since this. I must confess my mind is elsewhere. To tell the truth cousin my nights reman (sic) as before. Mr. Denis's stories of the murdered...

...even when I close my eyes, I can hear them. I see them in my mind and when I open my eyes they take shape. I lie still on my blankets and they come. Angry darkness growing in the corner of the room at first and then the form of my madness a figger (sic) of Satan's own design a shadow shapel (sic) like a man that wispers (sic) in my mind of the cold and blood on the snow. They hunger. I fere (sic) Wabojee (sic) was right I fere (sic)...

UNDATED LETTER #3

Constance:

I give this letter to Mr. Denis. He will mail it for me.
He is a good man I am ashamed to have spoken poorly of him befor (sic).
He and his brother crosst (sic) the ice to see me to take me back to the mainland with them but I canot (sic) go. Wabojee (sic) has said they will follow and they will hurt others as they hurt me. I took the licker (sic) Mr. Denis brang me though which caust (sic) him and his brother to laff (sic). They have gone now to gather wood for me as my injures (sic) make...

...forgive me. And forgiveness of you.

Your cousin,

IST 5

my month a

And after he left Marty asked
me what was wrong, that these last
few days, something was different.
Was something the matter? I was going
to tell her about everything right then
and there. I swear I was.

And then she said that I used to be
her best student, and she had planned
to recommend me for the Buckhalter
Prize, and honors placement, but after
these last few days...

So I told her nothing was wrong. I
told her I would buckle down, and
get back to work. I told her
tomorrow would be different.

Please God. Make tomorrow different

natural
found som
Kriegma

later...

Oh my God. I was sitting by the campfire just letting my eyes wander back and forth looking at the flames, looking away from the flames, up at the sky, back down at the ground, not focusing so the patterns wouldn't start, and I looked into the forest towards the dig site, and then it just came to me — bam — just like that.

There's a reason these islands are so deserted.

It's not that nobody lives here, or nobody ever lived here. People tried to live here. They really tried. A lot of people tried. Pierce, the Ojibwe, the Copper culture people — they all tried, but they couldn't. And what if the reason the couldn't is because...

There was something else here already.

FROM: claire_morris@kriegmoor-psychiatric.org
DATE: 9/24/04
RE: HA-09

Understand you've been spending a lot of extra time with this patient, doctor, and while I applaud the thoroughness of your approach, I must remind you of the other patients currently under your supervision. They are in need of your time and energy as well.

Thank you.

-- Claire

CLIENT: KRIEGMOOR
PATIENT (PT): DARRELL COVEY
THERAPIST (TH): DR. CHARLES MARSH
DATE OF SESSION: 9/24/04
SYSTEM PARAMETERS: LANGUAGE DETECT/ENGLISH LINE RETURN DELAY/3 SECONDS
SILENCE THRESHOLD: -5.4 DB FILE FORMAT: MS WORD

SESSION TEXT (CONTINUED)

1 TH: ask you this, then. Are the voices always with you?
2 PT: No. They go away sometimes.
3 TH: And how do you feel when they go away?
4 PT: I don't like it.
5 TH: Why not?
6 PT: Because I'm alone in my head then and I remember all the bad things. Who I
7 used to be. How I used to hurt people.
8 TH: Sometimes it's good to look back at the past, confront what you did.
9 PT: I don't like to do that.
10 TH: The past has unpleasant associations for you.
11 PT: Yes.
12 TH: Can I tell you something Darrell? The past has unpleasant associations for me,
13 too. The trick is to take what happened and learn from it. Move on.
14 PT: Leave here, you mean?
15 TH: Move on with your life. Someday leave here, yes.
16 PT: Oh I don't know. I don't know if I could ever leave here.
17 TH: Don't you want to go home?
18 PT: It's up to them. Whatever they want.
19 TH: They. The voices?
20 PT: That's right. They like it here.
21 PT: What's the matter doctor?
22 TH: Just checking something in your file...bear with me.
23 TH: Hmmm. That's strange. It's not in here.
24 PT: What?
25 TH: Your date of admission. The whole front half of the file seems to be missing.
26 PT: Is that bad?
27 TH: It's not good. I'll have records check into it.
28 PT: Records?
29 TH: The records department. They keep track of -
30 PT: Can you buy the records?
31 [PAUSE]

MEDLOG AUTOMATED TRANSCRIPTION SERVICES
SESSION INFORMATION

CLIENT: KRIEGMOOR PSYCHIATRIC
PATIENT (PT): JACOB HELLINGER
THERAPIST (TH): DR. CHARLES MARSH
DATE OF SESSION: 9/24/04
SYSTEM PARAMETERS: LANGUAGE DETECT/ENGLISH LINE RETURN DELAY/8 SECONDS
SILENCE THRESHOLD: -5.4 DB FILE FORMAT: MS WORD

SESSION TEXT (CONTINUED)

1	TH: Hi Jake. How are you doing today?
2	PT: Not so good.
3	TH: What's the matter?
4	PT: I keep seeing blood.
5	TH: Where do you see blood?
6	PT: On the walls.
7	TH: I don't see any blood Jake.
8	PT: It's gone now.
9	TH: Where did it go?
10	PT: I don't know.
11	TH: Okay. Where did the blood come from, Jake?
12	PT: The monsters made it.
13	TH: What monsters?
14	PT: You know.
15	TH: Jake, I'm looking at some notes from your mother here. She said that when you
16	were growing up, you used to love that book Where the Wild Things Are. Do
17	you remember that?
18	PT: Yes.
19	TH: Do you remember what happens in the book?
20	PT: Yes.
21	[PAUSE]
22	TH: Go on.
23	PT: Max is bad so he can't have any dinner. Then he goes to see the monsters.
24	Then he comes home.
25	TH: Do the monsters hurt him?
26	PT: No. He gets away. Can I watch TV now?
27	TH: TV time is in the early morning, Jake. You know that.
28	PT: Just an animal show. Nothing violent. No monsters.
29	TH: Jake.
30	[PAUSE]
31	PT: Okay
32	TH: Good. Now why don't we get back to what we were talking about before.

MEDLOG 1.2

CLIENT: KRIEGMOOR PSYCHIATRIC
PATIENT (PT): KARI HANSEN
THERAPIST (TH): DR. CHARLES MARSH
DATE OF SESSION: 9/25/04
SYSTEM PARAMETERS: LANGUAGE DETECT/ENGLISH LINE RETURN DELAY/8 SECONDS
SILENCE THRESHOLD: -5.4 DB FILE FORMAT: MS WORD

SESSION TEXT (CONTINUED)

1   TH: if you drank a lot?
2   PT: No.
3   TH: Had you gotten drunk before?
4   PT: A couple times.
5   TH: When was the last time, prior to the dig?
6   PT: I don't know...wait, a couple of my friends had a party for the 4th of July.
7   I guess then.
8   TH: And you never had a reaction like this to alcohol?
9   PT: No.
10 TH: No hallucinations, or blackouts, or -
11 PT: Nothing like that, no.
12 TH: All right. And this was the first time you'd ever taken any sort of drug?
13 PT: Yes. That's right.
14 TH: I'm including pot, or amphetamines, or -
15 PT: I told you, it was just that one time. Just because...
16 TH: Because of Johnny Reardon. Not wanting to look stupid.
17 PT: Yes.
18 [PAUSE]
19 TH: You're embarrassed.
20 PT: It was a stupid thing to do.
21 TH: We all do stupid things when we're infatuated...it's the nature of the beast.
22 PT: I guess.
23 TH: Oh it's true. Believe me. I speak from experience.
24 PT: Really? Like what?
25 TH: Well...
26 [PAUSE]
27 PT: Come on Dr. Marsh. You know all about me. I don't know anything about you.
28 TH: I don't think my past is really relevant here. Let's stay focused on -
29 PT: Come on.
30 TH: Well...
31 TH: In college...
32 PT: Ah.

33	TH: Yes I was in college once too. Believe it or not.
34	PT: I believe it. You're not that old.
35	TH: Thank you.
36	PT: So?
37	TH: There was a girl. Naomi Spatz. I –
38	PT: Naomi Spatz?
39	TH: Yes.
40	PT: Wow. I never heard of anyone named Naomi.
41	PT: Sorry. Go ahead.
42	TH: Junior year. I arranged my course schedule so that she and I were in several
43	classes together.
44	[PAUSE]
45	PT: Well...that's kind of a big deal.
46	TH: It was. My father couldn't understand my sudden interest in Romance
47	Languages. I ended up graduating on completion – I had to take extra courses
48	the summer after commencement.
49	PT: So what happened?
50	TH: What do you mean?
51	PT: Did you go out with her? With Naomi?
52	TH: No. She found me a little bit ah – too intellectual, I suppose.
53	PT: Yeah. That happens. Some people just want to party all the time. I mean – in
54	college. Always trying to get you to do things you don't want to.
55	TH: I suppose that never changes.
56	PT: No.
57	[PAUSE]
58	PT: You're not married are you Dr. Marsh? I mean, I don't see a ring but sometimes
59	people these days don't always wear rings. Not that it's really any of my busi-
60	ness but -
61	TH: No. I'm not married.
62	TH: I was, but...
63	[PAUSE]
64	PT: What happened?
65	TH: It's a long story. Let's just say I allowed my work to interfere with my personal
66	life.
67	PT: Oh. I'm sorry.
67	TH: That's all right. It's several years ago now so -
69	PT: I guess that's kind of what happened with me too. With Johnny and the X. I let
70	my personal life interfere with my work.
71	TH: I suppose that's true.
72	PT: Yeah.
73	TH: Well I think now we've both learned our lesson.
74	PT: Yes.
75	[PAUSE]
76	PT: I guess we have.

and a subsequent review of K's medical records bore out the anecdotal testimony from her diary: blood tests done at the time of her admission showed minute traces of the drug MDMA within her system, levels consistent with the dosage she'd described taking. But while K's initial reported reactions to the drug (elevated heartbeat, body temperature) were not unusual[31], the persistence and intensity of her subsequent hallucinations were deviant, more consistent with those associated with stronger hallucinogens such as LSD.

K's diary descriptions of her initial 'trip,' in fact, reminded me of nothing so much as the 'acid flashbacks' publicized by media celebrities in the 1960s — George Harrison of the Beatles, Timothy Leary, Danny Rasmussen of the Paisley Diamonds — and the claims made by those people for the consciousness-expanding powers of hallucinogenic drugs in general and LSD in particular. In retrospect, it seems obvious that my subconscious was already making the proper links, making the deductions that would move me forward to the next phase of my project.

My conscious mind, however, was still focused on my patient. I had managed to overcome her initial reticence (dating back, I already suspected, to an overly aggressive therapeutic approach taken by her previous clinician, Dr. Peter Ferguson), and establish a strong personal rapport with "K," in the process thoroughly familiarizing myself with the details of her case. Now, it was time to engage her more fully in the therapeutic process, to confront her with truths the she perhaps would rather not

---

[31] MDMA is a synthetic drug, produced within laboratories from methamphetamine and is based upon naturally-occurring stimulants within a variety of plants such as vanilla, dill, and nutmeg. The drug acts upon serotonin levels within the body and is categorized as a hallucinogenic amphetamine.

BAYFIELD HEIGHTS
PREPARATORY

...04

...n
...iatric Institute

...sh:

...our query of last month. We do indeed have spare cop...
...; I'm happy to enclose one for you, compliments of the sc...

...picture of Kari, chosen by herself, as well as text she wrote...
... She was a member of the swim team (pictures to be foun...
...as well as a frequent contributor to the school newspaper. I...

...ng along two articles that she wrote as well for your inform...

...ope all this proves helpful in your treatment. Please pass alo...

...cerely,

Brandon Attley
Vice-Principal

MEDLOG AUTOMATED TRANSCRIPTION SERVICES
SESSION INFORMATION

CLIENT: KRIEGMOOR PSYCHIATRIC
PATIENT (PT): KARI HANSEN
THERAPIST (TH): DR. CHARLES MARSH
DATE OF SESSION: 9/25/04
SYSTEM PARAMETERS: LANGUAGE DETECT/ENGLISH LINE RETURN DELAY/3 SECONDS
SILENCE THRESHOLD: -5.4 DB FILE FORMAT: MS WORD

SESSION TEXT (CONTINUED)

1 TH: do you know anyone like that?
2 PT: No.
3 TH: You're lucky. Very lucky. My aunt - my father's older sister Carlene, she had
4 Alzheimer's. It just - It ate her up. It progressed so fast. This had to be twenty
5 years ago - before they had some of the treatments - the medications - that
6 they have now. Near the end - she couldn't even remember her own name, and
7 this woman - she was an English teacher, over at the Woodruff school, in Rice
8 - she was the smartest person I ever knew in my life. Broke my heart to see
9 her that way. It was horrible. But you know something Kari? The end wasn't the
10 worst part. The worst part was the beginning, when she realized what was hap-
11 pening to her. She'd get lost halfway through a conversation, and get this look
12 in her eyes...she saw herself losing touch with reality, and knew there was noth-
13 ing she could do to stop it. I'll never forget that look.
14 TH: I'm going to be frank with you, Kari. Sometimes, when you and I talk -- I see the
15 same look in your eyes. Helplessness... hopelessness. Is that how you feel?
16 [PAUSE]
17 TH: Kari?
18 TH: It's okay to say yes. The important thing here is to be honest. I can't help you if
19 I don't know what you're thinking.
20 [PAUSE]
21 PT: Yes. That's how I feel.
22 TH: I can understand why. You've been on so many different medicines - all the
23 major anti-psychotics - haloperidol, chlorpromazine, zyprexa, seroquel...and
24 you've talked to so many doctors...and none of it made any difference, did it
25 Kari?
26 PT: No.
27 TH: But there's a crucial difference between your case, and my aunt's. The objec-
28 tive reality in her case was a physical disease. A deterioration of the brain tis-
29 sue. There was no cure for that. The objective reality in your case is different,
30 isn't it. Do you follow me Kari?
31 TH: The objective reality in your case is not a life-threatening disease. It's these
32 hallucinations. They're what we have to deal with. Now I don't know that we

33   can cure them, but I think what we can do - what I hope, actually, we've started
34   to do already - is lay a foundation for you to cope with them. To understand
35   what they are, and what they're not. Talking about all these stories - about
36   Pierce, the Ojibwe...I think you understand now where your fears are coming
37   from, and...
38   [PAUSE]
39   TH: That's all right.
40   PT: I'm sorry.
41   TH: I know these are hard things to talk about. You're being very brave.
42   PT: By crying?
43   TH: No. By telling the truth. Telling the truth is the hardest thing to do sometimes.
44   PT: Thank you. You're a nice guy, Dr. Marsh. You're the first person who's really lis-
45   tened to me in a long time.
46   TH: That's my job.
47   [PAUSE]
48   PT: Dr. Marsh? Can I ask you...what's your name? I mean, your first name?
49   TH: Charles.
50   PT: That's funny. That was my dad's name, too.
51   TH: I know.
52   PT: It's a nice name.
53   TH: Thank you.
54   PT: Everybody called my dad Chuck, though. Do people - what do they call you?
55   TH: Charles. Pretty much everyone calls me Charles.
56   PT: Charles.
57   TH: Yes.
58   [PAUSE]
59   TH: Kari - do you want to tell me why you were crying before?
60   PT: I can't say.
61   TH: Why?
62   PT: Because you'll think I'm crazy. But you think that already, don't you?
63   TH: Kari, I don't -
64   PT: I mean, why else would I be here if I wasn't crazy? I mean you know what I did
65   I had a breakdown I went nuts that's why they put me here, that's why -
66   TH: Kari. Kari, listen to me. I don't think you're crazy. I don't think you're crazy at all.
67   You have a medical problem, a problem we can solve -
67   TH: Why are you crying now?
69   PT: Because you're wrong.
70   TH: I'm wrong?
71   PT: Yes. It's not a medical problem at all.
72   [PAUSE]
73   TH: All right. If it's not a medical problem, what is it then?
74   PT: It's them.
75   TH: Them.
76   PT: The shadows. They're real, Dr. Marsh. I swear to God they're real.

MEDLOG 1.2

MEDLOG AUTOMATED TRANSCRIPTION SERVICES
SESSION INFORMATION

CLIENT: KRIEGMOOR PSYCHIATRIC
PATIENT (PT): KARI HANSEN
THERAPIST (TH): DR. CHARLES MARSH
DATE OF SESSION: 9/26/04
SYSTEM PARAMETERS: LANGUAGE DETECT/ENGLISH LINE RETURN DELAY 8 SECONDS
SILENCE THRESHOLD: -5.4 DB FILE FORMAT: MS WORD

SESSION TEXT (CONTINUED)

1   TH: but Nurse Somosi said she sat with you the whole time.
2   PT: Yes.
3   TH: So...
4   TH: I don't mean to harp on this Kari, but if she was there and didn't see
5   anything...what does that suggest to you?
6   PT: I don't know.
7   TH: You want to know what it suggests to me?
8   PT: That I'm crazy.
9   TH: Kari...
10 PT: That I'm seeing things. But I'm not. Why can't you believe me?
11 TH: It's not a question of believing you, Kari, it's a question of treating a medical
12   condition
13 PT: WHY CAN'T YOU BELIEVE ME!
14 [PAUSE]
15 PT: I'm sorry. I'm so sorry.
16 PT: What's happening to me.
17 [PAUSE]
18 TH: It's late. Why don't we stop here for now and pick up tomorrow?
19 PT: I guess. [PAUSE]
20 PT: Dr. Marsh?
21 TH: Yes Kari?
22 PT: Could we just talk for a minute about something else? Something that has noth-
23   ing to do with all this?
24 TH: I'd rather you rest, Kari. You seem very tired today.
25 PT: I am tired but please - please won't you just sit for a minute?
26 TH: Well...all right.
27 PT: Thank you.
28 TH: So what should we talk about?
29 PT: It's September, isn't it?
30 TH: That's right. September 24.
31 PT: The Apple Festival must be soon then.
32 TH: I think it is. I've seen some banners around town.

SESSION TEXT (CONTINUED)

33   PT: Do you go?
34   TH: When I was younger...every year.
35   PT: Me too. I used to work at one of the booths - for Hauser's?
36   TH: Ah. Great apple pie.
37   PT: The best.
38   TH: Apple butter, too.
39   PT: Sure.
40   TH: What? What's so funny?
41   PT: I was just thinking about my dad.
42   TH: Go on.
43   PT: I'll never forget - before the divorce, I remember walking through the festival
44   with him, he had this bowl of apple chili, and he kept wanting me to try some.
45   TH: Apple chili?
46   PT: Yeah. He loved it. Sounds terrible, right?
47   TH: Not a combination I would have thought of.
48   PT: Me either.
49   TH: How was it?
50   PT: I never had any. Never did get around to trying it.
51   [PAUSE]
52   TH: Okay. I want you to go to sleep early tonight, Kari. Get some good rest, and we
53   can talk again tomorrow.
54   PT: I'll try. I really will.
     TH: Goodnight Kari.
     PT: Goodnight.

MEDLOG 1.2

MEDLOG 1.2

MEDLOG AUTOMATED TRANSCRIPTION SERVICES
SESSION INFORMATION

CLIENT: KRIEGMOOR PSYCHIATRIC
PATIENT (PT): KARI HANSEN
THERAPIST (TH): DR. CHARLE...
DATE OF SESSION:
SYSTE...

MEDLOG AUTOMATED TRANSCRIPTION SERVICES
SESSION INFORMATION

CLIENT: KRIEGMOOR PSYCHIATRIC
PATIENT (PT): KARI HANSEN
THERAPIST (TH): DR. CHARLES MARSH
DATE OF SESSION: 9/27/04
SYSTEM PARAMETERS: LANGUAGE DETECT/ENGLISH LINE RETURN DELAY/8 SECONDS
SILENCE THRESHOLD: -5.4 DB FILE FORMAT: MS WORD

SESSION TEXT (CONTINUED)

1 TH: might be something we could work out, yes. No promises, though. I'll have to
2   talk to the director, and your mom as well about it - all right?
3 PT: Okay.
4 TH: Good. Now - I want to go back to what we were talking about before. About
5   what happened last night. I want you to tell me everything that you felt, every-
6   thing that you saw.
7 TH: Do you think you can do that?
8 PT: I'll try.
9 TH: Good. Let's start with you going to bed. What time was that?
10 PT: I don't know. Maybe nine, ten o'clock?
11 TH: The hall lights go out at ten. Was it before that, or after?
12 PT: After. No, wait. Before.
13 TH: Were you thinking about anything in particular then?
14 PT: Not really. A couple things.
15 TH: Such as...
16 PT: Well, the Apple Festival. I was pretty excited about going to that. Maybe going
17   to that.
18 TH: Okay. Anything else?
19 PT: Not that I can think of.
20 TH: So you weren't worried about going to sleep? Scared that you might wake up
21   and have another episode?
22 TH: Kari?
23 [PAUSE]
24 PT: Yes. Yes, I was scared.
25 TH: I would think so.
26 TH: Thank you again for being honest with me Kari.
27 PT: Do we have to do this?
28 TH: It's important, yes. So I experience what you experienced. So I can help you.
29 [PAUSE]
30 TH: Let's continue. So you fell asleep. And then...
31 [PAUSE]
32 TH: What happened after you fell asleep, Kari? Did you dream?

SESSION TEXT (CONTINUED)

33 | TH: No dreams at all?
34 | PT: No, I mean...I didn't fall asleep.
35 | TH: Not at all?
36 | PT: No. Not at all.
37 |

KRIEGMOOR
PSYCHIATRIC INSTITUTE

INTERNAL CORRESPONDENCE - NOT FOR EXTERNAL USE OR DISSEMINATION

TO: c_marsh@kriegmoor-psychiatric.org

FROM: a_blackburn@kriegmoor-psychiatric.org

DATE: 9/27/04

RE: HA-09

Regarding the above patient, I have asked night staff to observe and forward you reports on her sleep patterns for upcoming week. FYI, anecdotal testimony from staff re: seems to indicate nocturnal hallucinatory episodes not just this week but since week of 9/12 have been occurring both more frequently and with greater intensity.

For what it's worth, doctor, my experience has been that such developments frequently precede a breakthrough in treatment. I do hope that will be the case here as well.

-- Blackburn, Supervisor Nursing Staff

TO: c_marsh@kriegmoor-psychiatric.org

FROM: c_lapierre@kriegmoor-psychiatric.org

DATE: 10/4/04

RE: HA-09

Hi doctor, I'm new on the ward, I did overnights last Tuesday and
Wednesday? Ms. Blackburn sent around a note saying you wanted some details
on the trouble this patient's been having sleeping. Don't know how many
details I can give you, the poor girl was just sitting up in bed wide
awake all night long, it seemed, both nights. I know standing orders are
not to use sedatives unless your present and I can understand that given
how high her dose is right now, but...well, I don't mean to speak out of
turn but she needs some kind of help, I think.

- Cathy LaPierre

**KRIEGMOOR**
PSYCHIATRIC INSTITUTE

INTERNAL CORRESPONDENCE - NOT FOR EXTERNAL USE OR DISSEMINATION

TO: c_marsh@kriegmoor-psychiatric.org

FROM: l_francisco@kriegmoor-psychiatric.org

DATE: 10/6/04

RE: HA-09

The supervisor said you were looking for details about this patient's
insomnia: a check of my records reveals that I worked third shift Friday
last week. Patient was awake during all bed checks, 1:15, 3:15, 5:15.

EDLOG 1.2

MEDLOG AUTOMATED TRANSCRIPTION SERVICES
SESSION INFORMATION

CLIENT: KRIEGMOOR PSYCHIATRIC
OTHER (O): MS. INGRID HANSEN IN RE: PATIENT HA-09
THERAPIST (TH): DR. CHARLES MARSH
DATE OF SESSION: 10/8/04
SYSTEM PARAMETERS: LANGUAGE DETECT/ENGLISH LINE RETURN DELAY/8 SECONDS
SILENCE THRESHOLD: -5.4 DB FILE FORMAT: MS WORD

SESSION TEXT (CONTINUED)

1 O: that just as you have a schedule to keep, Doctor, I have one I'm required to
2   adhere to as well. So I don't appreciate having to wait for half an hour.
3 TH: I understand, and I apologize, Mrs. Hansen. I -
4 O: She's worse, doctor.
5 TH: Yes, she is.
6 O: I've never seen her like this before. She won't even look at me. Won't even talk
7   to me.
8 TH: We have her on some pretty strong medication right now - she's probably feel-
9   ing that quite a bit. I would say that if you want to stay a couple more hours,
10   she should fairly coherent.
11 O: I can't stay. I have a meeting. But I wanted to make sure to speak with you.
12 TH: I'm glad. I feel that your daughter and I are really establishing -
13 O: You've been talking about what happened on the island.
14 TH: Excuse me?
15 O: Dr. Morris has shown me a few of the transcripts. You've been talking about the
16   island, and all those ridiculous stories she and those people from the college
17   were reading.
18 TH: Well...yes, but that's so she can see where her hallucinations - the ideas for her
19   hallucinations - came from.
20 O: I want you to stop talking about those things. They're clearly aggravating her
21   condition.
22 TH: Mrs. Hansen, I don't think my reviewing the case history with your daughter is
23   responsible for the deterioration in her condition.
24 O: Then what is?
25 TH: That's what we're trying to figure out. It may simply be the natural progression
26   of her condition.
27 O: But it's only been since you started seeing her that this has happened. Doctor,
28   you'll forgive me for speaking bluntly, but I am a cause and effect person. It's
29   what I do every day of the week with my business. It's what allows me to accu-
30   rately analyze and forecast trends for my customers. And right here, right now,
31   I see a definite cause and effect. You bring up these ridiculous stories again,
32   which my daughter has spent two years trying not to think about, and she gets

33	worse. Therefore -
34	TH: But if you'll allow me to explain -
35	O: Are you going to let me finish?
36	TH: Yes. Go on.
37	O: Thank you. Now where was I? Yes. Those stories. I must tell you, doctor, I'm
38	not happy about this. Not happy at all.

KRIEGMOOR
PSYCHIATRIC INSTITUTE

INTERNAL CORRESPONDENCE - NOT FOR EXTERNAL USE OR DISSEMINATION

TO: c_marsh@kriegmoor-psychiatric.org

FROM: don_gilder@kriegmoor-psychiatric.org

DATE: 10/11/04

RE: PATIENT HA-09

Hello, Dr. Marsh. I'm one of the shift managers in C and D wings - I think we met the first day you were here, when the director was bringing you around. Anyway, I ran into Althea, and she said that you were looking for specifics regarding HA-09s sleeping habits, or really, lack thereof.

We had two nurses call in sick last Saturday, and so I ended up on C myself, working the overnight. First time I went by HA-09s room, she was lying in bed, asleep or pretty close to it (can't say for certain, but I think this was around 10:30, right after I came on), but about half an hour later I was on the second floor, when I hear this blood-curdling scream, and I knew right away it was your patient (not the first time this has happened). By the time I got downstairs, she was huddled in one corner of the room, pointing at the wall. Took me about twenty minutes to calm her down.

It happened again an hour later, and this time, I had to leave my only other help on the ward with her. She was pretty close to hysterical and to tell you the truth, I don't think she ever went back to sleep. It was a tough night all around, by the way - the kid (HE-31, he's yours too, isn't he?) was up a lot, we ended up having to give him something to help sleep as well.

Hope this info helps.

Don

MEDLOG 1.2

MEDLOG AUTOMATED TRANSCRIPTION SERVICES
SESSION INFORMATION

CLIENT: KRIEGMOOR PSYCHIATRIC
PATIENT (PT): JACOB HELLINGER
THERAPIST (TH): DR. CHARLES MARSH
DATE OF SESSION: 10/11/04
SYSTEM PARAMETERS: LANGUAGE DETECT/ENGLISH LINE RETURN DELAY/8 SECONDS
SILENCE THRESHOLD: -5.4 DB FILE FORMAT: MS WORD

SESSION TEXT (CONTINUED)

1 TH: what happened to scare you Jake?
2 PT: It was just like in the book.
3 TH: Where the Wild Things Are?
4 PT: Yes.
5 TH: Tell me.
6 PT: I was Max. I was in the forest and the monsters were hunting me. I hid from
7 them but they found me. And they killed me.
8 TH: That sounds terrible Jake.
9 PT: That's why I screamed.
10 TH: I can understand that.
11 PT: They put their knives in me and they cut me up and I watched them cut me up.
12 TH: The monsters had knives?
13 PT: Yes. Big knives and they had...
14 TH: What is it Jake?
15 PT: They wore masks. The monsters wore masks.
16 TH: Okay.
17 PT: You know what I think Dr. Marsh? I think the monsters were people. They were
18 people wearing masks.
19 TH: This is a very disturbing dream you had Jake.
20 PT: But it wasn't a dream. It was real. Just like in the book.
21 TH: Let's take a step back, Jake. Why were the monsters hunting you?
22 TH: Because of something you did?
23 PT: No.
24 TH: Then why?
25 [PAUSE]
26 PT: Because they were hungry.
27 TH: They were hungry.
28 PT: Uh-huh. They were hungry and they wanted to eat me. And when they caught
29 me that's what they did. They cut me up into little pieces and they ate me. They -
30 TH: All right Jake. Easy. Easy.
31 [PAUSE]
32 TH: I think that's enough for today, don't you?

SESSION TEXT (CONTINUED)

1	TH: Kari? Can you answer me please?
2	PT: I don't know.
3	TH: Did you sleep at all - let me put it that way.
4	PT: Yes.
5	TH: But you had another episode.
6	PT: Yes.
7	TH: Another bad one.
8	PT: Yes.
9	TH: Can we talk about it?
10	[PAUSE]
11	TH: I don't mean to sound like a broken record, but the more I know about what
12	you're thinking - before this happens, while it happens, and afterwards - the
13	more I can help you. You understand that, don't you?
14	PT: Yes.
15	TH: So can we talk about it?
16	PT: You don't believe me.
17	TH: I've said this over and over again - it's not a question of me believing you, it's a
18	question of me understanding exactly what it is that's happening.
19	[PAUSE]
20	TH: Why don't you want to talk to me about this Kari?
21	PT: I don't see the point.
22	TH: The point is to help you get better.
23	[PAUSE]
24	PT: The Apple Festival is over, isn't it?
25	TH: Yes Kari. The Apple Festival is over.
26	[PAUSE]
27	TH: I'm sorry I couldn't get permission for us to go, but your mother felt -
28	PT: Fuck my mother.
29	[PAUSE]
30	PT: I'm sorry.
31	TH: I understand your frustration Kari. I know how much you wanted to go.
32	PT: But I need to be better.

SESSION TEXT (CONTINUED)

33	TH: Yes. You need to be better. Which means we need to talk about this. We need
34	to...
35	[PAUSE]
36	PT: What?
37	PT: Is something the matter?
38	TH: No. It's just - something just occurred to me, that's all. A way to help you talk
39	about things more freely, perhaps.
40	PT: I'm all for that.
41	TH: Yes.
42	PT: So...
43	[PAUSE]
44	TH: Kari - have you ever been hypnotized?
45	PT: For real?
46	TH: Yes.
47	PT: You mean like 'you are getting sleepy, very sleepy' kind of hypnotized?
48	TH: Yes. That's exactly what I mean.
49	PT: No.
50	TH: Do you have any preconceived notions about hypnosis

INTERNAL CORRESPONDENCE - NOT FOR EXTERNAL USE OR DISSEMINATION

TO: c_marsh@kriegmoor-psychiatric.org
FROM: claire_morris@kriegmoor-psychiatric.org

DATE: 10/12/04
RE: HA-09

Please excuse the delay in getting back to you on your request. I've been thinking about this and consulting with various other staff members as well. Our conclusion: under normal circumstances, the technique is contraindicated for schizophrenics. However, as you point out, these are hardly normal circumstances.

You have the authority to proceed with this technique for three sessions, at which point we will re-evaluate patient's condition/your progress. Please exercise all due caution.

-- Claire

SESSION T...

CLIENT: KRIEGMOOR PSYCH...
PATIENT (PT): KARI HANSEN
THERAPIST (TH): DR. CHARLES MARSH
DATE OF SESSION: 10/13/04
SYSTEM PARAMETERS: LANGUAGE DETECT/ENGLISH LINE RETURN DELAY/3 SECON...
SILENCE THRESHOLD: -5.4 DB FILE FORMAT: MS WORD

SESSION TEXT (CONTINUED)

1 TH: close your eyes, and just relax. Can you feel your right hand Kari?
2 PT: Sure.
3 TH: Feel the fingers of your right hand now. The pinky, the ring finger, the middle
4 finger, forefinger, thumb...feel the blood flowing to them, flowing through them.
5 Concentrate on that feeling - the pulsing, the life going through your hand.
6 Concentrate on that hand, your right hand. The weight of the fingers, of the
7 blood, the bone, the muscle, you're aware of all of it. Your fingers are very
8 heavy. Very, very heavy. Thick. It would take a lot of energy to move them,
9 they're so heavy. So very, very heavy.
10 [PAUSE]
11 TH: Your whole hand is heavy now. So heavy, in fact, that you can't even lift it. But
12 that's all right. You're very relaxed very much at peace. Very content, even if
13 you can't lift your hand.
14 [PAUSE]
15 TH: You can't lift your hand Kari, can you?
16 PT: No.
17 TH: No, of course not. But you're comfortable lying in bed anyway. Very content.
18 Very relaxed. It's almost as if you're going to go to sleep now, as if it were night.
19 But it's not, you understand that don't you? It's one-forty-four in the afternoon,
20 and you're in the middle of a therapy session with me. Isn't that right?
21 PT: Yes.
22 TH: And who am I?
23 PT: Dr. Marsh. Charles.
24 TH: That's right. I'm Dr. Marsh. And you're Kari Hansen, and we're just going to talk
25 about a few things now. Okay?
26 PT: Okay.
27 TH: You're very relaxed, Kari. That's very good. I see a book here next to your bed
28 - Iron Lake. Can you tell me about this book?
   PT: It's a mystery. My mother brought it for me when she came.
   ...you're reading it now. Is it good?
   ...won't gotten very far.
   ...rnoon ahead of you, after our session.

(left fragment, partial text visible along page edge:)

...CC...
...pen...
...bo...
...light.
...etely c...
...e's lig...
...t they...
...dark. I'...
...red. I'm...
...I are ha...
...re are no...
...e, okay?
...me your ha...
...n not going...
...content. I'm...
...you to hold...
...e lying in this...
...t's dark in you...
...at happens ne...
...ve works right...
...am for a minute j...
...y -
...lax.
...ari.
...med - what did you...
...that we went to the...
...ream.
...e, yes. We were hap...

33	PT: Yes.
34	TH: And tonight.
35	PT: Yes.
36	TH: Do you read at night?
37	PT: Sometimes.
38	TH: What about last night? Did you read then?
39	PT: I tried.
40	TH: But you couldn't.
41	PT: No.
42	TH: I read last night, you know. Some things that Walt McKinnon at the historical
43	society sent me.
44	PT: Walt.
45	TH: You remember him?
46	PT: Yes.
47	TH: He wanted me to say hi to you. He wanted to know how you were doing.
48	PT: Not good. I'm not doing good at all.
49	TH: Shhh. That's all right Kari. You're relaxed. You're at peace. You're very, very
50	content.
51	TH: Let's talk a little bit more about last night. You ate dinner.
52	PT: Yes.
53	TH: And then...
54	PT: I watched TV but there was nothing on, so I read that book.
55	TH: You tried to read.
56	PT: Yes.
57	TH: But you couldn't.
58	PT: I couldn't concentrate.
59	TH: Why not?
60	[PAUSE]
61	PT: Because I could feel them.
62	TH: Go on.
63	PT: I could sense them, hiding behind the walls. In the walls.
64	TH: They're behind the walls?
65	PT: Not really. They're someplace else entirely but that's how they get here. They
66	come through, or sometimes they use the corners and come around.
67	TH: And are they there now? Behind the walls?
67	PT: Yes.
69	TH: Which wall?
70	PT: All of them. All the walls, and the ceiling, and the floor. Everywhere. They're
71	everywhere, all the time, they're watching and waiting for their chance to -
72	TH: Okay. Just relax Kari. Let's take a minute. You're doing great, let's just stay
73	relaxed.
74	PT: I'll try. I really will try, Dr. Marsh.
75	PT: It's just hard when they're right there, watching. Always watching.
76	PT: I wish I knew why. I wish I knew what they wanted.

CLIENT: KRIEGMOOR PSYCHIATRIC
PATIENT (PT): KARI HANSEN
THERAPIST (TH): DR. CHARLES MARSH
DATE OF SESSION: 10/13/04
SYSTEM PARAMETERS: LANGUAGE DETECT/ENGLISH LINE RETURN DELAY/3 SECONDS
SILENCE THRESHOLD: -5.4 DB FILE FORMAT: MS WORD

SESSION TEXT (CONTINUED)

1 TH: and what happened next?
2 PT: I put down the book.
3 TH: And then?
4 PT: I shut out the light.
5 TH: So it's completely dark in your room now.
6 PT: Yes. No - there's light coming from the hall.
7 TH: Of course. But they dim the lights at night, don't they?
8 PT: Yes. It's very dark. I'm scared.
9 TH: Don't be scared. I'm right here. Even though in your mind it's night, remember
   that you and I are having this session in the middle of the afternoon. The sun is
   shining. There are no shadows in the room, it's very bright, and you're very safe
   here with me, okay?
   PT: Okay.
   TH: Here. Give me your hand - your left hand. There. You feel that? I'm right here
   with you. I'm not going anywhere. So relax. Your bed is very comfortable.
   You're very content. I'm here. You can picture me sitting beside you, yes?
   PT: Yes.
   TH: Now I want you to hold that image in your mind, and think back again to last
   night. You're lying in this bed, and you've put your book down, and shut off the
   light. And it's dark in your room.
   PT: Yes.
   TH: Tell me what happens next.
   PT: The sedative works right away. I can't keep my eyes open. And then I'm asleep
   and I dream for a minute just a minute and then I wake up and they're right
   there, they -
   TH: Shhh. Relax.
   TH: Relax, Kari.
   TH: You dreamed - what did you dream about?
   PT: I dreamt that we went to the Apple Festival, and ate apple chili.
   TH: A nice dream.
   PT: Very nice, yes. We were happy.
   TH: And then...

33	PT: I woke up.
34	TH: Relax. You're here with me. You feel my hand?
35	PT: Yes.
36	TH: Good. Hold tight. It's like we're at the Apple Festival, isn't it? Like in your
37	dream?
38	PT: Yes. It's just like my dream. We're holding hands and walking through the festival.
39	TH: But now you're waking up.
40	PT: I don't want to wake up.
41	TH: It's all right, I'm still here. Now your eyes are opening. What do you see?
42	PT: My room.
43	TH: Describe it to me.
44	PT: I see the light from the hall reflected on the tv screen. The metal rail on the bed
45	the red numbers on the clock.
46	TH: What time is it?
47	PT: 1:40.
48	TH: What else?
49	PT: Someone is talking.
50	TH: One of the nurses.
51	PT: I think so. He's down the hall very far away I can barely hear him. He's arguing
52	with someone, I think. He wants more from them. A lot more.
53	PT: The moon is out.
54	PT: I feel them watching me.
55	TH: The shadows.
56	PT: Yes.
57	TH: Where are they?
58	PT: Under the tv - where the wires are.
59	TH: You see them?
60	PT: Not yet. But they're coming. They're looking for the way in.
61	TH: The way in.
62	PT: To our world.
63	TH: Where are they coming from Kari?
64	PT: I don't know. Someplace else. Oh God.
65	PT: They're coming now they're making the door.
66	TH: Tell me what they look like.
67	PT: They don't have any shape until they get here. Then...
67	[PAUSE]
69	TH: What is it Kari?
70	TH: What do you see?
71	PT: The reflection on the TV - it's gone. They're blocking the light.
72	PT: They're here.
73	TH: What do they look like?
74	PT: They're all over the room. Everywhere. Flying around me like black clouds like
75	bats...
76	PT: They're angry.

33	TH: Why are they angry?
34	PT: I don't know. But they're very, very angry. They want to hurt me again.
35	TH: How do they hurt you Kari?
36	PT: They swallow me up and cut me and stick things into my skin.
37	TH: They did this last night?
38	PT: Yes. There they are. Oh God it's happening again...
39	TH: Okay Kari. You can open your eyes.
40	PT: Why are they doing this to me? I didn't do anything. This is wrong.
41	TH: Kari listen to me open your eyes.
42	PT: It wasn't me I swear it wasn't me -
43	TH: KARI!
44	[PAUSE]
45	TH: There. That's all right, I'm here.
46	PT: Oh God.
47	TH: Shhh. It's okay. You're safe.
48	PT: No I'm not.
49	TH: The shadows are gone Kari and I'm here.
50	PT: But you won't be here tonight and they'll come again. They'll come again and
51	they'll hurt me again.
52	TH: They can't hurt you Kari. They're not real.
53	PT: Please stay with me tonight Dr. Marsh. Please.
54	TH: I know what's happening to you is terrifying. I know how real it all seems to
55	you. But the hallucinations -
56	PT: They're not hallucinations. They're real. They're real and they hurt me. They -
57	TH: Kari.
58	PT: What?
59	TH: What is that?
60	PT: What?
61	TH: There. On your arm.
62	[PAUSE]
63	TH: Could you roll back the sleeve of your gown for me please?
64	[PAUSE]
65	TH: Where did those marks come from Kari?
66	TH: Who did this to you?
67	TH: Stay right here. I'm going to get a nurse.
67	
69	
70	[TRANSCRIPT ENDS]
71	
72	
73	
74	
75	

KRIEGMOOR
PSYCHIATRIC INSTITUTE

Red Cliff Parkway
Bayfield, WI 48544

MEDICAL WARD

INCIDENT REPORT

DATE OF INCIDENT: 10/13/2004
DATE OF REPORT: 10/14/2004
REPORTING PHYSICIAN: G. YANAGISAWA
PATIENT: HA-09

Details: Tissue bruised and swollen along inside of patient's upper right arm, lower right leg. Multiple points of impact running parallel to major circulatory structures, evidence of repeated probing of contact points by sharp, needle-like objects.

Treatment: Impact points did not break skin, discoloration should fade, bruising heal naturally in a relatively short period of time.

Commentary: Possibility exists bruising is an allergic reaction to drug protocol, given pattern of marks, though this would be highly atypical. My opinion: wounds are most probably self-inflicted, given patient's current psychological condition. A plea for attention.

G. Yanagisawa 10/14/04

KRIEGMOOR
PSYCHIATRIC INSTITUTE

INTERNAL CORRESPONDENCE - NOT FOR EXTERNAL USE OR DISSEMINATION

TO: c_marsh@kriegmoor-psychiatric.org
FROM: a_blackburn@kriegmoor-psychiatric.org
DATE: 10/14/04
RE: HA-09

I know you're new here, so I'm going to forgive the suggestion that a staff member might have been involved in any way with the above patient's injuries.

I will alert all personnel, in particular third shift, to maintain a careful watch on this patient to insure no further such incidents occur.

-- Blackburn, Supervisor Nursing Staff

TO: c_marsh@kriegmoor-psychiatric.org

FROM: p_ferguson@kriegmoor-psychiatric.org

DATE: 10/18/04

RE: HA-09

You have my sympathies, doctor. Reading the transcripts of your sessions with HA-09 brought back all the difficulties I had in dealing with this particular patient.

I was indeed primary on her case from date of admission (8/29/03) to 9/8/04. As you noted, we did not file transcripts of all sessions, and of course my memory is far from perfect. Nonetheless I can say with a reasonable degree of certainty that the severity of HA-09's hallucinations varied not just from week to week, but sometimes day to day. We had sessions where she would be virtually catatonic, unable to answer even the simplest of questions, and sessions where she would not only be able to converse at length but actively participate in diagnosis of her condition. We were never able to correlate severity of hallucinatory episodes with any identifiable factors; medication, sleep quality, menstrual cycle, anything. It was puzzling, it was frustrating, it was why we eventually classified her schizophrenia as treatment-resistant.

What I'm seeing in your transcripts differs only in the active hostility of said hallucinations; that is, to my recollection, unique in the patient's case history, as is, of course, the cutting - obviously self-inflicted, as Dr. Yanagisawa suggested. You may want to consider a change in drug protocol - just a thought.

Let me know if there's anything I can do to help.

- Peter

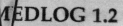

MEDLOG 1.2

MEDLOG AUTOMATED TRANSCRIPTION SERVICES
SESSION INFORMATION

CLIENT: KRIEGMOOR PSYCHIATRIC
PATIENT (PT): KARI HANSEN
THERAPIST (TH): DR. CHARLES MARSH
DATE OF SESSION: 10/18/04
SYSTEM PARAMETERS: LANGUAGE DETECT/ENGLISH LINE RETURN DELAY/3 SECONDS
SILENCE THRESHOLD: -5.4 DB FILE FORMAT: MS WORD

SESSION TEXT (CONTINUED)

1	TH: want to talk about what happened. About your injuries.
2	PT: I told you what happened.
3	TH: The shadows did this.
4	PT: Yes.
5	TH: And is this the first time they've done something like this? The first time they've
6	huut you?
7	TH: Kari?
8	PT: Yes.
9	TH: Why now? Why would they do this now?
10	PT: I told you. They're angry.
11	TH: Why?
12	PT: I don't know. I think...it might be because of the arrowheads.
13	TH: The ones you found on the island?
14	PT: Yes.
15	TH: Does that make sense, Kari? That happened almost one year ago. Why would
16	they be angry now?
17	PT: I don't know.
18	TH: Kari - understand that I don't want you to get upset, but I have to ask this. Are
19	you hurting yourself?
20	PT: Am I what?
21	TH: Are you doing this to yourself? These marks?
22	PT: You think I would do that?
23	TH: Would you?
24	PT: Fuck you.
25	TH: Kari...
26	PT: I can't believe you could say that to me.
27	TH: I didn't mean -
28	PT: Just go away.
29	[PAUSE]
30	TH: I can't go away Kari. I'm your doctor. Taking care of you is my job. I have to --
31	PT: Well you're not doing a very good job, are you?
32	[PAUSE]

33	TH: No. I don't suppose I am.
34	TH: All right, Kari. We'll talk again tomorrow.
35	PT: Wait.
36	PT: Dr. Marsh?
37	TH: Yes?
38	PT: I'm sorry.
39	PT: I think you're doing a good job. I know I'm not such an easy patient.
40	TH: You're doing your best, Kari. I know that.
41	PT: And I'm telling you the truth. I always tell you the truth.
42	TH: I appreciate that.
43	PT: But you still don't believe me.
44	TH: About the bruises? No.
45	PT: I wish I could prove it to you.
46	TH: Can I tell you something Kari? There's a part of me that wishes you could too.
47	[PAUSE]
48	TH: Well. I'll see you tomorrow Kari. I hope you have a good night.
49	PT: Come back later.
50	TH: Excuse me?
51	PT: Come back later and I'll prove it to you. Come back tonight and I'll show you
52	they're real.
53	[PAUSE]
54	TH: Kari. I can't do that. You know I can't do that.
55	PT: Please. Please Dr. Marsh. Charles.
56	[PAUSE]
57	PT: Please.
58	TH: I'm sorry. I can't.
59	TH: Goodnight Kari.
60	
61	**[TRANSCRIPT ENDS]**
62	
63	
64	
65	
66	
67	
67	
69	
70	
71	
72	
73	
74	
75	
76	

CLIENT: KRIEGMOOR PSYCHIATRIC
OTHER (O): MS. INGRID HANSEN IN RE. PATIENT HA-09
THERAPIST (TH): DR. CHARLES MARSH
DATE OF SESSION: 10/19/04
SYSTEM PARAMETERS: LANGUAGE DETECT/ENGLISH LINE RETURN DELAY/6 SECONDS
SILENCE THRESHOLD: -5.4 DB FILE FORMAT: MS WORD

SESSION TEXT (CONTINUED)

1 O: I have a number of concerns.
2 TH: As do we all.
3 O: I trust the director has shared mine with you.
4 TH: We've talked.
5 O: I wanted to reinforce what she said. I want you to understand the depth of my
6   concern. My daughter's formed quite an attachment to you doctor.
7 TH: Yes. I'm aware of that.
8 O: I'm not sure it's entirely appropriate.
9 TH: Mrs. Hansen. You understand that these things happen all the time, that -
10 O: Excuse me. I'm not a child. Don't talk to me like I'm a child.
11 TH: I'm sorry.
12 O: I understand that these things happen a lot. I don't give a good goddamn
13   about any of those other times it's happened frankly. This is the only thing that
14   matters to me - what's happening between you and my daughter.
15 TH: Nothing untoward is happening, I can assure you of that.
16 O: I know that. If I thought any different, I would be suing you and this institution
17   seven ways to Sunday. I've made my willingness to do just that very clear to
18   the director.
19 TH: I'm sorry you felt you had to do that. You know Kriegmoor's reputation, Mrs.
20   Hansen. What the institution stands for, its history -
21 O: I know your history as well Doctor.
22 TH: Excuse me?
23 O: I know about Texas. About Richard Lattimore.
24 TH: I see.
25 O: My daughter is the world to me, Dr. Marsh. I make it my business to find out
26   about the people she comes in contact with.
27 TH: I have nothing to hide. I've made my peace with the past.
28 O: Have you? I'm glad to hear it. Because of course, I would be concerned if you
29   were using my daughter's case to restore your professional reputation. Treating
30   her like an experiment.
31 TH: I'm not. Your daughter is not an experiment to me, Mrs. Hansen. I promise you

SESSION TEXT (CONTINUED)

33 O: I'm glad to hear it.
34 [PAUSE]
35 O: Again, you'll forgive me for speaking bluntly doctor. But I don't believe in sugar-
36   coating the truth.
37 TH: I understand.
38 O: Good.
39 TH: You had some other concerns?
40 O: Of course. The cutting.
41 TH: We're all concerned about that.
42 O: It has to stop before she does permanent damage.
43 TH: I agree, which is why we've put her on the T-86.
44 O: But it's not helping.
45 TH: Not yet, no, but I feel -
46 O: Then we have to find something else don't we? Or something to supplement its
47   effect?
48 TH: I suppose so.
49 O: You suppose so. Do you have any ideas what we might do? Because I certainly
50   have some thoughts along those lines. I'm not a doctor, of course, but some
51   things do seem obvious to me.

MEDLOG 1.2

MEDLOG AUTOMATED TRANSCRIPTION SERVICES
SESSION INFORMATION

CLIENT: KRIEGMOOR PSYCHIATRIC
PATIENT (PT): KARI HANSEN
THERAPIST (TH): DR. CHARLES MARSH
DATE OF SESSION: 10/21/04
SYSTEM PARAMETERS: LANGUAGE DETECT/ENGLISH LINE RETURN DELAY/8 SECONDS
SILENCE THRESHOLD: -5.4 DB FILE FORMAT: MS WORD

SESSION TEXT (CONTINUED)

1 PT: don't need them, and I don't want them!
2 TH: Kari...
3 PT: Take them off.
4 TH: Just relax, Kari. Your mother —
5 PT: Fuck my mother! Take these off right now!
6 TH: I can't do that. I'm sorry.
7 [PAUSE]
8
9
10
11
12
13
14
15
16
17
18
19
20
21
22

KRIEGMOOR
PSYCHIATRIC INSTITUTE

Red Cliff Parkway
Bayfield, WI 48544

INCIDENT REPORT

DATE OF INCIDENT: 10/22/2004
DATE OF REPORT: 10/23/2004
REPORTING PHYSICIAN: G. YANAGISAWA
PATIENT: HA-09

Details: Repeat of incident (see 10/13/04 report)

Treatment: As per previous.

Commentary: Please maintain 24-hour watch!!!

G. Yanagisawa 10/23/04

be laughing or crying. I could
Sleep and I was

ver and

the

KRIEGMOOR
PSYCHIATRIC INSTITUTE

 INTERNAL CORRESPONDENCE - NOT FOR EXTERNAL USE OR DISSEMINATION

TO: c_marsh@kriegmoor-psychiatric.org, YANAGISAWA

FROM: a_blackburn@kriegmoor-psychiatric.org

DATE: 10/23/04

RE: HA-09

I appreciate everyone's concern for this patient, but of course having somebody in her room all day, every day simply isn't possible, as I've explained to her mother on more than one occasion. We just don't have the staff to do this.

In my opinion the restraints need to be utilized on a twenty-four hour basis until the cutting stops.

Blackburn, Supervisor Nursing Staff

KRIEGMOOR
PSYCHIATRIC INSTITUTE

INTERNAL CORRESPONDENCE - NOT FOR EXTERNAL USE OR DISSEMINATION

TO: c_marsh@kriegmoor-psychiatric.org,
a_blackburn@kriegmoor-psychiatric.org

FROM: claire_morris@kriegmoor-psychiatric.org

DATE: 10/23/04

RE: HA-09

Until further notice patient is to be restrained at all times when not in presence of staff or support personnel.

(PT): KARI HANSEN
THERAPIST (TH): DR. CHARLES MARSH
DATE OF SESSION: 10/24/04
SYSTEM PARAMETERS: LANGUAGE DETECT/ENGLISH LINE RETURN DELAY/3 SECONDS
SILENCE THRESHOLD: -5.4 DB FILE FORMAT: MS WORD

SESSION TEXT (CONTINUED)

1 TH: the T is short for the manufacturer's name. Terence-Buttrell - they're one of the
2 big pharmaceutical companies. The 86, it's an abbreviation for the chemical
3 compound, that's all. Okay?
4 PT: No. I don't need any more drugs, doctor. Please.
5 TH: It's just for awhile - to help you sleep. It's very strong stuff - you may feel a little
6 groggy at first.
7 PT: It won't help.
8 TH: Kari…
9 PT: It won't help.

SESSION

1 TH: if you saw it on today's schedule, but there's a movie later in the auditorium.
2 Roman Holiday, with Audrey Hepburn. Did you ever see that?
3 TH: It's a great movie, Kari. Some beautiful shots of Rome.
4 TH: Might be good to get out of your room for awhile, distract yourself.
5 PT: I don't know. Maybe.
6 TH: I encourage you to go Kari.
7 PT: Are you going?
8 TH: Me?
9 PT: Yes. Are you going?
10 [PAUSE]
11 TH: No. No, I have work to do.

FROM: p_ferguson@kriegmoor-psychiatric.org
DATE: 10/25/04
RE: HA-09

Again I don't want to step on your toes, Doctor, but in my opinion the T-86 does not seem to be working for your patient. I have had some success with the new Orlander/Simons anti-hallucinogens, and I still have samples in my office, if you're interested.

- Pe
LIENT: KRIEGMOOR PSYCH
ATIENT (PT): DARRELL COVEY
THERAPIST (TH): DR. CHARLES MARSH
DATE OF SESSION: 10/25/04
SYSTEM PARAMETERS: LANGUAGE DETECT/ENGLISH LINE RETURN DELAY/3 SECONDS
SILENCE THRESHOLD: -5.4 DB FILE FORMAT: MS WORD

SESSION TEXT (CONTINUED)

TH: sorry I don't have more time to spend with you today Darrell. I'm running late.
PT: Who's Darrell?

DRAFT MATERIAL: NOT FOR PUBLICATION
ARTICLE TITLE: SHADOWS IN THE ASYLUM
AUTHOR: Charles Marsh, M.D., Ph.D.

At this point in my treatment of K, despite the optimistic face I
presented to her mother, I was in fact feeling quite disheartened.
The additional time and effort I had devoted to her case seemed in
vain; the personal rapport we had developed seemed irrelevant. Her
condition had worsened under my care. The certainty I had formerly
felt regarding the course of treatment
I had embarked on evaporated. Echoes of the Lattimore case, of the
ill-fated Predictives Calculus, occupied my mind. I began, once
more, to doubt my professional competency.

It was at this point in time — specifically on the evening of
October 22, 2004 — that I first obtained (and subsequently used)
stimulants from the hospital infirmary. My purpose in doing so
was two-fold: I intended to leave no stone unturned in pursuing
an effective therapy for K, and needed the additional time/energy
to continue researching cases similar to hers. Second, as the
director had pointed out, my work with other patients had suffered
as a result of my focus on K, and I was determined to right that
wrong.

I mention this not to excuse any of my subsequent actions (the
use of stimulants is a common enough practice among physicians, as
anyone who has worked in a hospital will attest to) but because of
what happened a few nights later, when I experienced an unforeseen
side-effect of that usage, when I entered K's room and stumbled
on to what seemed to me then (and I am certain, will seem to
the reader now) a most unbelievable truth. In that instant of
discovery, I was Isaac Newton, stunned by the fall of the apple,

27   ...went —
28   TH: You first.
      PT: I was just goin...

MENTION NAME OF DRUG
NYPUREDEN
USED IN AMTS CONSISTENT
W/PRESCRIPTION STANDARD

one

188 ...SERVICES

PATIENT (PT): KARI HANSEN
THERAPIST (TH): DR. CHARLES MARSH
OTHER PERSONNEL (OP): NURSE CATHY LAPIERRE
DATE OF SESSION: 10/25/04
SYSTEM PARAMETERS: LANGUAGE DETECT/ENGLISH LINE RETURN DELAY/8 SECONDS
SILENCE THRESHOLD: -5.4 DB FILE FORMAT: MS WORD

SESSION TEXT (CONTINUED)

1 OP: only wanted you. I'm sorry about the time, but –
2 TH: It's all right, Kristen. I was working anyway. Kari?
3 PT: Dr. Marsh.
4 TH: I'm here. Just calm down, I'm here.
5 OP: You want me to get a sedative, doctor?
6 TH: No, Kristen. That's all right. She seems better now. Kari? Are you feeling better?
7 PT: I guess so.
8 TH: Good. Why don't you close your eyes again, see if you can sleep a little –
9 PT: I'm not tired.
10 TH: It's late.
11 PT: I just – I don't think I could sleep right now.
12 OP: I'll get that sedative, doctor.
13 PT: No. Please. I just need to – I just want to relax a minute.
14 OP: Doctor?
15 TH: All right. No sedative. Do you want the TV on Kari, or –
16 PT: Could you sit with me a minute?
17 TH: I need to get back to work, I'm afraid. But maybe Kristen -
18 PT: No. You.
19 PT: Please. Just for a minute.
20 [PAUSE]
21 TH: Well. All right. Just for a minute.
22 OP: You need me here doctor?
23 TH: No thank you Kristen, you can go.
24 TH: Well.
25 TH: I spoke to your –
26 PT: I went –
27 TH: You first.
28 PT: I was just going to say – I ended up going to that movie the other day. The one
29   you told me about.
30 TH: Roman Holiday.
31 PT: Yes.
32 TH: Did you like it?

69

SESSION TEXT (CONTINUED)

12 PT: I don
13 TH: The o
14 PT: Yes.
15 TH: Does t
16   they be
17 PT: I don't k
18 TH: Kari - un
19   you hurt
20 PT: Am I wha
21 TH: Are you c
22 PT: You think
23 TH: Would you
24 PT: Fuck you.
25 TH: Kari...
26 PT: I can't belie
27 TH: I didn't mea
28 PT: Just go awa
29 [PAUSE]
30 TH: I can't go aw
31 PT: Well you're n
32 [PAUSE]

33 PT: Yes.
34 TH: It's one of my favorites. It was her first movie, you know. Audrey Hepburn. She
35   was quite young when she made it. Only eighteen, I believe.
36 PT: Wow.
37 TH: Yes. It's an impressive performance.
38 PT: No, I just meant…she's younger than me.
39 TH: Yes.
40 PT: I liked him. The guy.
41 TH: Gregory Peck.
42 PT: Yeah.
43 TH: Are you all right Kari?
44 PT: Yes. You were going to say before…
45 TH: I was going to say your mother called again. I spoke with her and we agreed
46   that -
47 TH: Your hands are shaking.
48 TH: Kari what is it? What's the matter?
49 PT: They're coming, Dr. Marsh. The shadows are coming now.
50 TH: Oh Kari.
51 PT: I'm going to prove it to you. That's why I wanted you to stay. To prove I was tell-
52   ing the truth. Wait - where are you going?
53 TH: To get the nurse. You shouldn't have -
54 PT: There. Oh God. You see?
55 PT: Do you see Dr. Marsh?
56 PT: Dr. Marsh?

the nurse back in.

and yet, as the transcript of this particular session will show,
I was temporarily speechless.

   I left K's room, and returned to my office. Everything was
exactly as I had left it: journals scattered everywhere, flipped
open to a variety of what I had thought relevant studies on
treatment-resistant schizophrenics, their common delusional
motifs, drug protocols, etc. The historical material Walter
McKinnon had supplied was on my desk as well, next to K's own
diary. My eyes were drawn to Pierce's words: he had spoken of
a figure of Satan's own design, of shadows shaped like men. I had
passed over them without a second thought earlier; they were,
obviously, the ravings of a madman.

   Now I saw them in an entirely different light.
Because in that instant I had sat at K's bedside, as she pointed
to the far wall, the world before me wavered, and suddenly
changed, as if a curtain had somehow been drawn. A film of first
grey and then absolute ebony appeared and was for a moment as
insubstantial as mist before taking on first weight, and then form.
The shape of a man. I remember blinking my eyes; surely
I had to be seeing things.

   And then the shadow moved, towards K at first, slowly, with
definite purpose, and she screamed my name, and then...it turned
towards me.

   Immediately, I sensed the anger K had spoken of. Conscious,
primal anger: perhaps rage would be a better word, rage directed
not just at my patient but at myself as well.

...even when I close my eyes, I can hear them. I see them in my mind and
when I open my eyes they take shape. I lie still on my blankets and they come.
Angry darkness growing in the corner of the room at first and then the form
of my madness a figyer (sic) of Satan's own design a shadow shapet (sic) like
a man that wispers (sic) in my mind of the cold and blood on the snow. They
hunger. I fere (sic) Wabojee (sic) was right I fere (sic)...

...of them came through the
wall. It came right through the tent wall
and it was in the tent with us, I swear
a stack of Bibles. A shadow, first
had no shape and then it flowed into
the shape of a man. A shadow shaped
like a man, just like Pierce wrote about.

God - What is wrong with me?

I opened my mouth to speak, but no words would come. I was terrified; beyond that, I was stunned. This was no trick of the light, no atmospheric phenomena. This was life, conscious, intelligent life of a specie whose existence I had never dreamed possible.

And as I marveled, the shadow came at me, and the anger I had sensed before multiplied a thousand-fold. Blackness loomed over me, and just as the old cliche would have it, my life, or at least portions of it, the worst portions, the portions I never ever allowed myself to think of, Texas and Lattimore and the calculus I had worked so hard on to such tragic effect flashed before my eyes. I lived it all, all over again, until at last, from what sounded like a long way off, someone spoke my name, and then a hand touched my shoulder. With that touch, it was as if a spell had somehow been broken.

I blinked. The shadow was gone. Kristen - the nurse - stood at my side. She asked if I was all right.

I said I was fine. I said I was going to call it a night. I turned to go -

And saw K in her bed, staring at me.

"You saw it," she said. "Didn't you? Dr. Marsh, you saw it!"

I left the room without another word.

I remained in my office the rest of the night, my mind on fire with questions, possibilities, theories. I read Pierce's letters again and again, along with the Ojibwe legends, transcripts of my ... questions with K, and ... ... common threads emerged — altered states of consciousness, glimpses of something that existed outside of normal human perception... it was fantastic, it was impossible, and yet... it was real. But even accepting, for the moment, its existence, how was it, why was it, that I was suddenly able to see this thing?

It was only as night turned to dawn, as the hospital began to come to life around me and I realized that I had stayed up the entire evening, that I remembered the Nypureden, and an answer to that question suggested itself.

The Nypureden contained traces of a psychoactive, as had the MDMA K had taken. In that respect, both were similar to hallucinogens, a class of drugs which I had studied during my graduate years in Providence, focusing at first on the work of Alexander Shulgin and Humphrey Osmond, and moving from their efforts to the writings of H.G. Wells, Aldous Huxley, and Raymond Laszlo, whose name has now been largely forgotten but who in his day wrote one of the most controversial works regarding such substances ever published. In it, he speculated on the consciousness-expanding effects hallucinogens might have on human perception. Used in the proper fashion, Laszlo declared, those substances would allow man to glimpse existence in its totality, to see beyond the curtain into the face of the infinite.

To him, in fact, these substances were not just drugs. They were doors, to a world beyond.

"Provocative...Highly Recommended"
- Booksellers' Journal

THE DOOR TO BEYOND

RAYMOND LASZLO

Expanding Human Perception Through Altered States of Consciousness

THE DOOR TO BEYOND

Since time immemorial, man has sought to commune with the higher powers, questing for truth, for power, for knowledge of his place in the universe. In this thought-provoking new book, combining history, scientific fact, and metaphysical speculation, Raymond Laszlo declares the existence of those powers an objective reality, and reveals the key to speaking directly with them.

PARTIAL CONTENTS

Out of the Past: Primordial Memory and Myth • Mystical Tradition • The Peyote Ritual • Baudelaire and Swedenborg • The Strange Case of Abraham Rusedski

RAYMOND LASZLO is a founding member of the Colloquium, an organization devoted to the exploration of truth in all matters scientific and philosophical. He lives and works in New York City.

A Note from the Publisher: this book does not condone the use of illegal hallucinogenic subs

Published By Red Lion

Part One   OUT OF THE PAST

Prefatory Remarks

The end of the millennium draws nigh, and reality changes beneath our feet. No longer solid, no longer certain, the very atoms that compose us and our surroundings are, we are told, mostly empty space. The particles within that space do not even exist until we ourselves take their measure, weigh them, account for their position. Matter itself is best thought of as a probability, rather than a constant, for these new physicists - the quantum theorists, as they call themselves - tell us we are active participants in the creation of the world we experience.

And the world we are creating is growing by leaps and bounds with each passing day. The universe itself is expanding, astronomers say, as measured by the new breed of telescope which uses not visible light but radio frequency to apprehend the distant reaches of the cosmos. Closer to home, mathematicians alert us to the existence of new dimensions with alarming frequency - a fifth, a sixth, a seventh, whole new planes of existence we previously knew nothing about. What are we to make of this brave new reality?

Let us say first of all that there are those to whom none of the deliberately provocative statements I have just made will be news. It is the least 'scientific' among us - the philosophers and painters, the writers and the dreamers, the musicians and the playwrights, the artists of this world, in short - who have known that there are, to borrow a phrase, more things in heaven and earth than dreamt of by any of the sciences. And indeed, how could it not be so, for the very tools man uses to take the measure of this world are

3

woefully inadequate to the task. Compare our ability to hear, or smell, or see with that of the "baser" animals – the percentage of audio frequencies, of the electromagnetic spectrum that we perceive is a very small part of a much, much larger whole, a whole whose size most cannot even begin to grasp. As Blake said:

> "If the doors of perception were cleansed
> Everything would appear to man as it is,
> infinite."

And the artist knows the infinite exists, for he is ever in pursuit of it, seeking to reflect the divine in his own creations.

The true artist, in fact, is driven to seek out this epiphany, and knowing that everyday life will not provide it to him, engages in behavior that viewed objectively can only be characterized as self-destructive, drinking to excess, ingesting drugs, etc. in pursuit of an altered state of consciousness in which he can experience the divine anew. The writer who speaks of being 'touched by the muse,' the painter who depicts 'the hand of God,' are speaking as those who have - to borrow a phrase - been blessed in such a way.

Which brings us to a second category of person similarly driven to touch the infinite, the man who perceives this world through the prism of religion. For him, glimpses of the divine involve not just apprehension of ultimate truth, but communication as well. He speaks to God, and God listens. God, in fact, often talks back. In order to achieve this communion with God, this epiphany, however, there are certain ceremonies that must be performed. Some of which involve behavior that viewed objectively can only be characterized as self-destructive (fasting, self-abuse), or rituals that over a span of centuries have lost all relevance to their original purpose (prayer, for example), that being the achievement of an altered state of consciousness in which the divine can be experienced anew.

And yet the men and women who indulged in these seemingly illogical, often self-destructive behaviors, were otherwise among the most important, accomplished, and significant figures within their particular societies, whose wisdom we still revere today. One must ask the question, then, how is it that they were so right about so much, and so wrong about the topic at hand? That they could have spent so much precious time and energy in search of something that so clearly did not exist?

I submit that they would have done no such thing.
I submit that they undertook these behaviors because they had every expectation of success. *I submit they performed these rituals because they worked.* These rites allowed the initiate to smash through the doors of perception, to see the world as it truly is – infinitely larger, more beautiful, and more terrible than the everyday reality we experience, and to

and I read on.

The morning turned to afternoon; I barely noticed. I let my phone ring through to voicemail, rescheduled what few sessions I had on my calendar, and further immersed myself in Laszlo's work. His initial chapters laid out the long, continuous history of man's usage of psychoactive substances to access the infinite and the intelligence that lurked behind the door he spoke of. And in some of those passages I found clues - hints - that sent me scurrying back to the source.

72.   HISTORICAL NARRATIVES OF THE LAKE SUPERIOR INDIANS

Taken down by hand on 19 March 1871 by Miss Annabelle Clare of Old Fort William, in that same town

My name is Michael Calais. I am French and Ashinaabe, my father was Jean Calais of Rice Village, my mother was born Calming Wind of the Lac d'Flambeau tribe but was known as Cristianne Calais after she married my father. I was raised in Rice Village until I was ten, when my parents were both killed. Then my uncle Thomas Larson of the Ashinaabe (also known as Broken Wing) who had moved to Red Cliff took me in. The story I will tell you now is of that time when I became a man, when the elders of the Red Cliff tribe prepared me to seek out Nanahozo, he who shaped the universe. I was taken from the village to the island of Ashuwagindaag Miniss, where I spent a fortnight eating no food, drinking only sips of water.

On the last day of my fast, as the sun rose above the lake, the clouds parted, and the true face of this world was revealed to me. In the lake I saw Nanahozo himself, in the sky I saw the shades of

---

like us all exactly the same but still... it doesn't seem right somehow. Not right at all... Not right at all. Like everything you're looking at is fake and there's something hidden behind it and if you could just find the curtain to lift up you'd see... what? I don't know. Nothing good I bet. Jesus Christ - listen to me. It's not even seven o'clock, but I am going to sle...

that's all.

I was lying in the tent last n to fall asleep last night, and that same feeling, like nothi real and if I looked too lor any one place... it was like th was melting away and I see... behind it? That's r exactly right, but it's the be come up with, and that's wh

and yet we can go back further still, let us say to the year 1500 B.C., to the world of the ancient Greeks, to that moment when civilization as we now know it emerged, to the first and greatest of all such rituals promising union with the divine: the Eleusinian Mysteries.

The Mysteries were the initiation rites for the cult of Demeter, the goddess of life, and her daughter Persephone. Details of the actual ceremonies involved, the words spoken, the relics used, were kept secret among the worshippers, and are now lost to us, yet we do know that, once again, there was fasting involved, and that the fast was broken by the drinking of the Kyreon, a fermented beverage of barley and pennyroyal which contained traces of the psychoactive ingredient LSA. In this manner – as in the 'vision quests' above – the doors were once again opened, and the initiate led into the Telesterion, the great hall of Demeter, prepared to meet his God.

And once again, here there is both transcendence and terror. Aristeides states that within the Telesterion, the initiates experienced 'the most bloodcurdling sensations of horror and the most enthusiastic ecstasy of joy.' Proclus saw 'terror' infused over the minds of the initiated. 'Entering into the secret dome,' Themestius said of the initiate, 'he is filled with horror and astonishment.'

What is it exactly that they saw?

Here the curtain of secrecy surrounding the Mysteries comes down, and permits us no further enlightenment. Unlike the Native Americans, who spoke colorfully (and, it must be acknowledged, confusingly) regarding their visions, the Eleusinian initiates leave us no records whatsoever. And yet given all the other similarities between these rituals, is it too much to draw a further parallel here? I think not. For the initiate here, as in the 'New World,' the mask of reality was ripped away, and they gazed upon the face of God, in all its terrible beauty.

CHAPTER 2
Primal Terror, Primal Shadow

The reader will recall our earlier discussion of Carl Jung, and his archetypal 'Shadow,' which he posits as the source for mankind's fear of the dark. Let us note now the actual anthropological evidence, which suggests our ancestors were in fact nocturnal creatures who welcomed nightfall as a chance to sneak safely down from the trees and forage for food. How are we to explain this dichotomy?

The historical record shows that by the time mankind transits from a nomadic, hunter-gatherer culture to an agriculturally-based society, his attitude towards the dark has already changed. I suggest now the cause of that change is to be found in the transcendental state mentioned above, that while in that state man encountered something, a presence, a terrifying

---

(surrounding clipped fragments)

...being so far forward in the mix. While Leonardson went back to work, the rest of the Diamonds - sans Rasmussen – left to grab some dinner. Danny and I decided to return to the lounge, where we parked ourselves in front of the fireplace, and continued our conversation.

* * *

How do you feel about the...

I think we'...

...wrote it while I was in Yorkville, a few months back.

Yorkville?

Part of Toronto. It's a – think of it as Canada's Berkeley. A hub. A destination for deserters, draft dodgers - a center for the whole anti-war movement.

Which...

...olved in.

...eople. Most of the ...ost of the young

...ition.

...believe we've ...ountry demon-...Cong, Ho Chi ...e Democrats,

...inute...

...being ...differ-...ists.

But ...too. ...our

The fact that it's gone on so lon... Nixon and Ho Chi Minh got t... and smoked the peace pipe, may... killing would stop.

Forgive my saying so, but again... sounds naive.

Maybe I shouldn't have said sm... the peace pipe. Maybe I should... said dropped acid.

You can't be serious.

Why? You ever done it?

No.

You ought to. Makes miscommunica... tion just about impossible.

How so?

You see behind the mask. You see the world as it truly is. See people for who - for what - they really are. Their essences. Their true selves. George [Harrison, of the Beatles] told me once - it's like you can suddenly see through... walls... everything comes clear... ...everything is so much bigger than you, that you're just a little part of a much larger world.

A lot of people have had bad experiences with acid.

Bad trips? Never had one. For me, each experience is more enlightening than the one before. Sometimes I feel like...

What?

Like I'm on the verge of discovering something profound about existence. That there's something else out there. something - some other kind of life - a

hig... inte... one

You... music

Yeah. we be... album.

Guess ... releasing

We still ... it's r... ouple sh... in some of

Any word y... happen?

Well...

We have to g...

It'll be soon. I...

...thaniel

...ed:

...ces.

but the man and his work had already been rejected (in corners, ridiculed) by the scientific community. His name was now spoken in the same breath as Velikovsky and Von Daniken - a charlatan, a fraud (accusations whose sting, I must confess, I had felt as well), a dilettante dabbling in areas he knew virtually nothing of. To take him seriously was tantamount to rejecting everything I had worked for, stood for, my entire life.

Still, his words rang true to me - his theories had the virtue of simplicity. My every instinct told me he was right.

But of course, as a scientist, I could not depend on instinct. Results - replicable, objective results - were all that counted.

I now refer the reader of this article to figure 6-A, the chart which appears on page [INSERT PAGE #], detailing the

KRIEGMOOR
PSYCHIATRIC INSTITUTE

Red Cliff Parkway
Bayfield, WI 48544

DR. CHARLES MAR
KRIEG-5R55479-P

This is Dr. Charles Marsh. It is 9:57 p.m, October 26, 2004. I am sitting at my desk at the Kriegmoor Psychiatric Institute, reviewing the case history of patient HA-09 - a diagnosed DSM-IV schizophrenic plagued by chronic, extremely vivid nocturnal hallucinations, the result of an accidental overdose of the drug MDMA. This patient's schizophrenia had been judged treatment-resistant - however, events of the last few days have caused me to theorize that the hallucinations she suffers from are, perhaps, not hallucinations at all. My purpose here this evening; an experiment which will test this theory.

I have with me 25 mg GCMD - brand name Nypureden - taken from the hospital's infirmary.

A similar dosage taken last night by myself produced -

Note to self for later incorporation into article. Refer to Laszlo's work here.

Also note: discuss historical material, Pierce, etc.

I have the tablets in my hand.

I must admit to feeling a bit nervous. More than a bit nervous, actually.

There are arguments against this course of action, I am well aware of that. Subjectivity of my observations, loss of experimental objectivity...

Enough temporizing.

I have taken the tablets. The time is 10:04 p.m. I'll work for the next few minutes.

next few minutes. The time is 10:04 p.m. I'll work for the
cablets. The time is 10:04 p.m. I'll work for the

Note to self: still no response from administration re: Darrell
Covey's records. Received additional materials new patient Nathaniel
Barron, clarification of charges pending against Mr. Barron.

The time is 10:15 p.m. Onset of drug-induced symptoms as expected:
excitement, slight nervousness, no noticeable perceptual differences.

I feel quite overheated actually. Removing my lab coat.

10:21, I still don't - can't see anything different. Maybe more
intense shades of light and dark. Difficult to say.

There is a painting on the far wall - a landscape, with a large
tree in the center of it. I have been staring at it for the last few
minutes. I now have the oddest sensation.

I feel something is staring back.

I think I see -

DR. CHARLES MARSH
KRIEG-SR55479-P04

KRIEGMOOR
PSYCHIATRIC INSTITUTE

Red Cliff Parkway
Bayfield, WI 48544

Someone's coming.

Dr. Morris.

Dr. Marsh. I thought I saw a light on. You're working late.

Yes. As are you,

Well, you know. I'm actually on my way home. Yourself?

Doing some dictation.

I see. That's Kari Hansen's file, isn't it?

Yes.

Charles, I'm concerned - are you all right?

I'm fine.

You're white as a sheet.

No I'm fine.

Very well. Do you have a minute?

Actually, I'm right in the middle of something. We could talk tomorrow.

I'd rather talk now, actually. In fact I must insist on it.

All right.

I need to speak with you about Kari — Ms. Hansen. About how much time
you're spending with her, how much energy you're putting into her
case. I have to tell you, her mother is concerned. I'm concerned.

I know.

Are you sure you're all right, Charles?

Fine.

The way you keep looking over my shoulder, I think maybe you're
expecting someone else.

Are you?

KRIEGMOOR
PSYCHIATRIC INSTITUTE

Red Cliff Parkway
Bayfield, WI 48544

INCIDENT REPORT

DATE OF INCIDENT: 10/26/2004
DATE OF REPORT: 10/26/2004
REPORTING PHYSICIAN: G. YANAGISAWA
PATIENT: DR. CHARLES MARSH

Details of Incident: Dr. Marsh collapsed while working after hours; collapse seems to have been brought on by nervous exhaustion. He regained consciousness approximately ten minutes after collapse, en route to medical ward. Patient was lucid, suffered no apparent damage from his fall.

Treatment: Enforced bed rest.

Commentary: Get some sleep!!!

G. Yanagisawa 10/27/04

from beyond those dimensions we are normally able to apprehend.
It pulsed with life. It had shape. It had purpose. Its anger was
real, its hostility real, its intelligence a visceral, undeniable
reality as well. It attacked me for a second time, and only the
presence of Dr. Morris, the touch of her hand on my shoulder as I
fell providing a physical anchor to this world, prevented me from
succumbing.

Dr. Yanigasawa had prescribed rest: I returned to my room at the
Lakeside Motel, and began committing my thoughts to paper. Those
initial pages of notes formed the rudimentary beginnings of this
article, and consisted largely of questions, starting points for
the research before me. First and foremost - what was this thing?
I could easily imagine the primitives Laszlo wrote of cowering in
their caves, in the corners of their makeshift shelters, in their
temples and places of worship as this thing - this intelligence
so unlike anything they had ever encountered - appeared and they
sensed - however briefly, however inaccurately - its desires, its
needs. They would have no name for it but God. What was I - a man
of science to make of it? Surely it was not divine, not in the
sense our ancestors had meant. Why its hostility? Intelligence to
me implied rationality: could miscommunication rather than evil
intent be at the heart of its actions? If so, then how to uncover
its true intent?

I returned again to Laszlo, to certain passages in his work
suggesting that other evidence existed of this intelligence
and its attempts to make itself known, attempts which were
particularly relevant to

MN 08933-0989

their movements restricted, their intellects dulled by endless,
monotonous days of planned `activities', their bodies subjected to
experimental treatments more befitting animals than humans, they
remain out of sight, out of mind, locked away precisely because they
have made the fatal error of telling others about their experiences.

I speak, of course, of the schizophrenic - more specifically, the
chronic, or treatment-resistant patient — who is characteristically
distinguished by the experience of hearing voices, a condition which
those few scientists (if we can consider the psychiatrist as such) who
do interact with them consider as something to be cured.

I would like to suggest that perhaps something else entirely is
happening, that the heightened state of awareness sought by the
artisan and acolyte comes to these people innately. That the voices
they hear come from beyond the door we have previously discussed,
and furthermore, that the words thus overheard provide us with hints
as to the true nature of that intelligence, hints that we shall now

SESSION TEXT (CONTINUED)

1 TH: Hello Darrell.
2 PT: Hi Dr. Marsh. How are you?
3 TH: I'm fine. You seem in a good mood today.
4 PT: I am. I feel good.
5 TH: Good.
6 PT: Like I knew I would.
7 TH: Darrell... that's distracting.
8 PT: Sorry. I don't mean to be distracting. I like you Dr. Marsh. The girls like you too.
9 TH: The girls. Who are the girls?
10 PT: You know.
11 TH: No, I'm afraid I don't. Who are they?
12 PT: It's right there in the file.
13 TH: I don't have your file, remember Darrell? We can't find your file.
14 PT: Oh yeah right.
15 TH: So who are the girls?
16 PT: Well they're my conscience.
17 [PAUSE]
18 TH: Are they the voices you hear Darrell? The girls?
19 PT: Yes. They are the sisters of righteousness.
20 TH: The sisters. You mean nuns?
21 PT: Nuns? That's funny.
22 TH: They're not nuns?
23 PT: No. Of course not.
24 TH: They're related?
25 PT: They're sisters.
26 TH: Blood relations, you mean.
27 [PAUSE]
28 TH: Darrell?
29 PT: I don't like that word. Blood.
30 TH: I'm sorry.
31 [PAUSE]
32 PT: Can we talk about something else now?

SESSION TEXT (CONTINUED)

33 TH: I think this is important, Darrell. I think –
34 PT: You ruined it.
35 TH: Excuse me?
36 PT: I was in a good mood and you ruined it.
37 TH: I'm sorry, but –
38 PT: I don't want to talk to you anymore.
39 TH: Okay. We don't have to discuss –
40 PT: I don't want to discuss anything.
41 [PAUSE]
42 TH: Darrell...
43 PT: Nothing

MEDLOG AUTOMATED TRANSCRIPTION SERVICES
SESSION INFORMATION

CLIENT: KRIEGMOOR PSYCHIATRIC
PATIENT (PT): NATHANIEL BARRON
THERAPIST (TH): DR. CHARLES MARSH
DATE OF SESSION: 10/26/04
SYSTEM PARAMETERS: LANGUAGE DETECT/ENGLISH LINE RETURN DELAY/3 SECONDS
SILENCE THRESHOLD: -5.4 DB FILE FORMAT: MS WORD

SESSION TEXT (CONTINUED)

1	TH: and you're from Minnesota originally.
2	PT: Yes, sir.
3	TH: Remember Nathan, you don't have to keep calling me sir.
4	PT: Okay.
5	TH: So you're used to this kind of weather.
6	PT: Yes, sir...Dr. Marsh I mean.
7	TH: Good. I made a note to myself here, Nathan, to tell you that on Saturday after-
8	noons, there's usually a football game showing in the lounge downstairs. Lot of
9	the staff, the residents here – they're big Badger fans.
10	PT: Okay.
11	TH: The Badgers – that's the University of Wisconsin team.
12	PT: I know.
13	TH: You miss playing football, Nathan?
14	PT: Yes sir, I do.
15	TH: You played...let me see here. Linebacker.
16	PT: That's right.
17	TH: You were a pretty good one too, I see. All-Conference last year, and I have a
18	letter from your coach here, he thought you were good enough to play pro.
19	[PAUSE]
20	TH: He also has some other things to say in the letter, Nathan. Some very nice
21	things about you, not just as a player, but as a person. I have a lot of nice let-
22	ters about you, from a lot of people. Professors, friends, your parents' friends...
23	[PAUSE]
24	TH: Did the Rodriguez boy play football?
25	PT: No.
26	TH: Had you seen him at any of the games?
27	PT: No.
28	TH: You didn't know him at all?
29	PT: No. But the Lord spoke to me of him.
30	TH: You said that at our last session too, Nathan. Do you want to explain it to me
31	now?
32	PT: Don't matter.

ARTICLE TITLE: SHADOWS IN THE ASYLUM
AUTHOR: Charles Marsh, M.D., Ph.D.

handwritten note: Are California

several other patients I was treating at the time seemed to me —
in light of Laszlo's suggestions — worthy of closer investigation.
But at the moment, the question uppermost in my mind was what to
do next regarding K. The reader of this article will understand
that at this point, though I was aware of the momentous nature of
my discoveries, my primary obligation was to my patient.

In any case, sharing my research with the director was not
likely to be an efficacious course of action. More than likely,
my thoughts would not only get me ridiculed, but fired. Suggesting
the director take Nypureden, or another hallucinogen was also
not likely to inspire belief on her part in my professional
competence. I was not close enough with any of the other doctors
at Kriegmoor to enlist their support, and because my sessions with
K were automatically recorded and transcribed, I couldn't even
share my news with her.

The only course of action open to me, I quickly realized, was to
continue on as I was doing. Treat K's continuing encounters with
this intelligence as hallucinations while I researched its true
nature, and in the meantime, do as little harm to her person and
psyche as possible. I resolved to have her restraints removed, the
potency of her sedatives reduced, and find a way to tell her that
I, at least, knew that she was as sane as anyone else[73].

But the very next morning, when I returned to my office, I found
an e-mail from the director waiting for me.

---

[73] Some days later, I did in fact, arrange for certain reading materials - my copy of
the Laszlo book, as well as Huxley's THE DOORS OF PERCEPTION - delivered to the patient
library.

TO: c_marsh@kriegmoor-psychiatric.org

FROM: claire_morris@kriegmoor-psychiatric.org

DATE: 10/31/04

RE: HA-09

I dislike delivering news in this manner, but I want to make sure you get this first thing in the morning.

Effective this date, I am removing you as primary on HA-09's case.

This decision comes after a series of at times contentious discussions with the patient's mother, as well as a long struggle with my own conscience. I want to assure you that I personally have no issue with your therapeutic skills, or your course of treatment. The problem is, as I'm sure you can guess, your relationship with the patient herself. Please don't mistake this for an accusation of questionable behavior on your part; the simple fact is that in my opinion the bond the two of you have developed prevents effective therapeutic work from taking place. It is in the patient's ultimate best interest, I believe, that another therapist work with her.

Please come see me when you get in, and we can talk about this further. We'll still want you to consult on the case, of course.

-- Claire

DRAFT MATERIAL: NOT FOR PUBLICATION

ARTICLE TITLE: SHADOWS IN THE ASYLUM

AUTHOR: Charles Marsh, M.D., Ph.D.

patient's best interest rang hollow in a way that only I (and of course, the reader of this article) could appreciate.

Swallowing my pride I requested permission to speak to K, to inform her of the switch in therapists personally, but the director demurred, feeling that Dr. Ferguson should be allowed to reestablish his own rapport with the patient. It was painful for me to read the initial transcripts of her sessions with Ferguson; not just because I saw in his approach a repudiation of all my hard work, but because of his callous refusal to acknowledge K's physical symptoms.

REF. JOHNSTON

DLOG 1.2

MEDLOG AUTOMATED TRANSCRIPTION SERVICES
SESSION INFORMATION

CLIENT: KRIEGMOOR PSYCHIATRIC
PATIENT (PT): KARI HANSEN
THERAPIST (TH): DR. PETER FERGUSON
DATE OF SESSION: 11/01/04
SYSTEM PARAMETERS: LANGUAGE DETECT/ENGLISH LINE RETURN DELAY/8 SECONDS
SILENCE THRESHOLD: -5.4 DB FILE FORMAT: MS WORD

SESSION TEXT (CONTINUED)

1 PT: but where's Dr. Marsh?
2 TH: I told you Kari, we all feel - the director, your mother, the other doctors here -
3   that it would be better if you and I talked about things for awhile. Just to get you
4   a fresh perspective on what's happening.
5 PT: It killed him, didn't it?
6 TH: What?
7 PT: The shadow, it killed him. It found him and it killed him, and you don't want to
8   tell me.
9 TH: Dr. Marsh is fine, Kari.
10 PT: Then where is he?
11 TH: As I said, we all feel it would be better - more helpful - for you, in the long run, if
12   you had another doctor for right now. And I think for us - you and I - it would be
13   better to focus on some of the issues that -
14 PT: Doesn't anyone care how I feel?
15 TH: Of course we do, but the most important thing is to get you better.
16 PT: I'm not crazy.
17 TH: Kari...
18 PT: He could tell you that I'm not crazy, because he saw it. I know he did.
19 TH: He saw what?
20 PT: The shadow.
21 TH: Kari, I can promise you Dr. Marsh didn't see any -
22 PT: Did he tell you that? Did Dr. Marsh tell you that?
23 TH: No, but --
24 PT: Then how do you know he didn't see it?
25 TH: I know.
26 PT: No you don't. Where is he? Where's Dr. Marsh? I want to talk to him.
27 [PAUSE]
28 TH: Kari, I understand your're upset. But do you remember what we talked about,
29   when we first met? How the mind can play tricks on you sometimes - how it
30   plays tricks on all of us? Makes us think we see things, think things are there
31   that aren't really -
32 PT: God. Why doesn't anyone believe me?

CLIENT: KRIEGMOOR PSYCHIATRIC
PATIENT (PT): KARI HANSEN
THERAPIST (TH): DR. PETER FERGUSON
DATE OF SESSION: 11/05/04
SYSTEM PARAMETERS: LANGUAGE DETECT/ENGLISH LINE RETURN DELAY/3 SECONDS
SILENCE THRESHOLD: -5.4 DB FILE FORMAT: MS WORD

SESSION TEXT (CONTINUED)

1 TH: so this drug should really knock you out - let you sleep the whole night through.
2 PT: It won't.
3 TH: I don't think that's a helpful attitude, Kari.
4 PT: I don't care what you think.
5 [PAUSE]
6 TH: All right. Let's both take a deep breath. Why don't we pick up where we were
7   before - the case studies I was talking about earlier, other kids who -
8 PT: Where's Dr. Marsh?
9 [PAUSE]
10 TH: Do you recall those case studies Kari?
11 PT: Do you recall Dr. Marsh? Dark hair, glasses, lab coat like yours...
12 TH: I don't appreciate your sarcasm.
13 PT: Well I don't feel appreciated either. Why doesn't anyone listen to me?
14 TH: I am listening.
15 PT: No you're not.
16 TH: You're asking me about Dr. Marsh and I'm telling you you can't see him right
17   now.
18 [PAUSE]
19 TH: I'm sorry Kari. I don't mean to yell. I really do want to get back to those case
20   studies, because as you see these are stories of people just like you, who went
21   through the same sort of things and at the end, came out fine.
22 PT: But they didn't.
23 TH: No they did. I could have some of them come here, tell you how they were able
24   to get past the hallucinations and -
25 PT: That's not what I'm talking about. They didn't go through the same things at all.
26   Not at all.
27 TH: What do you mean?
28 PT: This didn't happen to any of them, did it?
29 [PAUSE]
30 TH: You cut yourself again. Who do you think you hurt when you do this?
31 [PAUSE]
32 TH: I'm going to step outside for a minute, Kari. I'll be right back with Dr.

EDLOG 1.2

MEDLOG AUTOMATED TRANSCRIPTION SERVICES
SESSION INFORMATION

CLIENT: KRIEGMOOR PSYCHIATRIC
PATIENT (PT): KARI HANSEN
THERAPIST (TH): DR. PETER FERGUSON
OTHER PERSONNEL (OP): NURSE KRISTEN LAPIERRE
DATE OF SESSION: 11/09/04
SYSTEM PARAMETERS: Language Detect/English Line Return Delay/3 Seconds
SILENCE THRESHOLD: -5.4 DB FILE FORMAT: MS WORD

SESSION TEXT (CONTINUED)

1	PT: I want Charles.
2	PT: I know he's here.
3	PT: Please let me see him.
4	PT: Please.
5	TH: Shhh. That's it. Rest Kari. Rest.
6	[PAUSE]
7	OP: She's asleep, doctor.
8	TH: I can see that, thank you.
9	OP: Poor girl. She'll be out all night.
10	TH: Make sure the restraints stay on, please. All day tomorrow as well. Make a note
11	on her chart.
12	OP: They were on, doctor. I checked them -
13	TH: Well then how did she get those marks?
14	OP: I don't know.
15	TH: Are you suggesting someone on the staff made them?
16	OP: No, sir. I just…
17	TH: Then you have another explanation?
18	OP: No sir.
19	TH: No sir is right.
20	TH: Make sure the restraints stay on, is that clear?
21	OP: Yes doctor.
22	TH: This cutting has to stop.
23	
24	[TRANSCRIPT ENDS]
25	
26	
27	
28	
29	
30	
31	
32	

hinting that perhaps he could speak to the director, and plead my case, but Lucius felt uncomfortable intervening in such a manner. It was unbearably ironic. Just as I had finally come to understand the true nature of K's problem, I was cut off from all contact with her. The director and Dr. Ferguson were intransigent on this; despite my pleas for even an occasional visit, they were unmoved.

There was nothing I could do but acquiesce in their decision.

Over the next week, I walked through the common areas at times I was hopeful she might be there; she wasn't. I arranged my own patient schedule to pass her room, hoping to catch her eye while the door was open, but it was always closed. On the off-chance that we would meet accidentally, I carried in my pocket a note I had written on a single scrap of paper to let her know that I was in fact aware of exactly what was happening to her, but the note remained where it lay, in the pocket of my lab coat, unread.

I would have to focus my attention elsewhere, on my other patients, and hope that the information I thus gleaned would, as Laszlo's work suggested, eventually be of use in diagnosing the true nature of K's affliction.

KRIEGMOOR
PSYCHIATRIC INSTITUTE

From the desk of
Charles Marsh, M.D., Ph.D.

Kari--

Courage.

I know they're real.

- Charles

DLOG

MEDLOG
SESSION

CLIENT: KRI
PATIENT (PT
THERAPIST (
DATE OF SES
SYSTEM PAR

SESSIO

DLOG 1.2

MEDLOG AUTOMATED TRANSCRIPTION SERVICES
SESSION INFORMATION

CLIENT: KRIEGMOOR PSYCHIATRIC
PATIENT (PT): DARRELL COVEY
THERAPIST (TH): DR. CHARLES MARSH
DATE OF SESSION: 11/10/04
SYSTEM PARAMETERS: LANGUAGE DETECT/ENGLISH LINE RETURN DELAY/8 SECONDS
SILENCE THRESHOLD: -5.4 DB FILE FORMAT: MS WORD

SESSION TEXT (CONTINUED)

1 TH: how long you've been hearing these voices.
2 PT: Oh forever.
3 TH: Specifically...
4 PT: All day long. Since I got up.
5 TH: But not just today?
6 PT: No. Of course not.
7 TH: So how long?
8 [PAUSE]
9 PT: Forever. It seems like forever.
10 TH: Ten years?
11 TH: Darrell? Does ten years seem right? Too long?
12 PT: Why do you keep calling me Darrell?
13 [PAUSE]
14 TH: All right. I'll try not to call you that.
15 PT: Thank you.
16 TH: So what are some of the things the voices say to you?
17 PT: The girls you mean.
18 TH: Yes, the girls. What do they say?
19 PT: All kinds of stuff.
20 TH: Like?
21 PT: Well...they like to talk about the past. But I don't like that so much.
22 TH: Yes. We've discussed that. What else?
23 PT: I don't know.
24 [PAUSE]
25 TH: Darrell? Anything else they talk to you about?
26 [PAUSE]
27 PT: Sex. They talk about sex an awful lot.
28 TH: I see.
29 PT: They're really interested in it. I had my share though so you know - I don't focus
30   on it as much.
31 TH: Right.
32 TH: What else do you talk about?

SESSION TEXT (CONTINUED)

33   PT: Music.
34   TH: Okay.
35   PT: They like music. They like singing. They like me to sing for them too.
36   TH: So I understand. You do a lot of singing, the nurses tell me.
37   PT: It's not just me. It's the girls too. They love to sing. They know like a million
38   songs.

MEDLOG 1.2

MEDLOG AUTOMATED TRANSCRIPTION SERVICES
SESSION INFORMATION

CLIENT: KRIEGMOOR PSYCHIATRIC
PATIENT (PT): NATHANIEL BARRON
THERAPIST (TH): DR. CHARLES MARSH
DATE OF SESSION: 11/09/04
SYSTEM PARAMETERS: LANGUAGE DETECT/ENGLISH LINE RETURN DELAY/8 SECONDS
SILENCE THRESHOLD: -5.4 DB FILE FORMAT: MS WORD

SESSION TEXT (CONTINUED)

1   TH: there is no history of such in your family, Nathan. No mental illness.
2   PT: No sir.
3   TH: No. So let me jump back a minute to what you said at your trial. What you said
4   to me before. You said God told you about him - the Rodriguez boy.
5   PT: Yes.
6   TH: What did God say to you?
7   [PAUSE]
8   TH: Nathan?
9   PT: That's private sir.
10   TH: Let me ask you another question then. How do you know it was God talking to you?
11   PT: I know.
12   TH: Because...
13   PT: You might as well ask the dog how he knows to bark, Dr. Marsh. Because it is
14   evident, it is obvious, it is what is required.
15   TH: I don't understand, Nathan. Could you -
16   PT: You're not a believer sir, are you?
17   TH: Sit down please, Nathan.
18   PT: God is angry with you, Dr. Marsh. God wants me to punish you too.
19   TH: Sit down or I'm going to have to have you put in restraints.
20   [PAUSE]
21   TH: Thank you Nathan.
22   PT: I'm the instrument of God.
23   TH: I gather he's talking to you now.
24   PT: He walks with me, and he speaks to me. He stands by my side, he is the fist of
25   the falsely accused, the blade of vengeance, the sword of those –
26   TH: Yes. Nathan, I'm going to have to ask you again to please sit -
27   PT: He cannot be caged, Dr. Marsh, or contained. He is far greater than the things
28   of this world, and is first among those worlds that lie beyond. He has whispered
29   his name to me, his most secret name, and he has charged me with his duty.
30   TH: Sit down. This is the last warning I will give you.
31   PT: He is beyond your words, Dr. Marsh. Beyond your threats.
32   TH: You're making me very uncomfortable Nathan. I'm going to get the guard.

MEDLOG 1.2

MEDLOG AUTOMATED TRANSCRIPTION SERVICES
SESSION INFORMATION

CLIENT: KRIEGMOOR PSYCHIATRIC
PATIENT (PT): NATHANIEL BARRON
THERAPIST (TH): DR. CHARLES MARSH
DATE OF SESSION: 11/11/04
SYSTEM PARAMETERS: LANGUAGE DETECT/ENGLISH LINE RETURN DELAY/8 SECONDS
SILENCE THRESHOLD: -5.4 DB FILE FORMAT: MS WORD

SESSION TEXT (CONTINUED)

1 PT: that's how I was raised, Dr. Marsh. There is good and there is evil in this world
2 and when we find that evil we must stamp it out.
3 TH: And the Rodriguez boy was evil.
4 PT: He had done evil and became such.
5 TH: The voice told you this.
6 PT: The Lord told me this.
7 TH: How long has the Lord been speaking to you Nathan?
8 PT: Does that matter?
9 TH: It might.
10 PT: Not to me.
11 TH: Since you were a child?
12 PT: I was an innocent then.
13 TH: High school?
14 [PAUSE]
15 TH: High school, Nathan?
16 TH: What about when you were in college?
17 TH: I'm looking at your chart, Nathan. I see you were hospitalized for a concussion
18 last year, in November. You were hurt in a football game. Do you remember
19 that?
20 PT: Yes.
21 TH: Three weeks after that - December 4th - you were back in the hospital, com-
22 plaining of blurred vision. Headaches. The doctors were contemplating an oper-
23 ation at that point to relieve fluid build up in your brain.
24 PT: I refused them.
25 TH: Yes, I see that on your chart.
26 TH: Is that when the voices started Nathan?
27 PT: I woke on the morning of Christ's birth and the voice of the Lord was in my ear,
28 full of song and celebration.
29 TH: Is that a yes?
30 PT: Set me free now, Dr. Marsh.
31 TH: I'm afraid I can't do that, Nathan.
32 PT: Let me have you. Let me end your pai

FROM: don_gilder@krieg...

DATE: 11/12/04

RE: PATIENT HE-31

... your patient today, doctor...

ust an FYI before you see your patient today, doctor...

He barely slept last night – we couldn't get him calmed down at all, as
Kristen has probably told you already.

I wish I'd known you were working late, I would have had you come down and
talk to him.

MEDLOG 1.2

MEDLOG AUTOMATED TRANSCRIPTION SERVICES
SESSION INFORMATION

CLIENT: KRIEGMOOR PSYCHIATRIC
PATIENT (PT): JACOB HELLINGER
THERAPIST (TH): DR. CHARLES MARSH
DATE OF SESSION: 11/13/04
SYSTEM PARAMETERS: LANGUAGE DETECT/ENGLISH LINE RETURN DELAY/3 SECONDS
SILENCE THRESHOLD: -5.4 DB FILE FORMAT: MS WORD

SESSION TEXT (CONTINUED)

1   TH: it was the monsters again, I'm guessing. Is that right Jake?
2   TH: You don't want to talk about it?
3   PT: No.
4   TH: That's all right. I just want to make sure you're feeling okay now – no after-
5   effects from the sedative.
6   PT: I'm okay, I guess.
7   TH: Good. Because I think – just to help you sleep – we'll give you the same medi-
8   cation tonight.
9   TH: How does that sound?
10 [PAUSE]
11 TH: Jake? Are you all right?
12 PT: No.
13 TH: Tell me what's the matter.
14 PT: I'm scared.
15 TH: Of the monsters.
16 PT: Monster.
17 TH: Okay.
18 PT: Now it's just one. A big one. A mean one. An angry one. It chased all the oth-
19   ers away.
20 TH: Is this one going to eat you too?
21 PT: No. This one just wants to take me away. Take me to its island.
22 TH: Is this like the island in the book – the one that Max sails to?
23 PT: No. The island in the book is jungle. This island is different. It's cold and dark.
24   There's no light anywhere. No air. And they tie you up and keep you there so
25   that you die.
26 TH: That sounds terrible Jake.
27 PT: It is.
28 PT: That's why I'm scared. I don't want to go there.
29 TH: I don't blame you. But you know something Jake? There are no islands like
30   that. Not in real life.
31 PT: Okay.
32 [PAUSE]

33	TH: You don't sound convinced.
34	PT: Real life doesn't matter.
35	TH: Jake. It's disturbing to me to hear you say that. There's a big difference
36	between —
37	PT: There's no difference. Real life doesn't matter because the monster makes
38	it real. It touches me and it takes me to its island and when I'm there I can't
39	breathe. And I die.
40	[PAUSE]
41	TH: Is it trying to hurt you, Jake? Is that why it's taking you to its island?
42	PT: I don't know. Maybe.
43	TH: So maybe not?
44	PT: It's angry. That's all I know. It's very, very angry.
45	TH: How do you know that?
46	TH: Does the monster say things to you?
47	PT: No. I just…I know what it knows.
48	TH: I see.
49	[PAUSE]
50	PT: That's interesting. That's very interest—

MEDLOG 1.2

MEDLOG AUTOMATED TRANSCRIPTION SERVICES
SESSION INFORMATION

CLIENT: KRIEGMOOR PSYCHIATRIC
PATIENT (PT): DARRELL COVEY
THERAPIST (TH): DR. CHARLES MARSH
DATE OF SESSION: 11/14/04
SYSTEM PARAMETERS: LANGUAGE DETECT/ENGLISH LINE RETURN DELAY/3 SECONDS
SILENCE THRESHOLD: -5.4 DB FILE FORMAT: MS WORD

SESSION TEXT (CONTINUED)

1	TH: you've been here for almost thirty years now Darrell. Does that seem right to
2	you?
3	PT: I don't know.
4	TH: This is important Darrell. Because I don't have the records right now, the only
5	way I can -
6	PT: CDs.
7	TH: Excuse me?
8	PT: People still say records, but they're really CDs now. They're all CDs. Nobody
9	buys records anymore.
10	TH: I'm not talking about —
11	PT: It's too bad really. Records are better. They're bigger.
12	TH: Darrell…
13	PT: Plus they're analog. It sounds better than digital. It really does. Pete gave me a
14	CD player one year for Christmas but I had to throw it away everything sound-
15	ed so bad.
16	TH: I see.
17	PT: I used to have a lot of records. I don't know where they are now.

suggested that Laszlo's theories were correct, but I was dealing with such a small sample — two, at most three patients — that any conclusions I reached, any information I gleaned — would be, at best, suspect. I needed more data. I needed to be able to ask questions free of the restrictions that the automated recording systems imposed. And I needed these things immediately.

Because K was getting worse.

On Thursday, November 25th, at the Institute's Thanksgiving dinner, I saw her for the first time in close to a month. I had been receiving transcripts of her sessions with Dr. Ferguson, of course. He had been attempting yet again to find a pharmacologically-based cure for her hallucinations; their time together had degenerated into a series of rote question-and-answer sessions, with Ferguson trying to determine the effect of different medications on her condition. Her responses, mostly monosyllabic, I had taken simply for a lack of interest. I was thus completely unprepared for the marked decline in her condition.

She sat between her mother and another of the ward patients, at a table far from the administrative dais, wearing clothes clearly bought especially for this 'festive' occasion — a new blue dress, a white sweater buttoned at the breast — yet her manner, her mood, was anything but. Hands folded in her lap, she sat slightly hunched over, rocking gently in her seat, oblivious to everything going on around her. She had lost weight; her skin, despite the blush someone (her mother?) had hastily applied to her cheeks, looked sallow, and grey, and the circles under her eyes told me

her sight. I'll try not to call you that.

no better in the interim. Yet in her posture I saw something else as well. I was reminded of the huddled position HE-31 often took in our sessions together, knees drawn up against his chest, arms wrapped tight around them; the frightened child, withdrawing from the larger world.

K was scared. Even sitting here, among the crowd, she was scared.

And only I truly knew why; my heart went out to her.

It was at that precise moment that she turned, and our eyes met. And where before I had seen apathy and listlessness, I was now grateful to see the spark of life.

I smiled, she smiled back, and began to rise from her seat — And as she did, her mother stood as well, blocking my view. She put her hands on K's shoulders and forced her back into her chair. Then she turned and glared at me. I nodded hello, and returned to my own table.

When I turned back, sometime later, to try and catch K's eye again, she was gone.

Sometime after the director had spoken, after coffee and dessert was served but before dancing, I left as well, returning to my office to work through the night once more.

Over and over I reviewed the same transcripts, the same passages from Laszlo's work, the same pieces from the historical society, and felt the same frustrations build within me. I needed more material, and where was I to find it? Again, I felt a sense of the ironic; Laszlo had managed to interview over two hundred patients in the writing of his book, and here I couldn't even obtain the complete file for one of the three patients whose experiences might be relevant. Patient CO-18's records, despite my repeated inquiries, remained unavailable to me.

Or were they?

In the year between leaving Texas and assuming my position at Kriegmoor, I had become somewhat of an expert with computers. In clear violation of hospital policy, I now used that expertise to access the Institute's internal security systems and retrieve the codes necessary to enter the records building. I went there that very night, descending into the basement, where the hospital's archives - its paper records, those kept before the advent of the computer-based filing system we now used - were located. Dozens of cabinets, hundreds of drawers, thousands of files...

And, I quickly discovered, no trace of the specific folder I sought.

My frustration boiled over.

I kicked out at the nearest cabinet and an entire stack of folders, balanced precariously on the top of it - fell to the floor. Patient records spilled everywhere.

At which point I laughed out loud, realizing in that instant something that the more astute reader of this article will have deduced before. Laszlo may have had the experiences of two hundred patients to draw from, but I had thousands.

I pulled up a chair, and spent the remainder of that evening searching through the files of patients past and patients present.

I found much of interest

... PUBLICATIONS
... · Suite 1001 · New York NY · MU6-3453

PATIENT: Roy Jennings
ADMIT DATE: Dec 7, 1953

NOW ONLY
35 ...

Liége, ...
fair average huma...
"have belonged to a philosoph...
the thoughtless brains of a savage ...

FRANK LESLIE'S
ILLUSTRATED
NEWSPAPER

NEW YORK—FOR THE WEEK ENDING MARCH 1...

PRICE 10 CENTS ...

WESTERN
UNION

JOSEPH L. EGAN
PRESIDENT

...ED by STANDARD TIME at ...

16 457...

ROY JENNINGS
SENIOR EDITOR

10/25/53 —

Dunnington,
force will
I deny Ros...
They are her...
Indians tal...

10 / ...

🌲 LAKESIDE MOTEL
R... ...HTS WISCONSIN

🌲 LAKESIDE MOTEL
RED CLIFF PA...

🌲 **LAKESIDE MOTEL**
RED CLIFF PARKWAY BAYFIELD HEIGHTS WISCONSIN

...N DUNN...
...S LAKESI...

BRITTSEN DRUG & PHARMACY
36 MAIN BAYCLIFF

PATIENT HISTORY

Name of Patient: ~~John Doe~~ Roy Jennings
Date of Admitance: 12/7/53
Admitting Physician: Theodore Cotton

December 7 - Unidentified man, approximately forty to forty-five
years of age, smallish stature, dark-complectioned, black hair,
unshaven, ill-kempt, brought in by Wisconsin State Police early
a.m. Adjudged threat to self, others, making frequent, often in-
comprehensible statements. Initial diagnosis: paranoid schizophrenia. Administered thorazine, placed under involuntary restraint.
Belongings confiscated - seventy-eight dollars, a set of unlab-
eled keys, locked briefcase, a roll of aluminum foil.
December 7 - Night staff reports patient delusional, violent:
patient sedated and put in restraints.

December 8 - Repeat of previous evening's incident.

December 9 - Patient reluctantly responds to questioning. Patient
gives name as Roy Jennings. Insists he is not sick, gives New
York City address and phone number, also names and numbers of
several references: Lillian Skolnick, Robert Dunnington, Alan
Fitzgerald. States he is engaged in a 'critically important' scientific experiment. Demands return of his belongings, in particular his aluminum foil, and immediate release.

December 11 - Patient i.d. confirmed. Roy Jennings, aged thirty-
seven, unmarried, resident of New York City. Occupation: writer,
employed by Dunnington Publications Group. Spoke via telephone
to Miss Lillian Skolnick of Dunnington Publications, she identif-
ied Jennings by description, stated he had been sent to Wisconsin
September 15 on assignment for Dunnington Group, had resigned
from assignment and magazine early November, uncertain why. Personal history given by phone as well. Jennings graduated
Bronx Science, State University New York. Employed by Bardeen Fitzgerald Advertising NYC, rose to account executive 1947, left
September that year to work for Dunnington Publications Group,
1950 appointed senior editor. Residence 860 Greenwich Street, NYC.
Miss Skolnick passed on number of Jennings closest relative,
mother Anna Jennings of Bayside, New York, as well as Jennings
physician M. David Clements of New York City. Spoke via telephone
with Dr. Clements, who stated that patient has negative family
history of mental illness, no prior record of such illness. Unable
to contact Mrs. Anna Jennings this day.

December 12 - Unable to contact Mrs. Anna Jennings this day.

December 15 - Monthly patient review meeting; initial discussion of Jennings case. Diagnosis concurred by all attending.
Paranoid schizophrenia, several treatment options discussed.
Prognosis unclear, more information - history of illness, length,
time of onset, etc. - needed.

19 -
ious note
NAME OF PATIENT: Roy Jenni
DATE OF ADMITTANCE: 12/7/53
ADMITTING PHYSICIAN: T. Cotton
received via Dr. Cle   (mental).
              of illness   llpox/

Kriegmoor Lunatic Asylum

PATIENT HISTORY (CONT'D) FROM PREVIOUS PAGE

NAME OF PATIENT: Roy Jennings
DATE OF ADMITTANCE: 12/7/53
ADMITTING PHYSICIAN: T. Cotton

December 16 - Medical history received via Dr. C̶l̶o̶̶ firming patient has negative family history of illness (mental). No major illnesses (physic.) on record, innoculated smallpox/ polio/rubella, very good health. Vision 20/200L, 20/180R. Recent history of migraine headaches.

December 16 - Phone conversation with Mr. Robert Dunnington, owner Dunnington Publications Group. States Jennings had resigned employment November this year, citing desire to pursue his current assignment in more depth. Dunnington 'not entirely surprised' by Jennings committment to this institution, stating last article he wrote for magazine was full of 'wild speculation,' 'distortion of fact,' etc., had to be heavily edited for publication. Said material may be related to current delusions; Dunnington will have copy sent on.

December 18 - Spoke to Mrs. Anna Jennings, patient's mother. Mrs. Jennings is quite elderly, not able to grasp conditions surrounding her son's committment. Only other living relative is a nephew, Peter Heath, of Floral Park, Long Island. Unable to contact Mr. Heath this day.

December 19 - Material received from Mr. Robert Dunnington, as per previous note, enclosed to file.

DUNNINGTON PUBLICATIONS
575 Fifth Avenue · Suite 1001 · New York NY · MU6-3453

December 16, 1953

Dr. Theodore Cotton
The Kriegmoor Lunatic Asylum
Red Cliff Parkway
Bayfield, Wisconsin

Dr. Cotton:

First thing I want you to know is if this business with Roy
ever gets down to money, you just call my office, and I'll
see you get what you need right away, no questions asked. I
feel responsible here.

Now as I said to you, I was not entirely surprised to hear
this news, and I'm going to tell you why. I don't know if
you're familiar with the Dunnington name out there, but we're a
fairly large concern, we publish magazines on a very wide-ran-
ging variety of subjects. You're a man that wants a car magazine
we've got ROADWAYS. For the homemaker, we've got MODERN KITCHEN
AND APPLIANCE, and AMERICAN DECOR. For the sports fan, we've
got baseball magazines (AL and NL INSIDER) and a college football magazine (GRIDIRON, which is my favorite) and if you're a
clothes person, we've got RUNWAY and also NEW LOOKS. My point
is we deal in a wide range of topics, and we need writers who
can do the same. Versatility, that's the key, and Roy had that
in spades. He could write a lead quicker and better than anyone I ever met.

One of the magazines we do fairly well with is DESTINY, which we
push out to the sci-fi/supernatural crowd. It's a hard crowd
to please doctor, harder than you might think - they take this
stuff seriously. Very, very seriously, and so you need to write
for them in a serious way, even if you're writing about some
of the most ridiculous things you can imagine, Satan working
with the commies, aliens landing on earth thousands of years
ago, that sort of thing. Now Roy, he could do that too, one of
the few people we have here who could. So he did a lot of writing
for DESTINY, in fact he was the lead man on one of our more
popular columns for that magazine, EYE ON THE UNEXPLAINED, which
was what brought him out to Wisconsin in the first place. Because
I don't know if you're aware of it or not doctor, but there are
an awful lot of strange things that go on in your neck of the
woods. That's what Roy was working on. Except once he got out
there...well, he got way out there, if you know what I mean.
Started believing in the stuff he was writing. I do hope you can
help him find his way back; just from talking to you Doctor,
I feel like he's got a good chance, I really do.

Please keep me up-to-date on his condition. In the meantime,
Merry Christmas to you and yours. I'm taking the liberty of
enclosing a whole stack of magazines for your patients up
there; I hope they'll prove entertaining. And of corse, I'm
also passing on the copy of the DESTINY magazine we talked
about. The one with Roy's article. I hope that helps as well.

Very sincerely,

J. Robert Dunnington
President and Publisher

JRD/ds

Charting the Unkno

ALL NEW STORIES!

Charting the Unknown

DESTINY
MAGAZINE

NOW ONLY

35 cents

Nov. 1953

112 PAGES!

RAMA REVEALED
Inside the Temples of Sri Lanka

SHADOWS ON THE LAKE
Dark and inexplicable happenings
in the American Heartland

ROSWELL:
THE
OFFICIAL
REPORT

*what strange
darkness gathers
on Superior's shores...*

SHADOWS ON THE LAKE

by Roy Jennings

What we do know for certain is that, at
the time early French fur-traders had
pushed west from Huron into the
Superior region, the Chippewa tribe
were firmly ensconced in the area. For
approximately the

bottom, a number of
prop..
number of
custody of the
Society,

He, leader of
wan of the
d the tribe. Were
...the feathers might be

None can deny that there are places of power in this world.

Places where natural and supernatural energies align, collect, and concentrate themselves, where the mysterious, the inexplicable, and the fantastic are the order of the day, every day. The archeoastronomer speaks of leys, specific areas of this planet where measurable geophysical confluxes of energies occur. The ancients knew these places; they observed the fantastic events which occurred in them, and marked them as holy ground. On these leys, they built their temples, their shrines of worship. Think of Stonehenge, a circle of huge, pre-historic boulders some ninety miles west of London England, positioned just so by Druid priests to serve their ancient, awful rites; the Great Pyramid of Cheops, the most fantastic structure of Egypt's golden age; or the blood-stained ruins of Chichen-Itza, capital of the Mayan world.

Over the past few weeks, I have discovered another such place. A place of preternatural calm and beauty, isolated, virtually unknown, and yet with a history as colorful and suggestive of the paranormal as all those cited above. I speak of Wisconsin's picturesque Apostle Islands, an archipelego of surpassing beauty behind whose seeming serenity lurks a power beyond the ken of mortal man, a power whose presence, if one looks carefully enough, can be discovered to permeate the history of the entire region...

There are no historical records, of course, as to when exactly the area around what is now the Bayfield Peninsula was first settled.

Archaeological evidence has been found suggesting that native tribes were present in the Lake Superior region as long ago as five thousand years prior to the birth of Christ. What little we know of these first, unnamed settlers is intriguing; artifacts have been discovered suggesting they possessed sophisticated mining techniques far in advance of their contemporaries. Presumably their development in other areas - their culture, religious beliefs, etc. - was as advanced as well.

From the Indians that followed them into this region, we have a series of fantastical tales of 'those who came before us,' tales that suggest these first peoples were not people at all, but supernatural, almost God-like creatures. Some scholars have suggested, in fact, that most local Native legends such as the Windigo (see below), are based on stories of these settlers.

And yet long before the first Europeans came to North America, this mysterious people had disappeared without a trace, in a manner similar to the mysterious Anasazi of the Southwest, or the lost 13th tribe of the Hebrews. No doubt with the development of ever more sophisticated archaeological techniques, more clues to their fate will eventually be discovered.

What we do know for certain is that by the time early French fur traders had pushed west from Huron into the Superior region, the Chippewa tribe were firmly ensconced in the area. It is from this period - approximately the mid-1600s - that the supernatural makes is first appearance in the historical records, when a large number of the tribe were driven from their homes by the 'Windigo,' a demon that fed on the flesh of men. And in this instance...of children as well.

"It's a terrible story," Michael Pines, leader of the Red Cliff band of Chippewa, tells me over coffee one afternoon. "Happened on what we used to call Moningwanekaning Miniss - isle of the Golden-Breasted Woodpecker. Which is now Madeline Island. On a clear day you can see it from here - right on the lake there." Pines jerks his thumb in the direction of that lake, Superior, largest of the five great lakes, the single largest expanse of fresh water in the known world, the tiniest portion of which is visible just outside the window of the coffee shop we've arranged to meet in.

"The people had a real hard winter one year. No food. No food for them, and no food - some would say - for the demon. Windigo. So it took the nearest thing handy - the easiest thing it could find. The children. Killed over two dozen of them. Just about destroyed the tribe." Pines takes a sip of his coffee before continuing. "After that...the people couldn't stay there. Left the island entirely for a time. A long, long time."

I nod, already familiar with the story as it is included in most local history books, a number of which I read in preparation for this assignment, a number of which I have since obtained courtesy of the Bayfield Historical Society, just down the road from where Pines and I now sit. The coffee shop and the historical society are both located not in Bayfield proper but Bayfield Heights, a small community of quaint stores and shingled houses at the tip of Bayfield Peninsula, on a promontory overlooking the lake. The Red Cliff reservation, where Pines lives, is not far down the road, as is an impressive collection of buildings which form the Kriegmoor Asylum, one of the premiere such mental health hospitals in the country.

"Of course," Pines continues, "later on, some said that it was the Midiwewin - the tribe's medicine men - responsible for what happened to the children. Cannibalism. Killed those kids for food."

I nod again, having read those references myself.

"You think that's true?"

"Possible, I suppose. Anything's possible."

"What else could have killed them?" I ask, even as dozens of tales I have read over the past weeks pop into my mind. Stories of the strange shadowy creatures that inhabit the dark, wooded interiors of certain islands on the lake, none of which I share with Pines.

"What else could have done it?" Pines repeats, and then falls silent for a moment, thinking. "Well. My grandfather told me a story once," he says at last. "A story about something that happened to him, when he was a kid. Must have been (please turn to page 83)

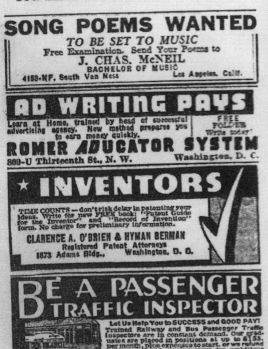
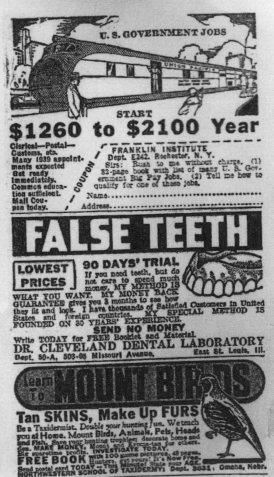

PATIENT HISTORY (CONT'D) FROM PREVIOUS PAGE

NAME OF PATIENT: Roy Jennings
DATE OF ADMITTANCE: 12/7/53
ADMITTING PHYSICIAN: T. Cotton

December 20 - Spoke with Mr. Peter Heath, patient's nephew, gave
verbal consent as patient's closest living relative for contin-
uation of involuntary committment.

December 20 - Patient became agitated when informed of Mr. Heath's
decision; further sedation necessary. Patient's briefcase forced
open. Contents include newspaper clippings, handwritten notes, extracts from books/magazines, various pieces of correspondence,
all hinting at debilitating nature and severity of patient psychosis.

Random sampling of material included in file for informational purposes.

LAKESIDE MOTEL
CLIFF PARKWAY BAYFIELD HEIGHTS WISCONSIN

NETTE - CALL WE
SHINGTON, D.C.
48-4100

A PUBLICATION OF L'INSTITUTE D'ANTHROPOLOGIE

Taken down by hand on 19 March 1871 by Mrs. Claudine
D'Passier of Old Fort William, in that same town

My name is Dark Eye, and I am a daughter of the Ashinaabe, which the saagn'aash [white man] called Chippewa. My
father was Green Thunder of the Beaver Band, my mother
Thin Deer, who died when I was very young of the smallpox.
I had two brothers who died of the same, who I do not remember. We lived then in what is now called the Wisconsin territory
[state] of the Americans. I do not remember very many things
from when I was a young girl.

As a maiden, I was given in trade to a Frenchman named
Charbon, a trader who was much older than I and did not treat
me well. I fled to live with the Great Chief Waubojeeg, and spent
many years then with him on La Pointe [Madeline] Island. This
was our sacred land, which the Midewiwin [medicine men] say
we came to from the Saltwater Sea. Those are years whose memory shines bright with me. I have many stories. One I will tell
you is of the year the summer did not come. The ice grew so
thick we could not find water to fish in. Food was scarce, and
many people died. A white man named Pierce came to us at
this time. He had been living on Ashuwaguindag Miniss. He
said food was scarce for him too but soon we learned a Wendigo had chased him from that island. I felt fear when I heard
this for the Wendigo was an evil spirit who ate human flesh. He
go had chased him from that island. I felt fear when I heard
My zhishay [uncle]who was Leaping Frog, told me stories
this for the Wendigo was an evil spirit who ate human flesh. He
was once a man but he had died of hunger. Now at
and was cursed to roam the earth until his
left of him was his shadow. and this shadow
The man Pierce begged the Midewiw
Midewiwin said they could do no
for this man because I heard
Waubojeeg said he had t
hurt the people. I do

...ness and personal fortunes were soon to take a drastic turn for the worse.

In 1891, Kriegmoor married the former Josephine Walker of New York City - a young woman almost forty years his junior. Within a year, the new Mrs. Kriegmoor was pregnant with their first child. For Kriegmoor, these events marked the fulfillment of a long-sought desire: he now had a family, and quite possibly, an heir to the vast fortune and commercial empire he had spent his lifetime building. Emboldened, Kriegmoor spent the next few months personally supervising the construction of a home for his new brood, to be constructed in a location both idyllic and practical; Hermit (sometimes called Austrian) Island, the site of one of Kriegmoor's busiest brownstone quarries. The lodge was built entirely from wood found on the island, and veneered in cedar; according to contemporary accounts, it was a strikingly beautiful home, featuring "balconies...entwined with the rustic beauty of cedar limbs... mantels...of brownstone, handsomely and artistically carved to represent the limbs of a tree." The house was finished in early 1892; unfortunately, before Kriegmoor and his new family could move in, fortune dealt the newlyweds a cruel setback.

Kriegmoor's young bride suffered a miscarriage; the resulting trauma sent her spiraling downward into a deep, deep depression. Kriegmoor brought her to the island, to show her the home he'd built for her, in hopes of lifting her mood, of perhaps encouraging her try again to start their family. Sadly, the house seems to have had the opposite effect on her; in a letter written to his wife's relatives on May 10 of 1892, he wrote:

...she will not leave her bed, will not explore the rooms of this manse I have built for her. A most fearful melancholy has set in, one that worsens with evening's approach. The night holds terrors for her. She claims to see things - phantom apparitions who liter- ally spring forth from the walls. Of course, it is her imagination. It is the tragedy of what has happened, the lost babe, that occupies her mind. Would that the doctors here could find some ___ calm her; would that your Dr. Paciuc wo___ ney from New York City to ___ ties, I have utm___

Reluctantly assenting, Kriegmoor then began a series of ultimately fruitless efforts to lease the Hermit Island residence (the home stood unoccupied until 1930, when it was finally torn down). On Josephine's return, the two of them rented a large colonial-style mansion in nearby Bayfield Heights, but sadly, were never again able to conceive a child.

Tragically, Mrs. Kriegmoor's depression soon returned, as did her hallucin- ations; her condition worsened so quickly that doctors feared to send her east again. In an undated letter to his mother-in-law, Kriegmoor wrote:

...at night, she carries on endless conversations with these phantoms; at times she appears terrified of them, at others to welcome their ap- pearance, as one would welcome a long-lost relative, from which I conclude that there are several of these creatures and among them - naturally - she has her favorites. Though of course, none of this is natural. She no longer eats, Julia. It is all I can do to put a cup of water to her lips and make her drink.

I am sorry. For Josephine's sake, I cannot consent to moving her ___ this time.

___ ease his wife's torment: he ___ tell you

the largest single piece of brownstone ever mined in the continental United States. However, the obelisk proved too expensive to transport to Chicago and so - like the house Kriegmoor had constructed for his wife - was never used.

At roughly the same time the obelisk was being built, Kriegmoor was also drawing up preliminary plans for an even more ambitious construction project - an asylum for the mentally ill. The earliest record of his intentions with regard to this institution come from a letter he wrote to a William Banks, an acquaintance of his in the New York construction industry, on December 12, 1894.

Dear William:

I have seen pictures of the building and it is magnificent. My congratulations to you and Stanford, and of course Mr. McKee as well. I am enclosing for your own information preliminary blueprints for the building we discussed in January. With regard to my rationale for this construction, it is tripartite: I believe that those unable, through no fault of their own, to function within our society deserve at the very least that which they would find in a state of nature; shelter, food, clothing. I have found a surfeit of such unfortunates here on the peninsula, who would benefit from such an institute. Of course, Josephine is one of them.

(I thank you for your concern in that regard, my friend; I must report, unfortunately, that her condition remains unchanged.) For all these reasons, I have moved construction of this facility to the forefront of the projects I plan to build within the next two years. I am hopeful I can rely on your firm to assist in this undertaking. You and I work well together, William: we are both men of an analytical, scientific bent. We see a problem, we do not stand about like old washer-women wringing our hands; we apply our skills and solve it.

I look forward to your prompt and hopefully affirmative

Cordially,

Herman Kriegmoor

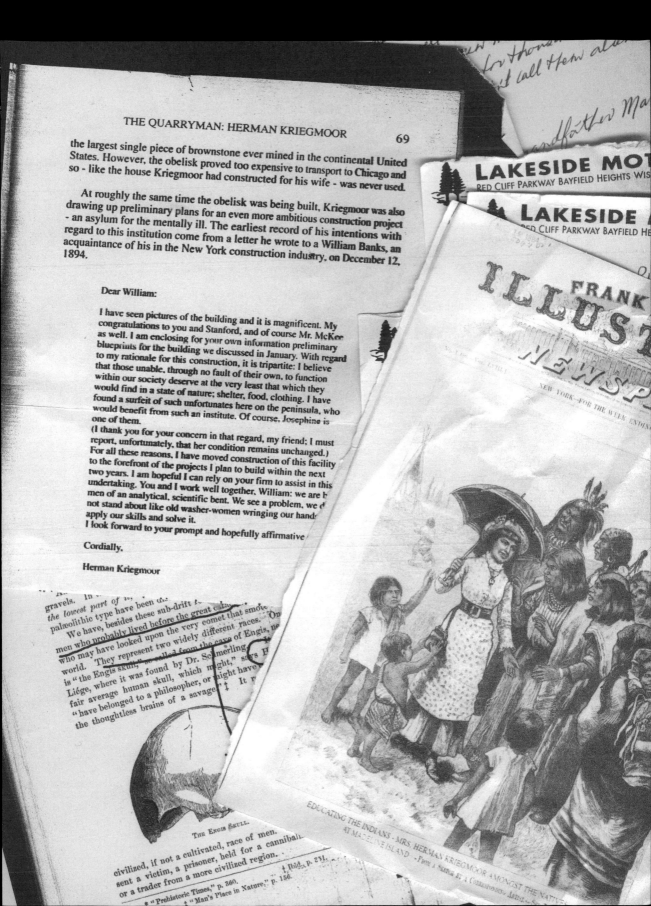

gravels. In the lowest part of it, the palæolithic type have been det...

We have, besides these sub-drift i... men who probably lived before the great extinct... who may have looked upon the very comet that smote... world. They represent two widely different races, ne... is "the Engis skull, so-called from the cave of Engis, ne... Liége, where it was found by Dr. Schmerling," says I... fair average human skull, which might have... "have belonged to a philosopher, or might have...the thoughtless brains of a savage..." It r...

THE ENGIS SKULL.

civilized, if not a cultivated, race of men. ...sent a victim, a prisoner, held for a cannibal... or a trader from a more civilized region.

† Ibid., p. 231.
* "Prehistoric Times," p. 360.   ‡ "Man's Place in Nature," p. 156.

EDUCATING THE INDIANS - MRS. HERMAN KRIEGMOOR AMONGST THE NATIVES AT MADELINE ISLAND - FROM A SKETCH BY A CORRESPONDENT ARTIST

WESTERN UNION

JOSEPH L. EGAN
PRESIDENT

SYMBOLS

DL=Day Letter
NL=Night Letter
LC=Deferred Cable
NLT=Cable Night Letter

Ship Radiogram

This is a full-rate Telegram or Cablegram unless its deferred character is indicated by a suitable symbol above or preceding the address.

ay letters is STANDARD TIME at point of origin. Time of receipt is STANDARD TIME at point of destination

The filing time sho

PM 6004

JFM35 RD 11

W.BUA181 GOVT PU=BH DC 16 457P=

OCTOBER 8 1953=

=R. DUNNINGTON DUNNINGTON PUB=

TO: ROY JENNINGS LAKESIDE MOTEL

IN RECEIPT THIS A.M. YOUR ARTICLE PART TWO SERIOUS PROBLEMS STOP
NUMBER ONE STOP YOUR ARTICLE SEEMS TO ADVOICATE EXPERIMENTS WITH
HALLUCINOGENS STOP NUMBER TWO ARTICLE ALMOST COMPLETELY DEPEN
DENT ON YOUR OWN EXPERIENCES HISOTORICAL SOURCES TAKEN OUT OF
CONTEXT STOP NUMBER THREE STOP AIR FORCE HAS DENIED ROSWELL
EVENT OCCURENCE STOP CALL SOONEST TO DISCUSS REWRITE STOP=

ROBERT DUNNINGTON PUBLISHER

ITS PATRONS CONCERNING ITS SERVICE

THE COMPANY WILL APPR

LAKESIDE MOTEL
RED CLIFF PARKWAY BAYFIELD HEIGHTS WISCONSIN

LAKESIDE MOTEL
BAYFIELD HEIGHTS WISCONSIN

LAKESIDE MOTEL
RED CLIFF PARKWAY BAYFIELD HEIGHTS WISCONSIN

BRITTSEN DRUG & PHARMA
36 MAIN BAYCLIFF
TILL 5:30 P.M.

GRUNDY PHARM
41 LAKE AVE.
TILL 8:00 P.M.

PINES' GRANDFATHER:
MARTIN PINES
BELANGER SETTLEMENT
3 HOUSES DOWN ON LEFT
FROM ENTRANCE

CHEVY ON BLOCKS IN FRONT
YARD

/27

Ad
of
Refus
WHY?

→ TALK TO

I was faint from
Hig

10/25/53 -

Dunnington — complete idiot. Of course Air
Force will deny Roswell — not the point.
I deny Roswell — little green men RIDICULOUS. But
They are here and have been for thousands of years.
Indians talked to them — didn't call them aliens But

10/26

Finally met Michael Pines' grandfather Martin
Old — 80's? Seems coherent.
He says on a Monday (6th?) on island was faint from
hunger — Slept — woke near quarry — felt something
watching him — Next night unable to sleep — felt
it again — then came it — darkness — no shape —
Pines is serious, tough old man, get scared as hell —
grandson cut talk short — get back later in week.

10/27

Long phone call with Frank Weller of U.S. Geological.
Admitted that surveys I sent him showing presence
of magnetite on Hermit Island appeared genuine —
Refused request for similar surveys New Mexico area
WHY? — ANSWER — THEY KNOW
→ TALK TO DUNNINGTON RE: possibility of reprinting
surveys in article!

10/28/93

Met w/ Maureen Wilma, official of Red Cliff
band of Chippewa (she calls Ojibwe) nation.
She repeated stories of her grandmother re: tribe
pre-contact (late 1600's) of "THOSE WHO CAME
BEFORE US"

2nd Meeting with Martin Pines - Thinks I am a skeptic
Wants me to duplicate his ordeal in order to
duplicate his experience. - But, I don't have time for an
extended fast - have to take short cut - what the drugs
are for -
We'll see - ?? what ?? - THAT'S THE QUESTION ??

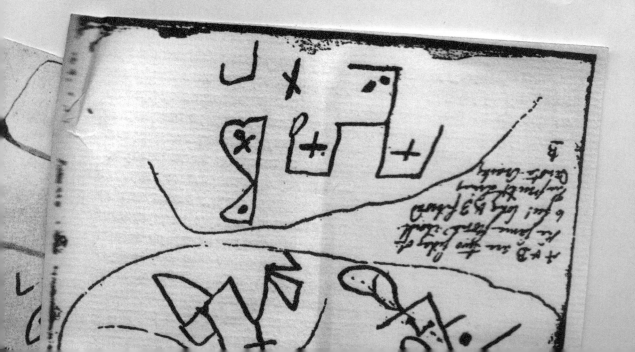

PATIENT HISTORY (CONT'D) FROM PREVIOUS PAGE

NAME OF PATIENT: Roy Jennings
DATE OF ADMITTANCE: 12/7/53
ADMITTING PHYSICIAN: T. Cotton

December 20 - Discussion w/Dr. Selwyn, Dr. Randall - in light of
patient's continued delusional behavior, consensus to begin
electroshock therapy.

December 21 - Patient became agitated, violent when informed of
ECT decision; Nurse Bradford and myself both injured in struggle
to restrain him (Nurse Bradford broken wrist, myself puncture wound)
following said notification. Patient injured as well, strained left
shoulder ligament. Patient placed in restraints treated in infirmary.

December 21 (p.m.) - Initial electroshock session takes place:
80 volts for one second duration, followed by a second charge of
30 volts for five seconds.

December 22 - Patient is unresponsive. Depressed mood state noted.

2nd electroshock session takes place. 30 volts for fifteen seconds
duration, followed by 15 volts for ten seconds.

December 23 - 3rd electroschock session. 39 volts for 15 secs, 30
volts 10 seconds.

December 25 - Staff Holiday. Marsden, M.D., in attendance.
Multiple electroshock sessions, as above.
Increased listlessness
Stimulants prescribed

January 12 - No outbursts since 12/21. Straitjacket harness removed. Moved into General Ward 5.

January 12 - Group therpay session. Patient was unresponsive.

January 26 - Book Room Incident (see accompanying report)

DATE OF INCIDENT: January 26, 1954
PLACE OF INCIDENT: Book Room
PATIENT: Roy Jennings
SUPERVISING NURSE Edna Morton

Being a record of what happened this morning during the
Ward 5 patients scheduled recreation period

After we served breakfast, I and orderlies Mankiewicz and Stone
and Nurse Frye led all eleven patients from Ward 5 into their
recreation area. Mrs. Neagley and Mr. Hart played their check-
ers and the others watched the television. Except Mr. Jennings,
who went into the book room. I would say acting in a suspicious
way. He kept looking around to see who was watching him. I pre-
tended not to be. He finally pulled a book down off the wall, and
walked over to one of the chairs by the window. He kept his back
to me, but kept looking over his shoulder. He was doing something
so I walked behind him and asked to see what he was reading.
From the look he gave me, I knew something was wrong. I tried to
take the book away from him, but he screamed and hit me.

Mr. Stone, the orderly, got him under control. We got the book.
It was an old spy novel. Someone-I believe it likely to be Mr.
Jennings - had ripped out a big chunk of the inside pages and
made a little space to hide things inside the book. What he had
been hiding was all these little scraps of silver paper, he must
have gotten them from the garbage cans. The inside of gum wrappers,
I think. Aluminum foil. Mr. Jennings bit Mr. Stone when I announced I was going to throw the silver paper away and that he would
not be permitted to have exercise period.

That is my report.

Kriegmoor Lunatic Asylum

PATIENT HISTORY (CONT'D) FROM PREVIOUS PAGE

NAME OF PATIENT: Roy Jennings
DATE OF ADMITTANCE: 12/7/53
ADMITTING PHYSICIAN: T. Cotton

January 27 - Dr. Cotton in attendance. A breakthrough of sorts;
after the book room incident (see attached report), patient this
a.m. at last agreed to discuss details of his psychosis rather
than undergo additional electroshock treatments. In summary:
Mr. Jennings believes malevolent creatures from another dimension seek to control his brain. Remarkably detailed psychosis
multiple pages of notes (compiled by patient at my suggestion)

My name is Roy Jennings, and IXX*XXXXXXX I'm as sane as the
next man, maybe more sane, in fact, if the next man lives here
on the lake, because I understand the true nature of things
here. The things he fears, I know what they are. Not that I
expect the next man, or any man to believe me, certainly not you
Dr. Cotton. I know why you wanted me to type all this down on
paper, it's so I can get these things out of my head and onto
the page so you can pick them apart, so you can show me the
error of my ways. Cure me. But you don't understand, doctor, the
drugs have taken me to a place from which there is no way down,
where the doors are always open, where they are there every night
where they talk to me, whisper things that only I can hear, confide their needs, their desires, share their very thoughts with
me. The foil protects me from them; it silences their voices,
their mental emanations. I believe you could measure these emanations if you had the right equipment this is the experiment
I was engaged in when the police took me in. I believe it likely
the government the US government and possibly other governments
as well is engaged in siXXXmilar experiments. I talked to a
Colonel Deveraux an Aif Force press liaison in Washington; he was
unwilling to respond to any of my questions especially when I
mentioned the word Roswell. But Roswell is a smokescreen doctor.
There are no flying saucers, no little green men. But there are
things lurking in the cornersxwxxkxx waiting for the sun to
go down for its radiations to lessen so that they can coalesce.

the Ojibwe, the French, the British, they were all primitives,
all equally so. Of course they called them Gods, what else could
they be? The idea of life existing elsewhere not just on other
worlds but in other dimensions within our own universe was be-
yound their conception. But it's not beyond ours.

DOCTOR - open your mind! Look at the historical record.

Who built the pyrmamids? The Egyptians didn't every reputable
scientist agrees. It's the same here the same with the Copper
Culture people who made those implements that suggest technology 5000 years in advance of what was possible. Who made them,
doctor? Can you answer that?

I CAN.
It was them.They lived here once. They congregate here; the magnetite is key: the magnetite accelerates the bonding process
and allows them to coalesce. Places of power - this is one right XX
here. The surveys show it. When they brush against me when they
touch me I see pictures in my mind their memories their lives the
things they did this place not as it is now but as it was then
hundreds maybe even thousands of years ago. Some mean us no harm
the wish only to share knowledge but there are those who are evil &

3 PT: No. This one just wants to take me away. Take me to its island.
4 TH: Is this like the island in the book—the one that Max sails to?
5 PT: No. The island in the book is a jungle. This island is different. It's cold and dark.
6   There's no light anywhere. No air. And they tie you up and keep you there so
       that you die.
7 TH: That sounds terrible, Jake.
8 PT: It is.
9 PT: That's why I'm scared. I don't want to go there.
10 TH: I don't blame you. But you know something, Jake? There are no islands like
11   that. Not in real life.
12 PT: Okay.
13 [PAUSE]
14 TH: You don't sound convinced.
15 PT: Real life doesn't matter.
16 TH: Jake. It's disturbing to me to hear you say that. There's a big difference
17   between—
18 PT: There's no difference. Real life doesn't matter because the monster makes
19   it real. It touches me and it takes me to its island and when I'm there I can't
20   breathe. And I die.
21 [PAUSE]
22 TH: Is it trying to hurt you, Jake? Is that why it's taking you to its island?
23 PT: I don't know. Maybe.
24 TH: So maybe not?
25 PT: It's angry. That's all I know. It's very, very angry.
26 TH: How do you know that?
27 TH: Does the monster say things to you?
28 PT: No. I just … I know what it knows.
29 TH: I see.
30 [PAUSE]
31 TH: That's interesting. That's very interesting.
32 [TRANSCRIPT ENDS]

can't be certain, but ... different kinds of signals every instant of every day ...
different kinds of signals every instant of every day ... think
audio signals we can smell things and taste them and touch them. There
of us like a radio – those signals are the programs we're built to
receive. But there are other programs we're not capable of com-pre-
hending. They're out there. We just can't receive them normally. We
can't see into the infrared we can't hear everything that a dog can
and we can't see the aliens even though they're there, they're
broadcasting all the time. We have to expand our perceptions.

We have to open our minds.—

Pines did it with the fasting. I did it with the drugs.

But – here's the but – once you can see them, they can see you as
well. We become the signal. They are the receivers. They can come
through the door once you've opened it, whenevr they want they
see the door is wide it's the electroshock I think it helped
turn the switch and now I see them all the time there are so many
of them I hear them their voices muddled distorted some are angry
some are terrified they came to me last night and showed me how
they died chased in the woods cut in the dark eaten alive oh
god I felt it I bled in my mind on my bed the knives so sharp and

SESSION TEXT (CONTINUED)

1   TH: what happened to scare you Jake?
2   PT: It was just like in the book.
3   TH: Where the Wild Things Are?
4   PT: Yes.
5   TH: Tell me.
6   PT: I was Max. I was in the forest and the monsters were hunting me. I hid from
7   them but they found me. And they killed me.
8   TH: That sounds terrible Jake.
9   PT: That's why I screamed.
10 TH: I can understand that.
11 PT: They put their knives in me and they cut me up and I watched them cut me up.
12 TH: The monsters had knives?
13 PT: Yes. Big knives and they had...
14 TH: What is it Jake?
15 PT: They wore masks. The monsters wore masks.
16 TH: Okay.
17 PT: You know what I think Dr. Marsh? I think the monsters were people. They were
18   people wearing masks.
19 TH: This is a very disturbing dream you had Jake.
20 PT: But it wasn't a dream. It was real. Just like in the book.
21 TH: Let's take a step back, Jake. Why were the monsters hunting you?
22 PT: I don't know.
23 TH: Was it because of something you did?
24 PT: I don't think so.
25 TH: Did the monsters say anything to you?
26 PT: Yes. They said they were hungry. They said they were going to eat me.

Kriegmeer Lunatic Asylum

PATIENT HISTORY (CONT'D) FROM PREVIOUS PAGE

NAME OF PATIENT: Roy Jennings
DATE OF ADMITTANCE: 12/7/53
ADMITTING PHYSICIAN: T. Cotton

February 4- Dr. Cotton Attending. Agreement among review board:
patient psychosis is worsening, Wounds on his arms, obviously self-
inflicted, matching description of 'wounds' in obviously embel-
lished story, indicative of same. Electroshock treatments to be
resumed w/increased intensity, frequency, also Hydrotherapy 2x daily.
Wet Pack as needed.

Note to file: Unusual occurrence, Miss Marjorie Alexander,
recent symptoms include complaint of similar phantasms plaguing
her at night.

I plan to speak to her physician, Dr. Sinkiewicz, re: possible

CLIENT: KRIEGMOOR PSYCHIATRIC
PATIENT (PT): JACOB HELLINGER
OTHER (O1): SARAH HELLINGER IN RE: PATIENT HE-31
OTHER (O2): JOHN HELLINGER IN RE: PATIENT HE-31
THERAPIST (TH): DR. CHARLES MARSH
DATE OF SESSION: 12/04/04
SYSTEM PARAMETERS: LANGUAGE DETECT/ENGLISH LINE RETURN DELAY/3 SECONDS
SILENCE THRESHOLD: -5.4 DB FILE FORMAT: MS WORD

SESSION TEXT (CONTINUED)

1   TH: All right, Jake. I want to talk a little more about what happened the other night.
2   I want you to tell your parents what you told me.
3   [PAUSE]
4   PT: The monster came again and it took me to the island. Only now I know it's not
5   an island I know what it is.
6   TH: What is it Jake?
7   PT: I told you. It's Mars.
8   TH: The planet Mars you mean?
9   PT: Uh-huh.
10 [PAUSE]
11 O1: Jake honey what makes you think its Mars?
12 PT: It told me.
13 O1: What did it say?
14 PT: It doesn't say anything it's just there in your mind it shows you pictures.
15 O2: And it showed you pictures of the island.
16 PT: Of Mars. I told you Mars.
17 O2: Maybe it looked like Mars, honey, but -
18 PT: No. It was I know it was because -
19 TH: Okay. It's okay Jake.
20 PT: No. It's not okay. It's going to take me to Mars again. And you can't breathe on
21   Mars.
22 [PAUSE]
23 O1: You want to go to the cafeteria with me for a minute, Jake honey? Get some-
24   thing to eat?
25 PT: Okay.
26 [PAUSE]
27 O2: So what's going on Dr. Marsh? Where's he getting all this from?
28 TH: I really don't know.
29 O2: This is freaking me out, I have to tell you. What can we do?
30 [PAUSE]
31 TH: We can encourage him to keep talking about it. I think that's all we can do.

EDLOG 1.2

CLIENT: KRIEGMOOR PSYCHIATRIC
PATIENT (PT): JACOB HELLINGER
OTHER (O1): SARAH HELLINGER IN RE: PATIENT HE-31
OTHER (O2): JOHN HELLINGER IN RE: PATIENT HE-31
THERAPIST (TH): DR. CHARLES MARSH
DATE OF SESSION: 12/04/04
SYSTEM PARAMETERS: LANGUAGE DETECT/ENGLISH LINE RETURN DELAY/8 SECONDS
SILENCE THRESHOLD: -5.4 DB FILE FORMAT: MS WORD

SESSION TEXT (CONTINUED)

32	O2: God.
33	TH: Can I ask you a question Mr. Hellinger? Jake was originally brought here
34	because of this imaginary friend he was seeing -
35	O2: Uh-huh.
36	TH: How long exactly had he been seeing this friend before you brought him here?
37	O2: A long time. Since he could talk. God, maybe even before, I don't know.
38	TH: An innate condition. I see. Do you know what did the friend say to him?
39	O2: Huh? How would I know that? I mean - the friend wasn't real, doctor.
40	TH: Of course. What I should have said - what did Jake tell you the friend was saying?
41	O2: He didn't really say much about it, to tell you the truth. He was just
42	always...talking to it.
43	TH: Was the friend a boy, a girl -
44	O2: A boy. It had a funny name. I can't remember.
45	[PAUSE]
46	[PAUSE]
47	O2: Leaf Gee, something like that. A foreign name. I really couldn't pronounce it.
48	TH: A foreign name. All right.
49	TH: You live right near here, isn't that right Mr. Hellinger?
50	O2: Yeah. Right on the border with the old Belanger settlement. Near the reservation.
51	TH: I see.
52	O2: That's the only way we can afford this place. Because we're in state. Financial
53	aid.
54	TH: I understand. You know - being from around here, have you ever heard the
55	story of the Windigo?
56	O2: Well...sure. But what's that got to do with anything?
57	TH: I'm just wondering how that might tie in to what's happening to Jake.
58	O2: How? How would it tie in?
59	TH: I'm not sure.
60	O2: Well for Christ's sake.
61	TH: Science does not always follow the straight and narrow path, Mr. Hellinger.
62	Sometimes it takes us to unexpected places – twists in the road. I believe that

PATIENT HISTORY (CONT'D) FROM PREVIOUS PAGE

NAME OF PATIENT: Roy Jennings
DATE OF ADMITTANCE: 12/7/53
ADMITTING PHYSICIAN: T. Cotton

February 7 - Patient unable to use typewriter this day; inco-
herent during our discussion.

February 8 - Review board special meeting; Jennings condition discussed. Further treatment alternatives; subject of lobotomization
broached. Will research efficacy of operation among
similar schizophrenic patients.

February 12 - Nurse Sanderson reporting. During hydrotherapy
session this a.m., patient attempted to drown himself.

February 15 - Dr. Marsden in attendance. Night terrors of increased intensity noted; patient moved to iso Ward to minimize
disruptive effects on general population.

February 18 - Dr. Cotton attending. I had summoned an emergency
review board meeting this a.m. re: Jennings. Unanimous agreement:
Lobotomy our best option at this point. Operation to be performed
this a.m.

NOTE TO FILE: Miss Alexanders hallucinations continue. Very strange.
Coincidence?

Marks on her arm similar to those on Mr. Jennings. Query sent to Dr.
Margulies Boston Public re: possible contagious nature of Jennings'
psychosis (hysteria transmission). Contact between two patients?

MEDLOG 1.2

MEDLOG AUTOMATED TRANSCRIPTION SERVICES
SESSION INFORMATION

CLIENT: KRIEGMOOR PSYCHIATRIC
PATIENT (PT): NATHANIEL BARRON
THERAPIST (TH): DR. CHARLES MARSH
DATE OF SESSION: 12/05/04
SYSTEM PARAMETERS: LANGUAGE DETECT/ENGLISH LINE RETURN DELAY8 SECONDS
SILENCE THRESHOLD: -5.4 DB FILE FORMAT: MS WORD

SESSION TEXT (CONTINUED)

1 PT: the gates open, and he makes his wishes known.
2 TH: What does that mean?
3 PT: I am the door through which God has chosen to pass.
4 TH: Yes, but -
5 PT: God is angry with you, Dr. Marsh. And he grows angry with everyone here. He
6   speaks to them and they ignore his wishes. This will not stand.
7 TH: How do you know that?
8 PT: Who decides who lives and who dies? Who bestows the breath of life and then
9   takes it away? Only God, Dr. Marsh. Only God.
10 TH: I see.

Kriegmoor Lunatic Asylum

PATIENT HISTORY (CONT'D) FROM PREVIOUS PAGE

NAME OF PATIENT: Marjorie Alexander

February 13 - Dr. Sinkiewicz attending.

Second conference with Dr. Cotton; his theories as before.
Poppycock and tommyrot. Contagious psychoses, indeed.

February 19 - Dr. Sinkiewicz attending.

Brief session with Miss Alexander.

'They are in the walls'
'Spectral figures at my bedside when I awake'

Note for Nurse Frye:

Wet pack treatments, increase to 3x Daily
Hydrotherapy as necessary

NO DRUGS WITHOUT MY EXPRESS WRITTEN ORDER

The Kriegmoor Asylum For The Criminally Insane

Alphabetical listing of current patients accompanied by physican summary
- March 1908

KRIEG, HANS. Admitted July 8th 1907. Town of Cleveland. Age
65. German. Widowed. Youngest child 25 years old. Farmer. Fair
circumstances. Earliest symptoms noted after wife's death. Began
starving cattle...was so mean that family couldn't live with
him. Has destroyed or starved several hundred dollars worth of
cattle, claiming that witches were the cause.

KRIEGMOOR, JOSEPHINE. Admitted January 5 1894. Resident of
Bayfield Heights. Born New York City. Wife of Mr. Herman Kriegmoor. No children. 32 years old. Fair circumstances. First symptoms began several years ago. Acted queer, began hearing voices.
Believes demons surround her and keep things going wrong. Sees
them every night. Visions grew so severe hospitalization required. All therapies to this date ineffectual. Has declared wish
to die rather than continue in this state.

Note from Hospital Director Samuels: Mr. Kriegmoor wishes his wife
...

MEDLOG AUTOMATED TRANSCRIPTION SERVICES
SESSION INFORMATION

CLIENT: KRIEGMOOR PSYCHIATRIC
PATIENT (PT): JACOB HELLINGER
THERAPIST (TH): DR. CHARLES MARSH
DATE OF SESSION: 12/06/04
SYSTEM PARAMETERS: LANGUAGE DETECT/ENGLISH LINE RETURN DELAY/8 SECONDS
SILENCE THRESHOLD: -5.4 DB FILE FORMAT: MS WORD

SESSION TEXT (CONTINUED)

1 TH: it must have been scary for you last night.
2 PT: Uh-huh.
3 TH: You were there on Mars.
4 PT: Uh-huh.
5 TH: And then...
6 PT: I couldn't breathe.
7 TH: Okay. Jake, your chart says up until the time you were four years old, you had
8   an asthmatic condition. Sometimes you had trouble breathing then too. Do you
9   remember that?
10 PT: A little.
11 TH: Did this feel the same? Could this have been an asthma attack?
12 PT: I don't know. It's hard to remember.
13 TH: Give yourself a minute.
14 [PAUSE]
15 PT: I don't think so.
16 TH: Why not?
17 PT: The asthma was...I couldn't catch my breath. This was more like - there was no
18   air. I couldn't breath even though I tried and tried.
19 TH: Okay. I understand.
20 TH: Jake why do you think the monster wanted to hurt you?
21 PT: I don't know. It kept saying it was my friend.
22 TH: What exactly did it say?
23 PT: Martian is friends. Martian is friends. Over and over. But it's not my friend. It's
24   hurting me Dr. Marsh.
25 TH: I know.
26 PT: Dr. Marsh?
27 TH: Yes?
28 PT: Are there drugs you can give me? To help me sleep?
29 [PAUSE]
30 TH: Drugs.
31 PT: Yes.
32 TH: I don't know that drugs are such a good idea, Jake.

TO: c_marsh@kriegmoor-psychiatric.org

FROM: don_gilder@kriegmoor-psychiatric.org

DATE: 12/7/04

RE: PATIENT HE-31

Rough night last night again, poor kid. Both him and HA-09... must be something in the water, I guess.

TO: c_marsh@kriegmoor-psychiatric.org

FROM: p_ferguson@kriegmoor-psychiatric.org

DATE: 12/8/04

RE: Patient HA-09

Forgive the oversight. My fault entirely, I meant to bring you up to speed on what had happened with your former patient, though I'm sure you can understand paperwork was the last thing on my mind this morning, given the circumstances.

I will discuss the incident in session this afternoon; transcripts of that should provide you with all necessary information.

Best,

Peter

MEDLOG AUTOMATED TRANSCRIPTION SERVICES
SESSION INFORMATION

CLIENT: KRIEGMOOR PSYCHIATRIC
PATIENT (PT): KARI HANSEN
THERAPIST (TH): DR. PETER FERGUSON
DATE OF SESSION: 12/8/04
SYSTEM PARAMETERS: LANGUAGE DETECT/ENGLISH LINE RETURN DELAY/8 SECONDS
SILENCE THRESHOLD: -5.4 DB FILE FORMAT: MS WORD

SESSION TEXT (CONTINUED)

1 PT: it covered me like a blanket and right away I couldn't breathe.
2 TH: Okay.
3 PT: It was the weirdest most awful feeling not the kind of I can't breathe when
4 you're swimming underwater and you run out of air but like –
5 TH: Easy Kari.
6 PT: It felt like my whole body was just shutting down like all of a sudden my veins
7 were getting thinner and thinner they were too tight to let the blood go through
8 it hurt oh god it hurt so much. And then I couldn't breathe like I was taking in air
9 and gasping but it didn't matter. I still couldn't breathe!
10 TH: And this is the first time something like this has happened?
11 PT: Yes. Oh God it was trying to kill me.
12 TH: Listen to me Kari. Obviously something is causing the hallucinations to inten-
13 sify. It may be a combination of the new protocols we're using and the fact that
14 you, frankly, are not paying enough attention to your health. You have to eat
15 better. You have to sleep. You have to -
16 PT: Where's Dr. Marsh?
17 TH: Dr. Marsh is consulting on your case, as I told you. I speak to him quite often.
18 PT: What does he say?
19 TH: I don't think that it's appropriate for me to discuss that in this context, Kari.
20 What I can tell you is that Dr. Yanagisawa and I think what happened to you
21 was basically a panic attack. You know what a panic attack is?
22 PT: No.
23 TH: A panic attack is -
24 PT: I know what that is. I'm telling you that's not what happened.
25 TH: Kari. You got scared, you began hyperventilating, and -
26 PT: Of course I got scared. You would be scared too if you could see it the way it
27 comes out of the wall and then it's there and then it comes right at you and into
28 you and then -
29 TH: Kari -
30 PT: It makes me stop breathing it wants me to feel like what it is to stop breathing it
31 wants me to feel like what it is to die.
32 TH: Kari, this is all in your head, I'm afraid. No one's going to die here I promise you

SESSION TEXT (CONTINUED)

33 that.
34 PT: I don't want to die.
35 TH: Shh. You're going to be fine.
36 PT: What if I'm not? What if you're wrong?
37 [PAUSE]
38 TH: Kari...

TO: p_ferguson@kriegmoor-psychiatric.org
FROM: c_marsh@kriegmoor-psychiatric.org
DATE: 12/8/04
RE: HA-09

Doctor:

I'm greatly disturbed by not just the happenings of yesterday evening, but what I find in the latest transcripts of your sessions with this patient.

It is clear to me she has closed herself off to you, doctor. You need to open lines of communication with her once again. The easiest way to do this would be to openly discuss the shadows she refers to in the context of her injuries - ask her what she thinks they are, what they do and/or say to her, even discuss ways to physically prevent them from reaching her. Treat the symptoms for the moment, reestablish your rapport, and then reach for an absolute cure.

        - Dr. Marsh

TO: c_marsh@kriegmoor-psychiatric.org
CC: "review"<reviewboard@kriegmoor-psychiatric.org>
FROM: p_ferguson@kriegmoor-psychiatric.org
DATE: 12/8/04
RE: HA-09

I'm afraid I don't believe taking the approach you suggest will do anything other than encourage further delusions on the patient's part. Moreover, I must point you to the rather definitive instructions issued by patient's mother regarding the stories you mentioned above.

Thank you for your suggestions, in any case.

Peter

KRIEGMOOR
PSYCHIATRIC INSTITUTE

INTERNAL CORRESPONDENCE - NOT FOR EXTERNAL USE OR DISCLOSURE

TO: p_ferguson@kriegmoor-psychiatric.org
FROM: c_marsh@kriegmoor-psychiatric.org
DATE: 12/8/04
RE: HA-09

Dr. Ferguson:

You've misread my e-mail. I did not suggest discussing the stories, but rather the current hallucinations the patient believes responsible for her injuries. I would be happy to conduct interviews along these lines.

        - Dr. Marsh

KRIEGMOOR
PSYCHIATRIC INSTITUTE

TO: c_marsh@kriegmoor-psychiatric.org
       "review"<reviewboard@kriegmoor-psychiatric.org>

FROM: claire_morris@kriegmoor-psychiatric.org

DATE: 12/8/04

RE: HA-09

I've been following your correspondence, gentlemen. Dr. Marsh, in my
opinion the distinction you refer to above seems a very subtle one
and would not, I believe, hold up in therapy or meet with the mother's
approval. The current course of treatment seems to me the correct one and
we will continue with it as discussed.

I do appreciate your continuing interest in the case, and thank you for
your understanding.

-- Claire

DRAFT MATERIAL: NOT FOR PUBLICATION

ARTICLE TITLE: SHADOWS IN THE ASYLUM

AUTHOR: Charles Marsh, M.D., Ph.D.

her favorite, Dr. Ferguson. But I did understand; I was the only
one, in fact. It wasn't just K getting worse; it was everyone.
It was the past repeating itself: as with Jennings and Miss
Alexander, so with K and my other patients. This 'psychosis' — as
the physicians of fifty years ago had called it — was contagious,
and only I knew why.

In separate correspondence with the director, I guardedly
pointed out the similarities between K's recent 'panic attacks'
and the breathing difficulties the H_____ boy was experiencing,
hoping to be given the opportunity to speak with both directly.
Her response? She ordered the building's ventilation system
checked for possible obstructions. She insisted on waiting for the
results of such a check before taking further action.

And by then of course it was too late.

The H____ boy, physically much frailer than K, was unable

DATE: 12/10/04

RE: JACOB HELLINGER

It is with the deepest regret that I inform you of the death last night
of Jacob Hellinger. During his six months here, Jake became a special
favorite of the hospital staff; I know I speak for all of us when I say we
will miss him greatly.

Services will be held at the First Lutheran Church in Bayfield Heights
this coming Sunday. A scholarship has been set up in Jake's name at the
Prentice Elementary School in Wappinger Kill.

Notes of sympathy may be sent to the family in care of my office.

- Claire

MEDLOG 1.2

MEDLOG AUTOMATED TRANSCRIPTION SERVICES
SESSION INFORMATION

CLIENT: KRIEGMOOR PSYCHIATRIC
OTHER (O1): SARAH HELLINGER IN RE: PATIENT HE-31
OTHER (O2): JOHN HELLINGER IN RE: PATIENT HE-31
THERAPIST (TH): DR. CHARLES MARSH
DATE OF SESSION: 12/11/04
SYSTEM PARAMETERS: LANGUAGE DETECT/ENGLISH LINE RETURN DELAY/8 SECONDS
SILENCE THRESHOLD: -5.4 DB FILE FORMAT: MS WORD

SESSION TEXT (CONTINUED)

1 O2: I don't understand why this happened. He was fine up until these last few
2   weeks.
3 TH: To be frank, we don't know either, Mr. Hellinger.
4 O2: This new drug you had him on –
5 TH: The T-86.
6 O2: Yes. I've been checking with some doctor friends of mine. They say it's an
7   experimental drug.
8 TH: Well. It's new. I wouldn't say experimental.
9 O2: They said it's very powerful. That it can have a lot of side-effects. Maybe that's
10   what aggravated his asthma. Brought it back. Killed him.
11 TH: I don't think so, Mr. Hellinger. Jake displayed none of the other symptoms that –
12 O2: Sometimes I think you guys don't have a fucking clue about what you're doing.
13 O1: John!
14 O2: Well it's true. You go on the Internet you read all this stuff about doctors who
15   prescribe the wrong drugs, doctors who take out the wrong organs they stay up
16   all night working and take drugs themselves and then make mistakes and –
17 O1: John! That's enough.
18 O2: I don't understand. He was fine up until he came here. Until you started seeing
19   him.
20 O1: John...
21 O2: Fuck it.
22 [PAUSE]
23 O1: I'm so sorry.
24 TH: That's all right Mrs. Hellinger.
25 O1: It's just - Jake was very special to John.
26 TH: You don't need to apologize.
27 O1: But I want to explain. I have two children from my first marriage but Jake
28   is...was John's only child.
29 TH: Of course.
30 O1: He wanted to see his child grow up. And now - well, he's just angry. It's not you.
31 [PAUSE]

KRIEGMOOR

9/04 – 1/05

December 14 2004. 12:37 a.m.. A sudden Realization. The computer is networked. Therefore, the computer is vulnerable. Henceforth, all notes/thoughts related to article will appear in this notebook.

Tonight: Finished review of Von Daniken. Chariots of The Gods. Laughable. Not science at all. And yet...

The man is a tireless researcher. Unafraid to question accepted wisdom. Admirable. Of particular interest: evidence he gathered suggesting presence of 'super-intelligent' life forms on Earth thousands of years ago. An alien intelligence. Spec. mention Wandjina - the mouthless, shapeless creatures who haunt aboriginal desert.

Wandjina → Windigo. Coincidence?

6:32 a.m. An awful dream. Nightmare involving incident from my own past, a memory I wish to forget. The foreman's face, when verdict in Lattimore trial announced. Grim satisfaction. Job well-done.

Fool.

that a passive approach would no longer suffice. I needed to actively seek out this intelligence before it could do further harm.

I conceived of a series of experiments involving the measurement of certain energy fields associated with all living creatures, and - using the last of the monies I had set aside for legal fees with regard to the still-ongoing civil trial in the Lattimore case - purchased the equipment I needed. However, at virtually the same time, I received word that K had suffered another, even more severe 'panic attack.'

Anxious as I was to begin my work, I realized now that Dr. Ferguson, through his preconceptions regarding the proper course of treatment for K, was hurting her. Perhaps causing permanent damage. I could not allow him to continue.

Surreptitiously obtaining his network identity, I accessed the hospital computer system from a terminal in the Duluth airport, and composed several entries in his name regarding a number of female patients, including K. I arranged as well for the subsequent discovery of those messages. On December 27th, pending investigation into the charges against him, Dr. Ferguson was suspended from duty, and placed on administrative leave from the hospital. I do accept a portion of the blame for the events that followed, although of course the problems in his personal life obviously preceded the charges I'd manufactured. Nonetheless, as my father was fond of saying, you cannot make an omelet without breaking a few eggs, and I accomplished what I set out to achieve: Ferguson's removal from K's case, and my own subsequent installation as one of

MEDLOC

MEDL
SESSIO

CLIENT:

Kari-

CLIENT: KRIEGMOOR PSYCHIATRIC
PATIENT (PT): KARI HANSEN
THERAPIST (TH): DR. CHARLES MARSH
DATE OF SESSION: 12/30/04
SYSTEM PARAMETERS: LANGUAGE DETECT/ENGLISH LINE RETURN DELAY/3 SECONDS
SILENCE THRESHOLD: -5.4 DB FILE FORMAT: MS WORD

SESSION TEXT (CONTINUED)

1 TH: This is Dr. Charles Marsh. It is 9:42 a.m. I've arrived for my session with the
2   patient but she is still sleeping.
3 [PAUSE]
4 [PAUSE]
5 TH: She looks very peaceful. Very content.
6 [PAUSE]
7 TH: I note bruising on her throat. Query Dr. Yanagisawa. If -
8 PT: Dr. Marsh?
9 TH: Shhh.
10 PT: Oh god. Dr. Marsh is it really you?
11 TH: Yes. I'm glad to see you, Kari.
12 PT: No one believes me. You have to -
13 TH: Shhh.
14 PT: No no you have to listen you have to make them understand. You have to -
15 TH: I brought you something.
16 PT: What?
17 TH: This book. It's another one by the same author you were reading before - that
18   your mother brought you?
19 PT: Yes but -
20 TH: I actually bought it over the weekend. The author was signing at a store in the
21   Heights and I had him inscribe it for you. See?
22 PT: Dr. Marsh I don't want to -
23 TH: Kari, look. Look at what he wrote.
24 PT: Oh.
25 [PAUSE]

51
52
53
54
55
56
57
58
59
60

KRIEGMOOR
PSYCHIATRIC INSTITUTE

From the desk of
Charles Marsh, M.D., Ph.D.

Kari-
 Everything we say is recorded -
you know that. This is the only
way I can speak the truth
to you, and you to me. I know
what you're going through. I
know they're real. I am working
on a way to stop them - but in the

26   TH: That's nice, isn't it.
27   [PAUSE]
28   PT: Yes. Very nice.
29   TH: I'm glad to see you again Kari. I know you've been having a hard time these
30   last few weeks. I really want to hear what's been happening.
31   in the file but of course I want in your own w...
32   PT: Okay.

SESSION TEXT (CONTINUED)

33   TH: You can take your time. Think about it is that you want to say.
34   [PAUSE]
35   [PAUSE]
36   TH: Take your time.

1-1   11:20 a.m.

We begin today.

Experiments derive from transcripts : transcripts
suggest during encounters with this shadow a sharing
of consciousness takes place - shared thoughts. Thoughts
are electrical impulses, thus measurable.

Equipment is prepared

Test subject obtained from local animal shelter
Female cat 4 yrs old exc. health

(Note : see prev. experiments Schalken indicating
   significant degree of correlation between primate/feline
   responses cranial conditioning + perceptual acuity)

1:25 p.m.   As per Hernandez-Peon/ Galambos, cat was
     anaesthatized - canula was inserted into
     femoral vein (right leg) of the cat - used
     to administer local anaesthesia

     Cat placed into a Malnik Model 10
     stereotaxic frame.

1:39 p.m.   Minute incision made along sagittal suture
     of the skull. Inserted fine-gauge needle into
     lateral ventricles of brain. Watching for...

1:59 p.m.   Cat began suffering violent series of seizures
     at this point in time. Unable to arrest. Lethal
     dose of anaesthesia applied.

1-2-05 4:41 p.m. Animal shelter has refused
to give me a second cat.

1-3-05   12:58 p.m. Cat found at corner of
Blake and 2nd. Cat is male neutered approximately
8 yrs. old. Identifying tags removed.

7:25 p.m. Procedure as above performed.
No complications. Electrodes attached to appropriate
leads.

8:42 p.m. Cat given 1/24 tablet Nypureden.
9:50 pm Cat resting comfortably
11:12 p.m. Resting comfortably

"   "   - ex. - Cat appears wary
Watchful. I will be as well.

8:12 p.m. Additional 1/24 tab. Nypureden given

11:21 p.m. First concrete result - (HALLELUJAH!!)
Woke to find cat hissing
at apparently empty air - retreated to
corner of tub, hissing continued approx.
3 minutes.
Electrodes measure increased cortical
activity, diffuse locations in cerebellum

Unable to correlate cortical activity
w/ cerebellum spec. location - data
previously mapped areas of brain - is this
a new perceptual center - beyond my
field of expertise...

NOTE: I DID NOT SENSE ANY SORT OF PRESENCE AT THIS TIME

.4 mv - 1
.2 mv - 2   > TO MAP AGAINST PREVIOUS - SEE BACK →

1:14 A.M. Noticeable spike of activity in previously-mapped
perceptual areas as per Gambal/Bendickson

.4 mv - 1
.3 mv - 2
.25 mv - Δe —→ to do

Cat is frantic !!! Desperate to be free of
Malnik frame to
                 I am afraid it will detach electrodes.

2:40 a.m. I must have fallen asleep.
The cat is dead.

Laundry at 8:00 a.m.

MEDLOG AUTOMATED TRANSCRIPTION SERVICES
SESSION INFORMATION

CLIENT: KRIEGMOOR PSYCHIATRIC
PATIENT (PT): RONA BIDDERLEE
THERAPIST (TH): DR. CHARLES MARSH
DATE OF SESSION: 1/3/05
SYSTEM PARAMETERS: LANGUAGE DETECT/ENGLISH LINE RETURN DELAY/3 SECONDS
SILENCE THRESHOLD: -5.4 DB FILE FORMAT: MS WORD

SESSION TEXT (CONTINUED)

1   TH: it is a shock, yes.
2   PT: He was always such a gentleman, Dr. Ferguson was. Very well-spoken. Very
3   polite.
4   TH: Yes. Well he did manage to fool many of us too, Mrs. Bidderlee. Now seeing as
5   this is our first session, I thought -
6   PT: He dressed so well. You can always tell a lot about a person by how they
7   dress. His coat was always very clean. Very white. Cleanliness is important,
8   don't you think doctor?
9   TH: I do.
10   PT: Your coat for instance. It's very rumpled. Not presentable in my opinion. Does
11   the institute do your laundry?
12   TH: They do. It's rumpled actually because I was working late and -
13   PT: Were I in your shoes I would certainly complain about this. Because a certain
14   a portion of your salary goes to the staff responsible and you have a right to be
15   angry.
16   TH: I - yes, maybe you're right. I should say something.
17   PT: Most certainly. And is that a spot there? That red? Tomato sauce, I should
18   imagine. Now that may be your lunch, doctor. One wouldn't want to blame that
19   on the laundress though of course these days there are so many cleaners inca-
20   pable of dealing with the simplest stains. Now when I was a girl part of your
21   upbringing - oh dear.
22   TH: What is it?
23   PT: They're back.
24   TH: Who?
25   PT: The bugs. The roaches. Very small ones. All over the window. Do you see?
26   TH: No, I'm afraid I don't.
27   PT: Most disturbing. I have spoken with the maintenance staff about disinfecting
28   properly so this doesn't happen but as I said in this day and age sometimes the
29   achievement of a simple task such as a good thorough cleaning seems beyond
30   the capability of these people.
31   TH: Huh.
32   PT: Of course you know who I mean when I say these people.

SESSION TEXT (CONTINUED)

1 TH: And so if you had to sum up - all the different medications Dr. Ferguson gave
2 you - was there any -
3 PT: No. No difference. Ow.
4 TH: It hurts to talk.
5 PT: Yes.
6 TH: Do you want some water?
7 PT: Thank you.
8 TH: Just take a minute. Rest. We have plenty of time to talk.
9 [PAUSE]
[PAUSE]

KRIEGMOOR
PSYCHIATRIC INSTITUTE

From the desk of
Charles Marsh, M.D., Ph.D.

no
You don't have to say anyth...
I just wanted to tell you how...
felt - . how I've come to f...
about you over these last fe...
weeks

SESSION INFORMATION...

CLIENT: KRIEGMOOR PSYC...
PATIENT (PT): KARI HANSE...
OTHER (O): MS. INGRID HA...
THERAPIST (TH): DR. CLAI...
DATE OF SESSION: 1/4/05
SYSTEM PARAMETERS: LA...
SILENCE T...

SESSION TEXT (CONTINU...

1 O: is what the doctor and I d...
2 [PAUSE]
3 O: Kari. You must have had...
4 [PAUSE]
5 TH: Where did you get the foil...
6 PT: From the kitchen.
7 TH: When were you in the kitc...
8 [PAUSE]
9 O: Kari. Dr. Morris is asking y...
10 PT: Mom, please. Just [UNINT...
11 O: Oh your poor throat honey.
12 [PAUSE]
13 O: What's the matter now? Wh...
14 PT: It was working. It was worki...
15 [PAUSE]

KRIEGMOOR
PSYCHIATRIC INSTITUTE

From the desk of
Charles Marsh, M.D., Ph.D.

You found the foil I brought

Yes

Make a cap wear the cap tonight
it will help!

don't understand

The shadow is alive

Yes

The shadow is I believe a
measurable life force an energy
The cap will shield you
Kari   Trust me

MEDLOG 1.2

MEDLOG AUTOMATED TRANSCRIPTION SERVICES
SESSION INFORMATION

CLIENT: KRIEGMOOR PSYCHIATRIC
PATIENT (PT): KARI HANSEN
OTHER (O): MS. INGRID HANSEN IN RE: PATIENT HA-09
THERAPIST (TH): DR. CLAIRE MORRIS
DATE OF SESSION: 1/4/05
SYSTEM PARAMETERS: LANGUAGE DETECT/ENGLISH LINE RETURN DELAY:8 SECONDS
SILENCE THRESHOLD: -5.4 DB FILE FORMAT: MS WORD

SESSION TEXT (CONTINUED)

1	O: is what the doctor and I don't understand honey. Why?
2	[PAUSE]
3	O: Kari. You must have had a reason for doing this.
4	[PAUSE]
5	TH: Where did you get the foil?
6	PT: From the kitchen.
7	TH: When were you in the kitchen?
8	[PAUSE]
9	O: Kari. Dr. Morris is asking you a question.
10	PT: Mom, please. Just [UNINTELLIGIBLE]
11	O: Oh your poor throat honey.
12	[PAUSE]
13	O: What's the matter now? Why are you crying Kari?
14	PT: It was working. It was working and you took it away. Wh... y... take it away?
15	[PA...

TO: "support"<nursing@kriegmoor-psychiatric.org
FROM: claire_morris@kriegmoor-psychiatric.org
DATE: 1/4/05
RE: HA-09

Please make sure to check patient's room thoroughly for foreign objects prior to evening curfew. Thank you

KRIEGMOOR PSYCHIATRIC
PATIENT (PT): DARRELL COVEY
THERAPIST (TH): DR. CHARLES MARSH
DATE OF SESSION: 1/6/05
SYSTEM PARAMETERS: LANGUAGE DETECT/ENGLISH LINE RETURN DELAY:8 SECONDS
SILENCE THRESHOLD: -5.4 DB FILE FORMAT: MS WORD

SESSION TEXT (CONTINUED)

1	TH: what are you doing under the covers Darrell?
2	[PAUSE]
3	TH: Darrell?

TO:

FR

DA

RE

Pa:
doc
un
be

I:
m

KRIEGMOOR
PSYCHIATRIC INSTITUTE

From the desk of
Charles Marsh, M.D., Ph.D.

I'm so sorry

But it worked?

Yes

We need another kind of shield

What though?

Something with the same
insulating properties
Something to keep it far
away from you

Keep talking
I have an idea

ial and
received
nding the
unintended
ege.

TO: c_marsh@kriegmoor-psychiatric.org

FROM: claire_morris@kriegmoor-psychiatric.org

DATE: 1/08/05

RE: REQUEST FOR MAINTENANCE DETAIL

Painting the patient's room? For one thing, it's the middle of winter, doctor. For another, we have a series of color choices which are permitted under our agreement with the Landmarks Preservation Committee, and I don't believe the 'special' paints you refer to are among them.

If you truly believe a change in her surroundings would help, perhaps her mother could arrange some familiar pieces of art, or photographs.

- Claire

MEDLOG 1.2

MEDLOG AUTOMATED TRANSCRIPTION SERVICES
SESSION INFORMATION

CLIENT: KRIEGMOOR PSYCHIATRIC
PATIENT (PT): NATHANIEL BARRON
OTHER PERSONNEL (OP): NURSE DONALD GILDER
DATE OF SESSION: 1/8/05
SYSTEM PARAMETERS: LANGUAGE DETECT/ENGLISH LINE RETURN DELAY/3 SECONDS
SILENCE THRESHOLD: -5.4 DB FILE FORMAT: MS WORD

SESSION TEXT (CONTINUED)

1 OP:how badly she's hurt.
2 PT: I'm sorry for any pain I caused her. She is an innocent.
3 OP:She just wanted to give you a bath.
4 PT: I cannot bathe. The holy of holies is taken up residence within me.
5 OP:Within you?
6 PT: Yes. I cannot profane the flesh that he occupies.
7 OP:He's in you now?
8 PT: My body is his at his discretion. He comes and goes as he will.
9 OP:Sounds like a no. How about we get you in a bath, and if you feel him coming
10   on, you let me know, and we'll get you out of there right away?
11 [PAUSE]
12 PT: This is not a joking matter.
13 OP:Neither is the way you smell.
14 [PAUSE]
15 OP:Have it your way. I'm going to get a couple of the guards, and -
16 PT: You'd better get more than a couple.
17 [PAUSE]
18 OP:Christ. What is it with everyone around here these days?
19 [PAUSE]

CLIENT: KRIEGMOOR PSYCHIATRIC
PATIENT (PT): KARI HANSEN
THERAPIST (TH): DR. CHARLES MARSH
DATE OF SESSION: 1/10/05
SYSTEM PARAMETERS: LANGUAGE DETECT/ENGLISH LINE RETURN DELAY/8 SECONDS
SILENCE THRESHOLD: -5.4 DB FILE FORMAT: MS WORD

SESSION TEXT (CONTINUED)

1 TH: hard night.
2 [PAUSE]
3 TH: Can I see the marks?
4 [PAUSE]
5 TH: And the other arm too now?
6 PT: Yes.
7 TH: I'm so sorry.
8 TH: Dr. Yanigasawa wants to change your medication again. He thinks this is an
9   allergic reaction.
10 TH: He may be right Karl. We can't discount that entirely.
11 [PAUSE]
12 [PAUSE]
13 [PAUSE]
14 [PAUSE]

KRIEGMOOR
PSYCHIATRIC INSTITUTE

From the desk of
Charles Marsh, M.D., Ph.D.

Oh Kari
That's all right
Ya don't need to say anything today
Was it the same last night
Ya can jst nod
It was worse?
I'm sorry

I wish I could think of
something that would
stop the pain
Something I could do
Something that cald

K

Should it ... for conflict I ha... demagnetizes which ... evening so that it will generate ... t should act as a weapon against ... it. Should disrupt the e-m fields ... it. Like a phaser on Star ...

... this a.m. Alarm is ... ty minutes ... ctive / operational

Cotton in... population... done: the right...

NAME OF PATIENT: Roy Jennings
DATE OF ADMITTANCE: 12/7/53
ADMITTING PHYSICIAN: T. Cotton

Feb. 19 - Prefrontal lobotomy performed this a.m. by Dr. Sinkiewicz; myself and Dr. Carter assisting. Operation a success,
patient moved to infirmary to recuperate.

March 6 - Dr. Cotton in attendance. Mr. Jennings returned to
Ward 5 general population. Appears content. I hope so.

I hope we have done the right thing.

1-11-05 (CONT'D)
2:13 a.m.

There is no such radical procedure in
this day and age. Therefore...

I have taken the Nypureden myself. ← NOTE 1 TAB PRESCRIP

I am, insofar as is possible, sending out
peaceful thoughts to this intelligence, hoping
that it will understand I wish only to commune.
Communicate. However...

Should it become necessary, I have prepared
for conflict. I have obtained a powerful
demagnetizer, which I have modified this
evening so that it will generate an electric pulse
that should act as a weapon against this
creature. Should disrupt the e-m fields
which compose it. Like a phaser on Star
Trek, I suppose.

Equipment now positioned and ready.

wavelengths. Also... increase

I am looking at

3:10 a.m.
Slight increase in background e-m noise detected, mostly at extreme low-f wavelengths, invisible to unaided eye. Subliminal sense of disquiet.

My disquiet as above increases.

3:26 a.m. Now noted: measurable (.2") increase avg. over all e-m wavelengths. Also...

I am looking at the wall and seeing a doubling of the surface - a 2nd layer behind. I ~~fe~~ feel certain it is between those layers of wall - within the wall. Hiding?

5:00 a.m. Definitely hiding

6:00 a.m. Note: staff meeting this a.m. Alarm is set. I will sleep for ninety minutes while equipment remains active/operational

---

CC: "review"<reviewboard@kriegmoor-psych

FROM: claire_morris@kriegmoor-psychiatric.org

DATE: 1/12/05

RE: STAFF MEETING

I'm sorry you weren't able to join us this morning doctor. Please find the minutes from the meeting attached.

I want to second the appreciative comments from the review board re: your work these last few weeks. You've really been burning the midnight oil with Dr. Ferguson gone, and I want you to know how essential your contributions have been to our ability to continue functioning as an institution during this crisis.

And before I forget: administration has notified me of your request for Darrell Covey's records. We are in the process of obtaining those for you. I know how difficult it must be to treat this patient without that information in hand, and I would simply ask that you continue to do your best up until such time as we do obtain the missing files.

Thank you once more for all your hard work.

- Claire

LC ● 1.2

MEDLOG AUTOMATED TRANSCRIPTION SERVICES
SESSION INFORMATION

CLIENT: KRIEGMOOR PSYCHIATRIC
PATIENT (PT): DARRELL COVEY
THERAPIST (TH): DR. CHARLES MARSH
DATE OF SESSION: 1/12/05
SYSTEM PARAMETERS: LANGUAGE DETECT/ENGLISH LINE RETURN DELAY/3 SECONDS
SILENCE THRESHOLD: -5.4 DB FILE FORMAT: MS WORD

SESSION TEXT (CONTINUED)

1 TH: Good morning Darrell. You're out from under the covers I see.
2 PT: Yes. The girls wanted to see the sun.
3 TH: It is nice to see the sun again after all that snow, isn't it?
4 PT: Uh-huh. It's been a long cold lonely winter. It's been like years since it's -
5 TH: Darrell.
6 PT: Sorry. You want me to sing something else?
7 TH: I don't think so Darrell. Not right now. Maybe we could talk -
8 PT: About the past? About yesterday, when all my troubles seemed so far away?
9   That's the girls' favorite song.
10 TH: I don't think I need to hear -
11 PT: You're right. I don't want to think about yesterday cause that was a hard day's
12   night.
13 TH: So I understand from Nurse Gilder.
14 PT: There was a shadow hanging over me.
15 [PAUSE]
16 TH: A shadow.
17 PT: Yeah. Just like in the song.
18 [PAUSE]
19 PT: Yesterday. You know the song, right doctor Marsh? The part where Paul sings
20   there's a shadow hanging over me? I mean it's the most popular song ever writ-
21   ten. Lucky bastard. Scrambled eggs. Came to him in a dream.
22 TH: I'm sorry?
23 PT: So am I. A lot of money there. I don't dream like that.
24 TH: Tell me what happened last night Darrell. Tell me about the shadow hanging
25   over you.
26 PT: Over you. Gary Puckett. And the Union Gap. Right? You remember them? Why
27   am I losing precious sleep over you. Guy was like a foghorn doc what a voice.
28   He even talked that way we did a gig with him once. Hi guys. I'm Gary.
29 [PAUSE]
30 TH: The shadow, Darrell.
31 PT: It's a mean one. It's angry. I hid under the covers. The girls told me when it was
32   gone.

SESSION TEXT (CONTINUED)

33 TH: Do you know why it's angry?
34 PT: No. But the girls do.
35 TH: What do they say? Why is it angry?
36 PT: Ask them.
37 TH: But you're the one they talk to Darrell.
38 PT: They would talk to you too. If you could hear them.
39 TH: But I can't.
40 PT: Yes you can just take a couple tabs and you'll be right there with me.
41 TH: Couple tabs?
42 PT: LSD.
43 [PAUSE]
44 TH: Is that what you did Darrell? Dropped a couple tabs?
45 PT: More than a couple, doc.
46 TH: And that's when you started hearing the girls?
47 PT: No. That was later. After. You got your history all mixed up again.
48 TH: Yes. Yes I suppose I do.
49 TH: All right Darrell, why don't we-
50 PT: Why do you-

KRIEGMOOR
PSYCHIATRIC INSTITUTE

TO: c_marsh@kriegmoor-psychiatric.org

FROM: claire_morris@kriegmoor-psychiatric.org

DATE: 1-13-05

RE: CO-18

At long last, please find enclosed the missing files for this patient.
Forgive the delay: as directed by patient's legal guardian, in
consideration of privacy issues and patient's treatment-resistant status,
we had removed these files from general circulation and it has taken me
close to two months to clear your access to them.

As you'll see immediately, Darrell Covey is a pseudonym, which we
are compelled to use under the terms of an agreement made between my
predecessor and the patient's legal guardians.

The man you've been treating for these last few months is - or perhaps I
should say, was - Danny Rasmussen.

Author's Note

Rather than insert the entire contents of Mr. Rasmussen's patient file here, as it appears was Dr. Marsh's intention, I thought the reader would be better served by the following excerpted documents, which give a sense of not only who Mr. Rasmussen was, but the circumstances surrounding his admission to Kriegmoor.

KRIEGMOOR
PSYCHIATRIC INSTITUTE

PATIENT #: RAS-03
Rasmussen, Danny

ADMIT DATE:
11/24/72

CONFIDENTIAL
DO NOT CIRCULATE

1955

ADMT DATE: 1/29/03

WpH 955

For Week Ending February 12,

8:30 ② ⑧ ④ ⑤ ⑫ ⑬ HOLLY.
WOOD SQUARES—Game
COLOR Celebrity players: Barbara
Baum, Wally Cox, Danny Rasmussen,
Hackett, Dean Jones, Martin,
Rose Marie, Jan Murray,
Werner Hart, Peter

...Association of America
...million selling sin

ROCK...

THE PAISLEY DIAMONDS

featuring
BLIND LIGHT
and
KEEP ME

EVERHILL
HIGH FIDELITY

LOVEY-DO
COLD FEE
KISS ME
HI-HEEL
NO PL

"FACETS"

THE PAISLEY DIAMONDS

Danny Rasmussen: Lead vocals, guitar
Peter Cheadle: Bass, backing vocals
Rafe Hawkins: Guitars
Chad Carter: Drums
Dave Letour: Piano

Blind Light
Keep Me
Serena'
Rock of all Ages
Cold Time
I'm Not The One

SIDE

She Does It To Me
Basically, Perfectly
The Day
Guitar X
Strangers in the Morning

Write to THE PAISLEY DIAMONDS Fan C
c/o
Everhill Records
1221 Sunset Boulevard
Hollywood CA 90028

These are heady days for rock and roll - a lot of great new bands, great new sounds, great new songs. Fr San Francisco to London, from Detroit to New York City, the young people of the world are finding their voices and being heard. Shaking things up, culturally, politically, and of course, musically. Catching the sp of these times is why I started Everhill Records - to find exciting new sounds and give them a forum to m their mark. Funny thing, though - it wasn't in any of those big cities that I found the first act I knew I wante sign to Everhill. No, it was in (of all places) Cincinnati Ohio where I discovered a group making music tha knew right away deserved to be heard by all generations of entertainment lovers. The Paisley Diamonds - Danny, Pete, Rafe, Chad, and Dave - are barely out of their teens, but show a depth of talent beyond their years. All we had to do was put the boys in the studio and tell them to go to work. You hold the results of tl efforts in your hands. My advice to you is put the record on your turntables, and let the Diamonds shine.

-- Don Dunleavy, President
   Everhill Records

MEET THE PAISLEY DIAMONDS

They've been friends since Junior high school – now Danny, Pete, Rafe, Dave and Chad are this year's hottest new pop act – the Paisley Diamonds!

Full Real Name: Daniel Wade Rasmussen
Nicknames: Danny, Muss
Age: 23
Birthdate: October 12, 1946
Birthplace: Toughkenamon, Pennsylvania
Personal points: Brown hair, brown eyes, 5'7", 145 lbs.
Marital status: single
Parents names: Mother, Dorothy Rasmussen/ Father, William Rasmussen (deceased)
Brothers and sisters names: None
Instruments played: He's the singer!
Age entered show business: When I was born, my dad put a guitar in my hand
Hobbies: None - All I know how to do is music.

Favorites:
color: blue
food: yes
drink: that too
clothes: I used to like the Carnaby stuff, but now it's too much. I dig the SF vibe, fashion-wise.
singer: John Kay
group: Beatles
movie: "Born to Be Wild "
car: Thunderbird
actor: Robert Wagner
actress: Racquel Welch
city: San Francisco
Miscellaneous likes: Good food, good friends, good music.
Miscellaneous dislikes: People who judge a book by its cover
Personal ambition: to use my music to make the world a better place
Professional ambition: to improve every day

Full real name: Peter David Cheadle
Nicknames: 'Chopper'
Age: 22
Birthdate: May 2, 1948
Birthplace: New Haven, CT
Personal points: Black hair, brown eyes, 5'7", 160 lbs.
Marital status: single
Parents names: Bart and Lorena
Brothers and sisters names: Anthony, Nick and Christopher
Instruments played: Bass
Age entered show business: Played in school band - in high school
Hobbies: Reading comic books, listening loud!

Favorites:
color: Blondes
food: Mamoun's Falafel
drink: Ice cold beer
desert: yes
clothes: jeans and t-shirts; nothing fancy
singer: Joe Cocker
group: Stones
song: "Satisfaction"
car: My '67 Mustang
actor: Omar Sharif
actress: Elke Sommer
city: New York
Miscellaneous likes: sleeping late, H.R. Pufnstuf
Miscellaneous dislikes: Bad Pop Music
Personal ambition: to have fun
Professional ambition: to make the Paisley Diamonds the biggest band in the world

WPLJ 95!

WOOD SQUARES—Game
Celebrity players: Barbara Bain, Wally Cox, Danny Rasmussen, Buddy Hackett, Dean Jones, Martin Landau, Rose Marie, Jan Murray and Charley Weaver. Host: Peter Marshall.

DIAMONDS

Group to Headline w/ R...

ON '68 TOUR

aiders, Manifred Mann, Hermits

OVE OVER, DAVY JONES!
HERE COMES DANNY RASMUSSEN

deliver Paisley Diamonds fan mail to official band headquarters

Diamonds to Headline Happenings!

New teen acts tour to open in Duluth

RASMUSSEN #1 IDOL, TEEN BEAT SEZ

Singer passes Mick, Monkees in polls

HAPPENINGS!

★★★★★★

PAISLEY DIAMOND — KEEP ME b/w GUITAR X

POP

PAISLEY DIAMONDS — Blind Light
Everhill   1003 (S)

Cincy rockers debut for Don Dunleavy's new label is spot-on pop rock with catchy chorus and catchier fade. Label plans all-out push for this, their first major release, hoping to capitalize on lead singer Danny Rasmussen's teen idol marketability. More than a pretty face here though — song has substance too, making it a must add for FM tastemakers. Should break nationwide.

THE PAISLEY DIAMOND

Radio World

HOT 100

For Week Ending February 12, 1968

★ STAR performer—Sides registering greatest proportionate upward progress this week.

31	16	11	16	SUSAN
29	11	7	10	DIFFERENT DRUM
57	82	97	4	CHAIN OF FOOLS
34	37	43	8	YOU

81	99	—	3	LOVEY-DOVEY
49	56	66	6	COLD FEET
77	88	—	3	KISS ME GOODBYE
46	47	49	8	HI-HEEL SNEAKERS

TITLE	Artist	Label & Number
1	2	2	LOVE IS BLUE (L'Amour Est Bleu)	7
3	3	9	BLIND LIGHT

September 24, 1988

Klein, Stones Pal Up
Chess Bros. Pony Up
Diamonds Set To
Shine Again

Set To Shine

A Peek Inside the Paisleys Latest - Plus Conversations With Danny Rasmussen on Consciousness Expansion, Communist China and Three Chord Chaos

by Dan Zegart

Unless at some point over the next three months the impossible happens (the impossible being John, Paul, George, and Ringo all together in one room sans lawyers, accountants, and spouses), the biggest rock'n'roll story of the year is likely to be the upcoming release of War Dogs, *the long-awaited second album from the Paisley Diamonds. For those of you who like to keep track of such things, it's been more than two years since the group's first record,* Facets, *stormed up the charts, selling close to two million copies and generating a frenzy of media attention the likes of which hadn't been seen in this country since...well, John, Paul, George, and Ringo. There were appearances on Bandstand, Dick Cavett, and (infamously) Ed Sullivan, lengthy articles in* Life *and* Time, *and of course, seemingly non-stop coverage of lead singer Danny Rasmussen, pin-up pix posted next to his inflammatory statements, both on and off-stage. There was also the music:*

And then there was nothing.

At least, nothing we could see. There were occasional sightings (a bearded, brooding Rasmussen at Altamont, guitarist Rafe Hawkins at Big Pink, bassist/band founder Pete "Chopper" Cheadle at the Stones' Rock'n'Roll Circus) and media rumors (Cheadle and Rasmussen weren't talking , Hawkins had quit the band, Cheadle was dead, Rasmussen was dead, the entire band was dead),but as far as concerts, new songs, new records...nada.

For my own part, I had no doubt that the Diamonds would re-emerge eventually (having spent two long, messy weeks with them on the road in early '69, I knew that making music was what they were all about). So the call I received in July came as little surprise — the band had been in the studio for half a year, working on a new album, and they wanted to preview it for a select group of journalists - a very select group, in fact: myself, John Morthland of Rolling Stone

growling distorted guitar as only Rafe Hawkins can play it). I heard enough to conclude that War Dogs is going to be every bit the smash that the Diamonds (and Everhill Records) are expecting. The music is heavy, with a capital H - producer Len Leonardson has put Hawkins guitar right up with Rasmussen's vocals in the mix, and the bass and drums aren't far behind - but after Zeppelin, that's only to be expected. What's new here are Rasmussen's lyrics –biting, subversive stuff that more than ever belies his pop icon image. There's "Red World" – four minutes of Danny belting out his opposition to the war, sounding so angry you expect him to jump out of the speakers and bite someone's head off. Contrast that with "When You Say No," a gorgeous pop-rock anthem ala "All You Need Is Love" laying out in no uncertain terms the singer's views on drug use/abuse (more on that later on in this article, including a detailed recap of Rasmussen's

promoting War Dogs, and life in general.

- D.Z.

***

Congratulations. I think the record sounds amazing.

Cheadle: Wait till it's finished. (laughter)

How long have you been at it?

Cheadle: Since January –

Rasmussen: A lot longer for some of us. "Plastic Carson" - I started writing that back in summer '69, maybe a month or so before Woodstock.

How would you compare this record to FACETS?

Letour: It's much more spiritual, man. A whole different vibe - we collaborated a

Set To Shine

—Continued from Preceding Page

being so far forward in the mix. While Leonardson went back to work, the rest of the Diamonds - sans Rasmussen – left to grab some dinner. Danny and I decided to return to the lounge, where we parked ourselves in front of the fireplace, and continued our conversation.

* * *

How do you feel about the album?

I think we're getting there.

Which means?

Which means I hear that we have more work to do. All of us. I think the arrangements are there, it's just a matter of getting the performances. And then the colors, the textures – making sure they support the art.

You're talking about production?

Of course.

How do you like working with Lenny?

I respect his work ethic more than anything else. He's willing to stay in the room until it's right, no matter what. That's the way I am, too.

Some people are going to be surprised by what they hear. This record – it's not the straight-ahead rock'n'roll album FACETS was.

How could it be? It's been two years since that came out. A lot has changed since then.

Tell me about `Traitor's Gait.'

I wrote it while I was in Yorkville, a few months back.

Yorkville?

Part of Toronto. It's a – think of it as Canada's Berkeley. A hub. A destination for deserters, draft dodgers - a center for the whole anti-war movement.

Which you're very involved in.

Me and a lot of other people. Most of the country. Definitely most of the young people.

Talk to me about your position.

It's a pretty simple one. I believe we've spent a lot of time in this country demonizing the 'other' - the Viet Cong, Ho Chi Minh, the Republicans, the Democrats, the blacks, the Asians -

But playing devil's advocate a minute...

Sure.

Some people would say you were being naïve. That there are some real differences between us and the Communists.

Sure there are. I'm not denying that. But underneath it all, they're people too. There is no other. There's just your brother.

That's from 'Traitor's Gait,' isn't it?

It is. And it's what I believe. We're all the same, underneath. Nixon, Ho Chi Minh, Kissinger, the Soviets... all just human beings. I don't believe in evil. I believe there is a great potential for miscommunication in this world, though.

So the war is just a miscommunication?

The fact that it's gone on so long is. If Nixon and Ho Chi Minh got together and smoked the peace pipe, maybe the killing would stop.

Forgive my saying so, but again - that sounds naive.

Maybe I shouldn't have said smoked the peace pipe. Maybe I should have said dropped acid.

You can't be serious.

Why? You ever done it?

No.

You ought to. Makes miscommunication just about impossible.

How so?

You see behind the mask. You see the world as it truly is. See people for who - for what - they really are. Their essences. Their true selves. George [Harrison, of the Beatles] told me once - it's like you can suddenly see through walls... everything comes clear. You see that everything is so much bigger than you, that you're just a little part of a much larger world.

A lot of people have had bad experiences with acid.

Bad trips? Never had one. For me, each experience is more enlightening than the one before. Sometimes I feel like...

What?

Like I'm on the verge of discovering something profound about existence. That there's something else out there, something - some other kind of life - a

Recording WAR DOGS: below left, Chad harmonizing on 'When You Say No;' below, right, Rafe Hawkins rips it up on 'Hill 54;' and above, Pete 'Chopper' Cheadle, layin' it down on 'Plastic Carson'

higher intelligence - a different kind of intelligence - and I'm going to be the one to find it.

You sound more like a scientist than a musician. Or a philosopher.

Yeah. Yeah, I guess I do at that. Guess we better get back to talking about the album.

Guess so. When does Everhill plan on releasing?

We still have a lot of work to do before it's ready. I know we're a couple shows soon - work out the kinks in some of the material.

Any word yet on when those shows might happen?

There beard-mont, Pink, per" Roll and kins ead, nd w

Todd Graham Presents

HAPPENINGS!

FEATURING
THE PAISLEY DIAMONDS

SPECIAL GUESTS TO BE ANNOUNCED

★ ★

2 Nights Live at The Blue Rendezvous

NOV ★ ★ ★ ★
18/19

TICKETS
$5.00 $6.00 $7.50

POSTER BY LARS   *CO-PRODUCED BY DON DUNLEAVY

EVERHILL
ENTERTAINMENT

CONCERT TRAGEDY
Two Killed in Crowd Frenzy

by Sean Gillespie / Staff Reporter

Duluth, Minnesota - An overcrowded concert venue, a fanatical audience, a teen idol lingering teasingly close to his adoring fans - all these ingredients combined in disaster last night during the Happenings concert revue at the Blue Rendezvous. As the Paisley Diamonds launched into a performance of their hit "Blind Light," the crowd surged forward unexpectedly, crushing to death twin sisters Elizabeth and Susan Gadd of Columbus...

SHINING ON... A LITTLE LESS BRIGHTLY

Los Angeles, December 3 - You may recall that the last time the Paisley Diamonds were mentioned in this space, it was to announce that the band was taking a break from recording their long-awaited second album, 'War Dogs,' in order to allow singer Danny Rasmussen time to reflect on and recover from last year's concert tragedy in Duluth. Well, apparently Rasmussen's hiatus from the group is going to be permanent. According to sources JAMS spoke with earlier this week, the band has reluctantly returned to work on its second album without Rasmussen. The band has not replaced Rasmussen, those same sources said, but rather group founder Pete Cheadle has taken on most of the lead singing himself. More on this situation as it develop...

...ASMUSSEN IN HIDING

Manager Bobby Ciccarelli:
"Danny overcome with grief"

RANDOMLY NOTED

Just as this issue went to press, we received the news that Danny Rasmussen had been acquitted of all capital charges in the deaths of Elizabeth and Susan Gadd. The singer's attorney, John Fogel, issued the following statement to the press shortly after the verdict was announced.

"While we're pleased with the jury's decision here today, and look forward to hearing the judge's decision next week, we understand this pales in importance next to what happened to Elizabeth and Susan. On behalf of Danny and the Diamonds, we want to again offer our sympathy to the Gadd family. Danny in particular wants the girls parents to know that their daughters are always - always - in his thoughts."

CHEADLE CLAIM... RASMUSSEN FORCE... THEIR HAN...
Singer's Bizarre Behavio... Led To Teen Idol's Exi...

DRUGGED-OUT DANNY?
CELS
Secluded Singer Said...

EVERHILL RECORDS CANCELS DIAMONDS' CONTRACT

By Jeff Alley

At least the Paisley Diamonds will not have to suffer through the indignity of the dreaded sophomore jinx - the inevitable letdown when a group's follow-up to a smash first record is met with less than stellar acclaim.

That's because there will be no second album for the group - not, at least, on Everhill Records. The label unceremoniously dumped its one-time stars officially in a press release obtained by JAMS last weekend.

"It's never a happy day when you have to do something like this," the release quotes Don Dunleavy, Everhill's President, as saying. "But we think it's in everyone's best interest to have a fresh start. We love the Paisley Diamonds, and we wish them all the success in the world. But Everhill has to move forward as a company now."

"We feel disappointed, sure," said band manager Bobby Ciccarelli when contacted with the news. "Betrayed, even, a little bit. The Diamonds made Everhill, and Don knows it. We would have hoped for a little more support from the label."

Sources tell JAMS though, that there is considerable friction between Dunleavy and the band, who recently completed recording their second album with bass player Pete Cheadle moving over to handle lead vocal duties for the departed Danny Rasmussen. Band members have supposedly sued Rasmussen to deny him participation in any further earnings by the group. The situation is made even more complicated by the fact that the band, through Ciccarelli, is alleging improprieties in Everhill's royalty statements, irregularities that have supposedly cost the group members hundreds of thousands of dollars. According to court records, papers have already been filed that would, in effect, revoke Everhill's license to press more copies of the Diamond's records. Everhill, in return, has filed suit to prevent the Diamonds from signing with any other companies until their lawsuit is resolved. The practical effect of all these concurrent, competing lawsuits may very well be a complete withdrawal of all Paisley Diamonds product from the

market place (including the band's never-finished second record, War Dogs), which would mean that, unbelievable as it may sound, ten years from now no one will ever have even heard of the group.

Ciccarelli only laughed when the suggestion was put to him.

"The group's going through some tough times now, that's for sure. But that - no. The Paisley Diamonds will be around for a long, long time to come."

RANDOMLY NOTED —

Los Angeles, February 1973 - The curtain finally fallen.

Four years since the release of their first and only record, three years since their last public appearance, the Paisley Diamonds are no more. In a statement released to the press early last week, band founder Pete Cheadle finally confirmed the long-rumored split. "It breaks my heart to announce that the band has officially broken up. The Diamonds will always be like brothers to me, and I wish each of them all the best."

Cheadle, for his part, already has a solo album recorded, though record industry insiders who have heard it are singularly unimpressed. Guitarist Rafe Hawkins has begun working with a group of other musicians, including bassist James Jamerson and drummer 'Pistol' Pete Allen of Motown's Funk Brothers. Keyboardist Dave LeTour has gone to work for the Boston-based music technology company MXR, while drummer Chad Carter plans to leave the music business entirely. Partially-completed recordings from the band's War Dogs sessions are in legal limbo as well, with multiple parties laying claim to ownership.

As for one-time teen idol Danny Rasmussen....All attempts to contact him or any of his representatives remain, as of this writing, unsuccessful.

RASMUSSEN URGED

J.M. Petersen – Special to the Courier

CROWD ON,

Ma "Dan

WITNESSES TESTIFY

...DON

...SSEN
...Ciccarelli:
...e with grief

...AMONDS ALBUM
...ELEASE DELAYED YET AGAIN
...unleavy Said To Be Unhappy With New Recordings

MEDLOG AUTOMATED TRANSCRIPTION SERVICES
SESSION INFORMATION

CLIENT: KRIEGMOOR PSYCHIATRIC
PATIENT (PT): DARRELL COVEY / DANNY RASMUSSEN
THERAPIST (TH): DR. CHARLES MARSH
DATE OF SESSION: 1/13/05
SYSTEM PARAMETERS: LANGUAGE DETECT/ENGLISH LINE RETURN DELAY/8 SECONDS
SILENCE THRESHOLD: -5.4 DB FILE FORMAT: MS WORD

SESSION TEXT (CONTINUED)

1 TH: been here for thirty-three years, Darrell. Or Danny, rather. Which one would you
2   prefer?
3 PT: I don't care.
4 TH: Let's go with Danny then. The chart says you started hearing the voices in
5   February 1970.
6 PT: Was that when it was?
7 TH: That's what the records say.
8 PT: I guess that's right then. All I know, it was after Duluth.
9 TH: Duluth?
10 PT: The concert.
11 TH: I see...Yes. The tragedy. You must have been under a lot of strain then. A lot of
12   stress.
13 PT: I was freaked out.
14 [PAUSE]
15 TH: And that's when you started hearing the voices?
16 PT: Yeah. Of course. Obviously. I'm standing on the corner twelfth street and vine
17   and then the girls are there right in my ear. I thought I was going crazy. I ran
18   out into the street. I almost got hit by a car look out look out look out. I thought
19   it was the end.
20 [PAUSE]
21 TH: What did the voices - the girls - say to you then?
22 PT: Hi. They said hi. I freaked. But after awhile I got used to it. I understood. It
23   helped too - help me make some changes in myself, you see.
24 TH: I'm afraid I don't.
25 PT: I saw myself and I didn't like who I was. I didn't like the skin I was in.
26 TH: I still don't understand.
27 PT: They didn't think it was my fault but I knew it was. Of course they loved me.
28   Even after what happened they loved me that's why they came to me but when
29   I saw what I looked like back then prancing around on the stage like God's
30   gift...
31 TH: I'm a little lost Darrell. You saw what you looked like...on film?
32 PT: In my head. The girls showed me pictures in my head.

SESSION TEXT (CONTINUED)

33 | TH: Of you.
34 | PT: Of me and the band. Of what they'd seen before it all happened.
35 | TH: Before what happened?
36 | PT: Before Duluth.
37 | PT: Didn't we go over this already?
38 | [PAUSE]
39 | TH: Yes. Yes we did. What happened in Duluth.
40 | PT: The concert.
41 | TH: Yes.
42 | [PAUSE]
43 | PT: What's the matter doc?
44 | [PAUSE]
45 | TH: Danny - you said the girls were sisters?
46 | PT: They sure are. Twins actually. They're twins.
47 | [PAUSE]
48 | PT: Did I not say that before?

CONCERT TRAGEDY
Two Killed i

by Sean Gillespie / Staff Reporter

Duluth, Minnesota / An overcrowded concert venue, a fanatical audience, a teen idol lingering teasingly close to his adoring fans / all these ingredients combined in disaster last night during the Happenings concert revue at the Blue Rendezvous. As the Paisley Diamonds launched into a performance of their hit "Blind Light," the crowd surged forward unexpectedly, crushing to death twin sisters Elizabeth and Susan Gadd of Columbus,

RANDOMLY NOTED

Just as this issue went to press, we received the news that Danny Rasmussen had been acquitted of all capital charges in the deaths of Elizabeth and Susan Gadd. The singer's attorney, John Fogel, issued the following statement to the press shortly after the verdict was announced.

"While we're pleased with the jury's decision here today, and look forward to hearing the judge's decision next week, we understand this pales in importance next to what happened to Elizabeth and Susan. On behalf of Danny and the Diamonds, we want to again offer our sympathy to the Gadd family. Danny particular wants the girls parents to know that their daughters are always - always - in his thoughts."

Diamonds to
Headline

said food was scarce for him too but soon we learned a Wendigo had chased him from that island. I felt fear when I heard
this for the Wendigo was an evil spirit who ate human flesh.
My zhishay [uncle] who was Leaping Frog, told me stories of
this spirit when I was young to frighten me. He said the spirit
was once a man but he had died of hunger. Now all that was
left of him was his shadow, and this shadow was the Wendigo,
and was cursed to roam the earth until his hunger was satisfied.
The man Pierce begged the Midewiwin to help him. But the
Midewiwin said they could do nothing for him. I felt sorrow
for this man because I heard his cries of fear at night. But
Waubojeeg said he had to leave because the Wendigo might
hurt the people. I do not know what became of this man Pierce.

HISTORICAL
SOCIETY

Places	Historic Events

...even when I close my eyes, I can hear them. I see them in my mind and
when I open my eyes they take shape. I lie still on my blankets and they come.
Angry darkness growing in the corner of the room...

want what happened on
Madeleine Island back in the
1600s — all those kids getting
killed — the way Johnny tells
it... it's really creepy —
enough to keep you up at night

them. They lived here once. They congregate here; the mag-
is key: the magnetite accelerates the bonding process
lows them to coalesce. Places of power — this is one right XX
The surveys show it. When they brush against me when they
me I see pictures in my mind their memories their lives the
they did this place not as it is now but as it was then
ds maybe even thousands of years ago. Some mean us no harm

where the Wild Things Are?
T: Yes.
TH: Tell me.
T: I was Max. I was in the forest and the monsters were hunting me. I hid from
them but they found me. And they killed me.
H: That sounds terrible Jake.
: That's why I screamed.
: I can understand that.
They put their knives in me and they cut me up and I watched them
The monsters had knives?
Yes. Big knives and they had...
What is it Jake?
hey wore masks.

SESSION TEXT (CONTINUED)

1 PT: I felt what they felt the crowd closing in on them it happened so quick they
2 didn't really even have time to react.
3 [PAUSE]
4 TH: And then they died.
5 PT: They coalesced. They cast aside the chains of the body to become pure ener-
6 gy. Pure thought. Like the Organians. It's man's ultimate destiny you know. Do
7 you study Indian religion doc? The one ness we are all part of.
8 TH: Okay.
9 PT: I have to confess something sometimes the drugs you give me they hit just
10 right and the world melts away and we join. We become one. It's kind of like
11 sex.
12 [PAUSE]
13 PT: Sometimes I let them jerk me off too. Just to get that buzz.
14 [PAUSE]
15 TH: So...this shadow you saw the other night. Tell me more about that.
16 PT: It's a vengeance-seeker a ball of anger. That's how it coalesced.
17 TH: A vengeance-seeker?
18 PT: Uh-huh. That's what the girls said.
19 TH: What else did the girls say?
20 PT: They're scared. That is a dark hole of blackness from which there is no escape.
21 TH: Sounds like they're scared of it.
22 TH: Oh yeah. You bet.
23 PT: I don't understand. They're dead, aren't they?
24 [PAUSE]
25 PT: Oh yeah they're dead. But there are worse things than being dead, Doc.
26 Believe me.
27 TH: I don't know what you mean by that.
28 PT: Why do you keep calling me Darrell?

1 TH: talk a little bit more about the Rodriguez boy. About what happened.
2 PT: I took a lead pipe and broke his head open. That's what happened.
3 TH: Do you think about him at all?
4 PT: I see him on the ground. Prostrate before the avenging hand of god. Before jus-
5 tice.
6 TH: Do you ever hear him? In your head?
7 PT: I hear God Dr. Marsh. His voice is a bell ringing ever louder in my head calling
8 the faithful to heel. To worship and obey.
9 TH: You don't feel anything at all over what you did?
10 PT: Satisfaction. A job well done.
11 TH: Nothing more.
12 PT: Oh I feel a lot more, Dr. Marsh. I feel lot more all the time.
13 TH: Go on.
14 PT: You would have me speak of the God within?
15 TH: The voice within you — yes.
16 PT: I speak to you now, Dr. Marsh. In his name. Set me free. Let me have you. Let
17 me ease your pain as well. ... that would be a very smart thing to do now, would it?

AUTHOR: Charles Marsh, M.D., Ph.D.

these shadows were exactly that, what science had once termed the 'ectoplasmic aura' of a person — a physical manifestation of the memories, the energies, the very consciousness that inhabited their physical bodies and now, after the death of those corporeal vessels, existed as a separate, cohesive entity on its own.

This is the very essence of my discovery, that life continues after death.

The energies associated with these intelligences was theoretically measurable — which in retrospect is unsurprising, given that the process of memory formation within the brain involves the genesis and release of chemical energy. The reader of this article should not expect a lengthy explanation of such topics here, as they are outside my area of expertise, but the raw data I have gathered should provide a starting point for others more expert in matters neurobiological to draw on.

The nature of these intelligences thus established — and I shall continue using that term to refer to these entities, rather than the obvious 'ghost,' with all the baggage it carries - I now faced a new question. How to determine the identity and motive of the particular intelligence plaguing

1	O: my god when they called...
2	TH: I know.
3	O: I've taken a room at the motel near here. In case you need to reach me. In
4	case it happens again. Her heart actually stopped doctor.
5	TH: Yes.
6	O: How can she be so scared? What is so terrifying?
7	[PAUSE]
8	TH: I wish I could answer that.
9	O: You know I brought her ice cream.
10	TH: I know.
11	O: Peppermint stick from Hansen's. She didn't want any. That's her favorite flavor,
12	and she didn't want any.
13	TH: I'm sorry.
14	[PAUSE]
15	TH: I wish I could think of something else to say.
16	[PAUSE]
17	O: You know I'm missing a meeting now. A very important meeting with a very
18	important client. And you know what? I don't care. It doesn't matter.
19	[PAUSE]
20	O: I want to apologize to you Dr. Marsh. I know I'm overbearing sometimes.
21	Overprotective.
22	TH: It's a mother's instinct.
23	O: I see the way she reacts to you it's very positive.
24	[PAUSE]
25	O: Do you ever talk to the people from the dig?
26	TH: I have. But not for some time now, actually.
27	O: Next time you do - if you do tell them it's okay for them to come. If they still
28	want to see Kari.
29	TH: I will. I'm sure they'll be glad to hear that.
30	[PAUSE]
31	O: Tell me something Dr. Marsh. Is my daughter going to die?

TO: c_marsh@kriegmoor-psychiatric.org
FROM: g_yanagisawa@kriegmoor-psychiatric.org
DATE: 1/15/05
RE: HA-09

I don't understand it either.

To review, because of the physical damage being done to patient's airways
during the panic attacks - and the physical pain she was suffering because
of said attacks - we decided to significantly increase sedative dosage
prior to sleep in order to prevent any possible awakening and subsequent
recurrence of panic episodes.

That she could had similar attacks of such strength while sedated
is certainly unprecedented in my experience and speaks to the degree
which this particular hallucinatory reality has fastened itself to her
consciousness. Frankly, I'm stumped. I have contacted a friend of mine
from medical school who specializes in alternative healing methods
for psychiatric patients, and am waiting for response from her and any
possible suggestions. In the meantime, I don't think we have any choice
but to increase the amount of pain medication, despite any possible
addictive consequences, in order to keep patient as comfortable as
possible.

-- Gerry

MEDLOG 1.2

MEDLOG AUTOMATED TRANSCRIPTION SERVICES
SESSION INFORMATION

CLIENT: KRIEGMOOR PSYCHIATRIC
PATIENT (PT): KARI HANSEN
THERAPIST (TH): DR. CHARLES MARSH
DATE OF SESSION: 1/15/05
SYSTEM PARAMETERS: LANGUAGE DETECT/ENGLISH LINE RETURN DELAY/8 SECONDS
SILENCE THRESHOLD: -5.4 DB FILE FORMAT: MS WORD

SESSION TEXT (CONTINUED)

1	TH: Hi Kari.
2	TH: Don't try and talk. I'm just going to sit here for a minute. Hold your hand. Okay?
3	[PAUSE]
4	[PAUSE]
5	
6	TH: Would you like me to read you a story? I could do that if you want. What chapter are you in now in your book?
7	[PAUSE]
8	[PAUSE]
9	
10	TH: Or do you just want to sit?
11	[PAUSE]
12	[PAUSE]
13	TH: Whatever you want to do is fine.
14	[PAUSE]
15	[PAUSE]
16	
17	TH: Can I get you something to drink?
18	[PAUSE]
19	[PAUSE]
20	TH: The

KRIEGMOOR
PSYCHIATRIC INSTITUTE

From the desk of
Charles Marsh, M.D., Ph.D.

I'm so sorry
I should have been here with you
You're so young
Who have you known who would want
to hurt you so much?
So badly?
Anyone from your past who hated
you enough to do this
an old boyfriend?
Can you think of anyone?
Anyone who loved you and you
hurt them?
Anyone?
I'm looking at your records and I don't

EDLOG AUTOMATED TRANSC
SESSION INFORMATION

CLIENT: KRIEGMOOR PSYCHIATRI
PATIENT (PT): KARI HANSEN
THERAPIST (TH): DR. CHARLES MA
DATE OF SESSION: 9/19/04
SYSTEM PARAMETERS: LANGUAGE
SILENCE T

SESSION TEXT (CON

1 TH: so no clues as to
2   up and vanished
3 PT: No.
4 TH: Fascinating. We
5   a group of peop
6   group. Good fri
7 TH: What do you t
8   your friends?
9 TH: Kari, I'm look
10   not to permit
11   mentions th
12 PT: I know.
13 TH: How do yo
14 PT: I don't kno
15 TH: Do you w
16 PT: My mom
17 TH: It's okay
18 PT: I guess
19 TH: Kari. A
20 PT: Oh ye
21 TH: She ra
22 PT: Yes.
23 TH: Since your parents di
24 PT: My dad is dead.
25 TH: Were the two of you close?
26 PT: I didn't see him much.
27 TH: Sounds like you regret that.
28 PT: I guess. I could have been nicer to him. Should have been nicer.
29 TH: Do you think about him a lot?
30 PT: Sometimes. More now than I used to. But my mom and I are really tight. She
       looks out for me, my mom.
31 TH: Yes. Yes, I can see that she does.
32

MEDLOG AUTOMATED TRANSCRIPTION SERVICES
SESSION INFORMATION

CLIENT: KRIEGMOOR PSYCHIATRIC
OTHER (O1): SARAH HELLINGER IN RE: PATIENT HE-31
OTHER (O2): JOHN HELLINGER IN RE: PATIENT HE-31
THERAPIST (TH): DR. CHARLES MARSH
DATE OF SESSION: 12/11/04
SYSTEM PARAMETERS: LANGUAGE DETECT/ENGLISH LINE RETURN DELAY/3 SECONDS
SILENCE THRESHOLD: -5.4 DB FILE FORMAT: MS WORD

SESSION TEXT (CONTINUED)

1	O2: I don't understand why this happened. He was fine up until these last few
2	weeks.
3	TH: To be frank, we don't know either, Mr. Hellinger.
4	O2: This new drug you had him on –
5	TH: The T-86.
6	O2: Yes. I've been checking with some doctor friends of mine. They say it's an
7	experimental drug.
8	TH: Well. It's new. I wouldn't say experimental.
9	O2: They said it's very powerful. That it can have a lot of side-effects. Maybe that's
10	what aggravated his asthma. Brought it back. Killed him.
11	TH: I don't think so, Mr. Hellinger. Jake displayed none of the other symptoms that -
12	O2: Sometimes I think you guys don't have a fucking clue about what you're doing.
13	O1: John!
14	O2: Well it's true. You go on the Internet you read all this stuff about doctors who
15	prescribe the wrong drugs, doctors who take out the wrong organs they stay up
16	all night working and take drugs themselves and then make mistakes and -
17	O1: John! That's enough.
18	O2: I don't understand. He was fine up until he came here. Until you started seeing
19	him.
20	O1: John...
21	O2: Fuck it.
22	[PAUSE]
23	O1: I'm so sorry.
24	TH: That's all right Mrs. Hellinger.
25	O1: It's just - Jake was very special to John.
26	TH: You don't need to apologize.
27	O1: But I want to explain. I have two children from my first marriage but Jake
28	is...was John's only child.
29	TH: Of course.
30	O1: He wanted to see his child grow up. And now - well, he's just angry. It's not you.
31	[PAUSE]
32	TH: I understand. Any father would feel the same.

CLIENT: KRIEGMOOR PSYCHIATRIC
OTHER (O): MS. INGRID HANSEN IN RE: PATIENT HA-09
THERAPIST (TH): DR. CHARLES MARSH
DATE OF SESSION: 1/16/05
SYSTEM PARAMETERS: LANGUAGE DETECT/ENGLISH LINE RETURN DELAY/8 SECONDS
SILENCE THRESHOLD: -5.4 DB FILE FORMAT: MS WORD

SESSION TEXT (CONTINUED)

1 O: why are you asking me this, doctor? Charles has been dead almost twenty
2   years now.
3 TH: I think that - his death may have impacted Kari more than we originally thought.
4 O: What makes you think that?
5 TH: Some...recent developments in our sessions. Now - had recently before your
6   ex-husband killed himself had you spoken with him?
7 O: I don't know. As I said, it was more than twenty years ago.
8 TH: A week before he killed himself?
9 O: Perhaps. That seems about right.
10 TH: What was the conversation like?
11 O: It was tense, like most of our conversations. He always asked the same ques-
12   tion of me.
13 TH: Which was?
14 O: He wanted to see Kari. To try and change her mind...
15 TH: About?
16 O: Seeing him. She did not want to see him.
17 TH: Do you think your husband - was he mad at Kari for that?
18 O: I don't know. I suppose he could have been, though Charles was always reluc-
19   tant to truly express anger, if he felt any.
20 TH: He kept things inside himself.
21 O: Yes. What is the point of all this?
22 TH: I'm sorry. Just a couple more questions. So Charles never expressed any anger
23   towards Kari?
24 O: Not to her.
25 TH: But to you?
26 O: I suppose there was some anger there.
27 TH: All right. Thank you.
28 O: Dr. Marsh - you said recent developments in your sessions. I haven't seen any
29   transcripts to that effect.
30 [PAUSE]
31 TH: I shouldn't have said recent, I'm sorry. I misspoke. More like recent develop-
32   ments in my own mind. Things I've been thinking about. I was just going over

SESSION TEXT (CONTINUED)

33   some of Kari's records my own notes. Just trying to find something to grab
34   onto. Clues.
35 [PAUSE]
36 TH: I'm sorry. I didn't mean to get your hopes up.

1-16-05 ———→ why? Does Hansen realize what he is
(11:12 p.m.)   doing? Is rational thought possible
                  for him / these intelligences in general?
Rasmussen's experience suggests yes.*

So what does Hansen want?

He wants K. He wants her with him. Not what
  =   == =
I want. I want her here - with me. So...

(WE ARE ENEMIES) Melodramatic, but true...

11:30 p.m.   Nypureden taken - 4x normal dosage

2:15 a.m.   Demagnetizer is portable. I have circuited
            the Institute - no sign of Hansen.

3:15 a.m.   2nd circuit of institute. No Hansen, but...

Gilder saw me. Outside K's room. I made up a story.
  Not sure he believed. I may have to pay him to keep
  quiet. Or...

          4 p.m.   I have misplaced my pen. My
special pen, which I have been writing with for
almost two months now. I believe the cleaning staff
may have taken it.

6:32 a.m.   Nothing. Several circuits made of institute,
and no sign of Hansen. A frustrating evening, salvaged
only by a second reading of certain passages from
Cayce. Possession / spirit possession - is this communion
taken to its logical extreme? Barron? I wish I knew
more about the science involved. Had the time to evaluate
Cayce's claims in light of the historical evidence. When
I publish, perhaps.

1-18-05   9:00 a.m.   Angry memo from the director. Something
about my other patients. I am ignoring it for the
moment.

12:10 p.m.   I found

MEDLOG AUTOMATED TRANSCRIPTION SERVICES
SESSION INFORMATION

CLIENT: KRIEGMOOR PSYCHIATRIC
PATIENT (PT): DARRELL COVEY / DANNY RASMUSSEN
THERAPIST (TH): DR. CHARLES MARSH
DATE OF SESSION: 1/19/05
SYSTEM PARAMETERS: LANGUAGE DETECT/ENGLISH LINE RETURN DELAY/8 SECONDS
SILENCE THRESHOLD: -5.4 DB FILE FORMAT: MS WORD

SESSION TEXT (CONTINUED)

1 TH: come out from under the covers Darrell - Danny.
2 [UNINTELLIGEBLE]
3 TH: It's hard to hear you from under there. Please.
4 [PAUSE]
5 TH: Thank you.
6 TH: Danny? What's the matter? Why are you crying?
7 PT: The girls are dead.
8 TH: What do you mean?
9 PT: It killed them it was so angry it chased them and split them into millions of tiny
10   bits they're gone I was going to be with them forever and now they're gone
11 TH: Danny...
12 TH: Please come out from under the covers.
13 PT: Make it go away, Dr. Marsh. Please make it go away.
14 [PAUSE]
15 TH: I'm trying to do that, D...
16 T...

MEDLOG 1.2

MEDLOG AUTOMATED TRANSCRIPTION SERVICES
SESSION INFORMATION

CLIENT: KRIEGMOOR PSYCHIATRIC
PATIENT (PT): NATHANIEL BARRON
THERAPIST (TH): DR. CHARLES MARSH
DATE OF SESSION: 1/19/05
SYSTEM PARAMETERS: LANGUAGE DETECT/ENGLISH LINE RETURN DELAY/8 SECONDS
SILENCE THRESHOLD: -5.4 DB FILE FORMAT: MS WORD

SESSION TEXT (CONTINUED)

1 TH: you've stopped eating.
2 PT: Yes.
3 TH: Why?
4 [PAUSE]
5 TH: What do you expect to happen, Nathan?
6 [PAUSE]
7 PT: Why do you keep calling me Nathan?
8 [PAUSE]
9 [PAUSE]
10 PT: You know who I am, Dr. Marsh. You know what I want.
11 [PAUSE]
12 PT: Set me free. Let me ease your pain.

MEDLOG AUTOMATED TRANSCRIPTION SERVICES
SESSION INFORMATION

CLIENT: KRIEGMOOR PSYCHIATRIC
OTHER (O): MS. INGRID HANSEN IN RE: PATIENT HA-09
THERAPIST (TH): DR. CHARLES MARSH
DATE OF SESSION: 1/20/05
SYSTEM PARAMETERS: LANGUAGE DETECT/ENGLISH LINE RETURN DELAY/3 SECONDS
SILENCE THRESHOLD: -5.4 DB FILE FORMAT: MS WORD

SESSION TEXT (CONTINUED)

1 O: but I do feel responsible. I was the one who convinced the director to pull you
2   off the case. I should have let you continue.
3 TH: That's all in the past now. It doesn't do us any good to –
4 O: But you're the only one who's been able to reach her.
5 TH: You have to stay positive, Ms. Hansen. For Kari's sake.
6 O: I'm trying. But my poor girl...to see these things, coming after you night after
7   night after night, trying to kill you...it must be unbearable for her, don't you think
8   doctor?
9 [PAUSE]
  TH: Yes. Unbearable.

The Kriegmoor Asylum for The Criminally Insane
Bayfield Wisconsin

Alphabetical listing of current patients accompanied by physican summary
- March 1908

KRIEG, HANS. Admitted July 8th 1907. Town of Cleveland. Age
65. German. Widowed. Youngest child 25 years old. Farmer. Fair
circumstances. Earliest symptoms noted after wife's death. Began
starving cattle...was so mean that family couldn't live with
him. Has destroyed or starved several hundred dollars worth of
cattle, claiming that witches were the cause.

KRIEGMOOR, JOSEPHINE. Admitted January 5 1894. Resident of
Bayfield Heights. Born New York City. Wife of Mr. Herman Kriegmoor. No children. 32 years old. Fair circumstances. First symptoms began several years ago. Acted queer, began hearing voices.
Believes demons surround her and keep things going wrong. Sees
them every night. Visions grew so severe hospitalization required. All therapies to this date ineffectual. Has declared wish
to die rather than continue in this state.

Note from

PATIENT HISTORY (CONT'D)

Name of Patient: Roy Jennings
Date of Admittance: 12/7/1953
Admitting Physician: Dr. Cotton

March 9 - Dr. Cotton attending. I came in this a.m. to find
Mr. Jennings crying - hysterical about something. What?

March 10 - Nurse Frye recording in absence of regular medical
staff. Patient was in obvious distress this past night. Repeated
guttural screaming, necessitated sedation and application of
straitjacket harness.

March 11 - Dr. Marsden in attendance. Marks discovered this a.m.
on patient's arm - knife wounds? In file, previous suggestion of
similar occurrence. Puzzling: straitjacket harness had not been
tampered with.

3/11 p.m. - Cotton - allergic reaction? Will check w/nursing staff

March 12 - Mr. Jennings isolated in Ward 5 - Nurse Abramowicz
present. He was disturbing the other patients.

March 13 - Dr. Cotton attending. A terrible tragedy has occurred.

Mr. Jennings is dead. He killed himself early this morning, just
before dawn. Somehow broke free of his restraints and threw himself
out the window. This should not have been possible; not only
because of the restraints, but because of the operation. He should
not have had the initiative to do such a thing. I do not understand.
We must have erred, somehow, while performing the lobotomy. I am
heartsick.

I can only pray that at last, wherever he is, Mr. Jennings has found
peace.

*************FILE CLOSED*********

ADDENDUM TO FILE MARCH 18
Dr. Marsden reporting. Received note from Dr. Sinkiewicz, meant
for Dr. Cotton who is currently on leave. Relating to Miss
Marjorie Alexander. Her hallucinations have stopped.

MEDLOG AUTOMATED TRANSCRIPTION SERVICES
SESSION INFORMATION

CLIENT: KRIEGMOOR PSYCHIATRIC
OTHER (O): MR. ANTHONY BIDDERLEE IN RE: PATIENT BID-O3
PATIENT (PT): RONA BIDDERLEE
THERAPIST (TH): DR. CHARLES MARSH
DATE OF SESSION: 1/20/05
SYSTEM PARAMETERS: LANGUAGE DETECT/ENGLISH LINE RETURN DELAY/8 SECONDS
SILENCE THRESHOLD: -5.4 DB FILE FORMAT: MS WORD

SESSION TEXT (CONTINUED)

1	O: she has something she wants to say to you doctor. Go ahead mother.
2	PT: Well I really don't think it's my place.
3	O: Of course it's your place. Speak your mind. Isn't that what you always told me
4	speak your mind?
5	PT: Yes but I really don't feel comfortable doing this.
6	O: Mother -
7	PT: I'm sorry dear.
8	O: Mother -
9	TH: Excuse me - Mr. Bidderlee?
10	O: Yes?
11	TH: I'm sorry. I have a very short amount of time to spend with your mother today
12	and I don't think this is the best use of that time.
13	O: Which is exactly the problem.
14	TH: Excuse me?
15	O: You haven't spent more than ten minutes with my mother during any single ses-
16	sion all week. I don't think that's right.
17	TH: Well it is a very busy time here as I'm sure you know, and -
18	O: I understand that to be the case. But what I also know is that I'm paying a
19	good deal of money for specialized treatment here, and I'm not getting it. That
20	doesn't make me happy.
21	TH: Well -
22	O: Frankly doctor, I feel you should have a greater sense of duty to your patients.
23	Responsibility.
24	TH: Responsibility?
25	O: That's what I said.
26	TH: To my patients?
27	O: Yes.
28	[PAUSE]
29	TH: I see.
30	[PAUSE]
31	TH: Perhaps you're right.

1-2-05 1:34 a.m. →

Conclusions →

to take only those steps, those actions supported by
facts

Fact #1 - He wants Kari
Fact #2 - He will have Kari
Fact #3 - In the interim, other patients suffer
Fact #4 - In the interim, Kari suffers!

Therefore...

The interim must be shortened

Action must be taken. I must take it.

5:39 a.m.   Madness. Can I contemplate
doing such a thing? With one innocent life
on my conscience already? And if I were to

MEDLOG 1.2

MEDLOG AUTOMATED TRANSCRIPTION SERVICES
SESSION INFORMATION

CLIENT: KRIEGMOOR PSYCHIATRIC
PATIENT (PT): KARI HANSEN
THERAPIST (TH): DR. CHARLES MARSH
DATE OF SESSION: 1/22/05
SYSTEM PARAMETERS: LANGUAGE DETECT/ENGLISH LINE RETURN DELAY/3 SECONDS
SILENCE THRESHOLD: -5.4 DB FILE FORMAT: MS WORD

SESSION TEXT (CONTINUED)

1 TH: Hello Kari. I'm here.
2 [PAUSE]
3 TH: These are beautiful flowers - your mother sent them? That's nice. And some
4   from Johnny Reardon too. I see. That's a nice card. Did you enjoy their visit?
5 [PAUSE]
6 [PAUSE]
7 TH: That's good. Shall I read to you today? Or should we just sit?
8 [PAUSE]
9 TH: Let's just sit for a minute.

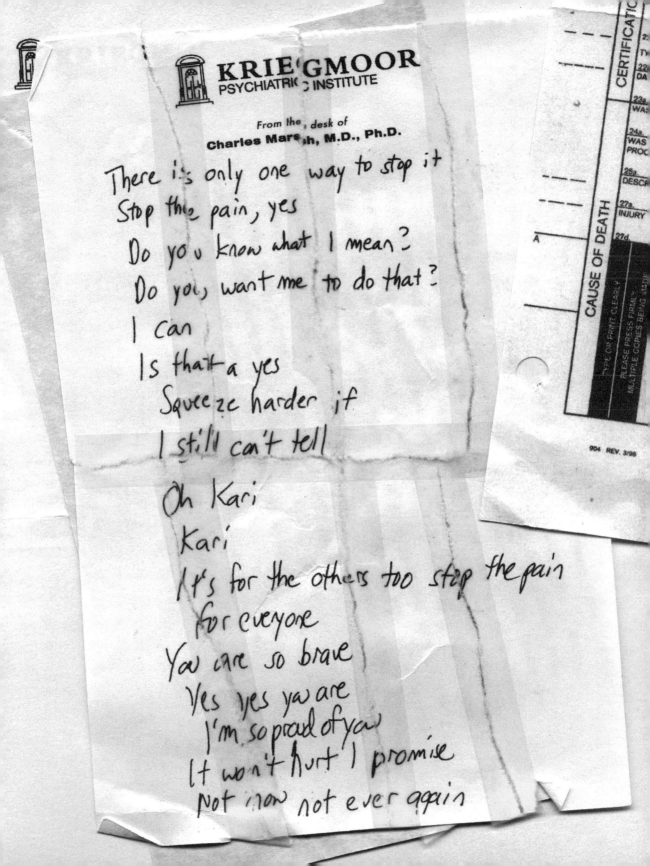

KRIEGMOOR
PSYCHIATRIC INSTITUTE

From the desk of
Charles Marsh, M.D., Ph.D.

There is only one way to stop it
Stop the pain, yes
Do you know what I mean?
Do you want me to do that?
I can
Is that a yes
Squeeze harder if

I still can't tell

Oh Kari
Kari
It's for the others too stop the pain
for everyone
You are so brave
Yes yes you are
I'm so proud of you
It won't hurt I promise
Not now not ever again

science is in that sense a religion; one believes, or one does
not. I was a believer; thus, once I had determined the identity
of this particular intelligence, once I realized that this
intelligence would continue to torment not just K but other
patients at the Institute until it was given what it wanted,
I had to act according to my creed, no matter my personal
feelings. I believe K understood this; I believe in her final
moments, she granted me not just permission to do what was
necessary, to end at last the pain that had tormented her for
so long, but blessed me with her forgiveness as well.

The reader may think this wishful thinking on my part; it is
nothing I can document scientifically, of course, though at some
future date communication with the deceased

INCIDENT REPORT

DATE OF INCIDENT: 1/22/2005
DATE OF REPORT: 1/23/2005
REPORTING PHYSICIAN: G. YANAGISAWA
PATIENT: HA-09

Details of Incident: Patient suffered accidental overdose of experimental drug T-86, resulting in immediate respiratory arrest and systemic heart failure.

Treatment: NA

Commentary: I am greatly disturbed by this incident. Many details as reported on Dr. Marsh's memo of earlier this a.m. do not seem to me to fit together into a coherent pattern. I do not suggest malevolent intent, this may be simple carelessness at work or an unintentional error but this sort of thing cannot happen in a place like Kriegmoor. As director of the medical ward I am ultimately responsible for making sure that all patients receive the proper drugs in the proper dosage at the proper time. I have mandated since my arrival a complete overhaul of our procedures in this area, an overhaul designed to insure this kind of tragedy never occurs.

Copies of this report have been sent to the hospital board, as well as Director Morris.

1-23-05   3:12 p.m.   I found sleep difficult last night.

I hope I have done the right thing.

To continue: p. 89, Once you're linked up to it, if you think, the Shadows respond. This quote, permission required probably from author and publisher? Consult an attorney I suppose, but only when pub is firm. They will bleed ya. I know an attorney named Biester

CLIENT: KRIEGMOOR PSYCHIATRIC
OTHER (O): MS. INGRID HANSEN IN RE: PATIENT HA-09
THERAPIST (TH): DR. CHARLES MARSH
DATE OF SESSION: 1/24/05
SYSTEM PARAMETERS: LANGUAGE DETECT/ENGLISH LINE RETURN DELAY/8 SECONDS
SILENCE THRESHOLD: -5.4 DB FILE FORMAT: MS WORD

SESSION TEXT (CONTINUED)

1	[PAUSE]
2	[PAUSE]
3	[PAUSE]
4	TH: I don't know what else to say, Ms. Hansen.
5	O: I know. I appreciate how much you...
6	TH: It's all right. Go on. It's all right.
7	[PAUSE]
8	O: Thank you doctor. You're a good man.
9	[PAUSE]
10	[PAUSE]
11	TH: At least she's at peace now.
12	O: Yes.
13	TH: I feel glad about that.
14	O: Excuse me?
15	TH: Not glad, of course. What I meant to say was comforted. That her troubles have
16	ended. That she doesn't have to -
17	O: Yes. I suppose you're right.
18	O: The funeral is tomorrow. Will you come?
19	TH: Of course.

TO: g_yahrgasurae kriegmoor-psychiatric.org
CC: c_marsh@kriegmoor-psychiatric.org
FROM: claire_morris@kriegmoor-psychiatric.org

DATE: 1-25-05

RE: Your Memo 1/23 - Further Response

We are discontinuing usage of the T-86, having concluded a no-fault agreement was concluded with the drug's manufacturer. As part of this agreement we are required to sign a non-disclosure form, copies of which are available on the internal web site document page. Please return via hand to my office when signed.

I have spoken with patient's mother regarding the circumstances of her daughter's death, and her strong wish, which I have decided to honor, is that after we have concluded our own in-house inquiry, the matter be dropped entirely.

Dr. Marsh has voluntarily placed himself on leave until that inquiry is concluded.

Claire

Red Cliff Parkway
Bayfield, WI 48544

January 31, 2005

Ms. Ingrid Hansen
Hansen Solutions
1309 W. 6th Street
Bayfield Heights WI 48989

Dear Ms. Hansen:

My sympathies once again. This is a difficult letter for me to write, but I believe you are owed the truth. Over the last few days of Kari's life, you and I grew close. I expect that had she lived, recovered, been released from Kriegmoor, we would have grown closer still. I appreciate the friendship and support you showed me during the hospital's investigation of the circumstances surrounding Kari's death. But I must tell you, Dr. Yanagisawa's initial conclusion was correct. I did indeed administer the T-86 incorrectly, and was responsible for Kari's death. Moreover, this was not an accident. This was an act of mercy. Let me explain. I have, for the last few months, been working on an article (at any moment now, you may read of its pending publication and clues to its contents in the press; it is, I believe, a revolutionary work). In this article

Author's Note

The letter above, found in the papers given to me by Dr. McCormick, was never sent.

Immediately following the death of Kari Hansen, hospital records show Marsh asked for and received a leave of absence, during which time he returned to Austin, Texas. He did speak with Lucius McCormick during this time, making vague allusions to the article he was writing. McCormick has few specific memories of their conversations, but recalls coming away from their meeting with the impression that all was not well with his former colleague.

On February 7, Dr. Marsh returned to Kriegmoor. From that date forward, though he continued seeing patients and resumed work on the experiments he had begun earlier, records of his own writing—his article—seem to disappear. I have been able to reliably date some small bits of paper—sometimes consisting of little more than sentence fragments—and have arranged them into a narrative that I believe accurately reconstructs the course of events that followed. My own theory is that at some point in early February, Dr. Marsh destroyed much of his own work himself. Ripped it to shreds.

As I have said earlier, things at Kriegmoor did not turn out as he expected.

LOG 1.2

MEDLOG AUTOMATED TRANSCRIPTION SERVICES
SESSION INFORMATION

CLIENT: KRIEGMOOR PSYCHIATRIC
PATIENT (PT): RONA BIDDERLEE
THERAPIST (TH): DR. CHARLES MARSH
DATE OF SESSION: 2/7/05
SYSTEM PARAMETERS: LANGUAGE DETECT/ENGLISH LINE RETURN DELAY/8 SECONDS
SILENCE THRESHOLD: -5.4 DB FILE FORMAT: MS WORD

SESSION TEXT (CONTINUED)

1 | TH: Good afternoon Mrs. Bidderlee.
2 | PT: Good afternoon Dr. Marsh. Welcome back. How was your vacation?
3 | TH: Well...I wouldn't exactly call it a vacation. Just some time away from work.
4 | PT: Well that's a vacation isn't it. The very definition of a vacation I would say.
5 | Where did you go? What did you do? I hope not to one of those theme resorts.
6 | Not a cruise ship. I find them terribly boring. Self-indulgent. Sit around all day
7 | and eat. Fat, fat, fat. You know fat is the leading killer of children in America
8 | today? Yes indeed. Portion size. Portion control. On those cruise ships -
9 | TH: It wasn't a cruise ship I went on, Mrs. Bidderlee. I went to -
10 | PT: Oh not a third world country. I hope not. So many diseases there. They don't
11 | clean their food properly. Hygiene is deplorable among those people.
12 | TH: You don't have to worry. I went to Texas.
13 | PT: Never been there. But I remember.
14 | TH: Remember...?
15 | PT: The Alamo.
16 | TH: Ah.
17 | [PAUSE]
18 | PT: Goddamn Mexicans. At least you got to see the sun, I expect.
19 | TH: Yes.
20 | PT: And it was warm.
21 | TH: Warmer than here.
22 | PT: Snowed every day this week here. Sunrise at 7:00 a.m., sunset at 3:00 in the
23 | afternoon. Oh dear.
24 | TH: What is it Mrs. Bidderlee?
25 | PT: Right there - by the window.
26 | TH: Roaches?
27 | PT: No, no. The shadow.
28 | [PAUSE]
29 | TH: The shadow.
30 | PT: Yes. Go away will you? Go away. Damned thing.

2-1-05   3:12 p.m.   Bidderlee's experience not unexpected
They live here, congregate here - the
shadows on the lake. One of the
Ojibwe children the murdered children
perhaps - a restless spirit, as it were.
But why Bidderlee? In the scheme
of things... unimportant. I will research
later. For now much work remains to do
on article. Writing, revision, rewriting, e-
Sitchin speaks of Anunaki and their
times with remarkable historical accuracy -
how is this possible? Biblical ⟶

⟶ references in detail...

Question is - how long can these energy patterns
remain before dissipating? 100 years? 1000? Longer??

    100 years?
    1000?
    Longer?

2-8-05   12:10 a.m.   And yet...

        Why Bidderlee? Why now?

DLOG AUTOMATED TRANSCRIPTION SERVICES
SSION INFORMATION

ENT: KRIEGMOOR PSYCHIATRIC
TIENT (PT): DARRELL COVEY / DANNY RASMUSSEN
ERAPIST (TH): DR. CHARLES MARSH
ATE OF SESSION: 2/8/05
STEM PARAMETERS: LANGUAGE DETECT/ENGLISH LINE RETURN DELAY/8 SECONDS
SILENCE THRESHOLD: -5.4 DB FILE FORMAT: MS WORD

SESSION TEXT (CONTINUED)

1 PT: I got a question.
2 TH: Okay.
3 PT: Can I go home now?
4 TH: Danny...I think you've made a lot of progress. But I think we have a lot to talk
5   about before you can leave the Institute. Don't you?
6 PT: I guess.
7 TH: That's right.
8 PT: Well then can I ask you a favor Dr. Marsh?
9 TH: Of course.
10 PT: Can you find my record collection?
11 TH: Uh...I can try. Is there someone I can talk to or –
12 PT: I need it soon. As soon as possible. I'm looking for one record in particular. A
13   record by the Monkees. You remember the Monkees?
14 TH: Yes.
15 PT: They did a movie it was called Head.
16 TH: I don't –
17 PT: A lot of people said they were tripping when they made it but I know better.
18   They knew what they were doing. I need the soundtrack album Dr. Marsh that's
19   what I'm looking for. The cover was made out of foil. Aluminum foil. I need that
20   album.
21 [PAUSE]
22 TH: The album's made out of foil?
23 PT: Yeah. You know about aluminum foil, right Dr. Marsh?
24 [PAUSE]
25 PT: I could use a few copies of the record, actually. If you can find them.
26 TH: Actually
27 PT: Your're a believer aren't you?
28 TH: Yes, Danny. I'm a believer, but –
29 PT: Not a trace. Of doubt in your mind.
30 [PAUSE]
31 TH: Danny. I'll see what I can do about the record, but as far as leaving goes...I
32   don't think that's a good idea.

MEDLOG AUTOMATED TRANSCRIPTION SERVICES
SESSION INFORMATION

CLIENT: KRIEGMOOR PSYCHIATRIC
PATIENT (PT): NATHANIEL BARRON
THERAPIST (TH): DR. CHARLES MARSH
DATE OF SESSION: 2/8/05
SYSTEM PARAMETERS: LANGUAGE DETECT/ENGLISH LINE RETURN DELAY/8 SECONDS
SILENCE THRESHOLD: -5.4 DB FILE FORMAT: MS WORD

SESSION TEXT (CONTINUED)

1	PT: Hello.
2	TH: Hello Nathan. How are you?
3	PT: I'm fine.
4	TH: Ready for us to take the tube out? Get some solid food in you?
5	PT: That won't be necessary. God is with me.
6	TH: Really?
7	PT: Yes. He is with me all the time now.
8	TH: And he's talking to you still?
9	PT: That's right.
10	TH: And what does he say?
11	PT: He wants you. You and your friends.
12	TH: Really?
13	PT: Oh yes. That's what he said. Marsh and his friends. Let me take you to him
14	doctor.
15	TH: I don't think so. I don't think in your condition you can even stand.
16	PT: I would manage. I've been thinking about this. The bed rail detaches. It would
17	be a simple matter. A handful of good solid blows. Four at most. Perhaps five
18	Six to be sure.
19	[PAUSE]
20	TH: You know Nathan I looked at Dr. Cutler's transcripts - the sessions you had
21	while I was gone? You didn't talk this way to him.
22	PT: Of course not. He is blind. He does not see the way you do. He does not kno
23	what you know. You have been to the edge of the infinite and he is bound to
24	this reality.
25	[PAUSE]
26	PT: I can take you further, if you let me. I can take you all the way to God.
27	[PAUSE]
28	PT: Set me free, Dr. Marsh. Let me ease your pain.
29	[PAUSE]

NSCRIPTION ...
TRIC
Y / DANNY
S MARSH

GE DETECT/ENG
E THRESHOLD:

KRIEGMOOR
PSYCHIATRIC INSTITUTE

TO: c_marsh@kriegmoor-psychiatric.org

FROM: claire_morris@kriegmoor-psychiatric.org

DATE: 2-09-05

RE: RECENT SESSION TRANSCRIPTS

In reviewing your work earlier this morning doctor I couldn't help but
notice a certain passivity in your manner, particularly during sessions
with some of the treatment-resistant patients. After events of the
last few weeks, this is of course understandable. Aggressive treatment
protocols, confrontational question and answer sessions are difficult
under the best of circumstances. I just want to say if you're feeling at
all that you came back too soon, you should feel free to take more time
as needed: we want you here, of course, but we want you here at full
strength.

- Claire

NTINUED

eady Dr. M

tute.
sign, Dann
plan to d
...
y I have l
ou do.
k
W
t.
las
angr
rive
ong.
t to si

have a comp
l right.
he maintena
What's the m
Well just look

revi

MEDLOG 1.2

MEDLOG AUTOMATED TRANSCRIPTION SERVICES
SESSION INFORMATION

CLIENT: KRIEGMOOR PSYCHIATRIC
PATIENT (PT): RONA BIDDERLEE
THERAPIST (TH): DR. CHARLES MARSH
DATE OF SESSION: 2/09/05
SYSTEM PARAMETERS: LANGUAGE DETECT/ENGLISH LINE RETURN DELAY/8 SECONDS
SILENCE THRESHOLD: -5.4 DB FILE FORMAT: MS WORD

SESSION TEXT (CONTINUED)

1 PT: well I'm certain of that. Hearing voices - what do you take me for, doctor? I cer-
       tainly would have let you know if I was hearing voices.
2 TH: I'm sorry.
3 PT: Because I'm not a crazy woman you know. Do I look like a crazy woman? Of
       course not. I take a great deal of pride in my appearance doctor.
4 TH: Yes I know you do.
5 PT: I may be eighty-seven years old but you know I can keep up with people half
       my age. You know I swim twenty laps in the pool each day doctor. You know
       just because a woman is old doesn't mean she's dead.
6
7
8
9
10 TH: Uh...
11 PT: How old are you Dr. Marsh?
12 TH: I'm forty-one.
13 PT: Forty-one. Well. There you have it.
14 TH: Yes.
15 PT: Do you have a bathing suit?
16 TH: Do I what?
17 PT: A bathing suit. We'll have to go swimming sometime. Oh for god's sakes. There
        it is again. That damned shadow.
18
19 [PAUSE]   ...t the Mexicans in with some bleach, Dr. Marsh - shall we? A good

SESSION TEXT (CONTINUED)

1 PT: I really think I'm ready Dr. Marsh.
2 TH: Ready?
3 PT: To leave the Institute.
4 TH: That's a healthy sign, Danny. Maybe later we can talk a little about some of the
5   things you might plan to do when you leave. Where you might live, how you'd
6   support yourself...
7 PT: Oh I have money I have lots of money.
8 [PAUSE]
9 TH: Yes I imagine you do.
10 PT: And I really think I'm ready to leave. I want to leave.
11 TH: Yes. I can tell. Why is that Danny?
12 PT: You know.
13 TH: I'm afraid I don't. Why don't you tell me?
14 [PAUSE]
15 PT: It yelled at me last night, Dr. Marsh.
16 TH: It?
17 PT: Yes. It's very angry Dr. Marsh. It's still very angry.
18 [PAUSE]
19 PT: So will you drive me home? Cincinnati? They built a new interstate. I don't think
20   it'll take too long.
21 [PAUSE]
22 PT: I promise not to sing in the car Dr. Marsh if you'll take me. Please. I really want
23   to go home.

---

after we die.

Cf. Pullman, The Subtle Knife

Malone calls it Shadow!!!

2-09-05   6:12 p.m. Spoke on the phone w/
Mark Dunner editor American Psychiatrist re:
my article. Reaction similar to Lucius's friend
Barbara Rosenfeld of Clinician. Very intrigued.
When I am finished, send it on. Sounded
enthusiastic. And yet...

I detected a note of hesitation in his voice,
I think. Perhaps I am imagining it. I know he
published on Lattimore, on the calculus. Is he
gunshy? Perhaps. We'll see. Another week, another
revision, then I should be finished. Then I will

MEDLOG 1.2

CLIENT: KRIEGMOOR PSYCHIATRIC
PATIENT (PT): RONA BIDDERLEE
THERAPIST (TH): DR. CHARLES MARSH
DATE OF SESSION: 2/10/05
SYSTEM PARAMETERS: LANGUAGE DETECT/ENGLISH LINE RETURN DELAY/3 SECONDS
SILENCE THRESHOLD: -5.4 DB FILE FORMAT: MS WORD

SESSION TEXT (CONTINUED)

1   PT: There you are, Dr. Marsh.
2   TH: Yes, here I am.
3   PT: Hmmm.
4   TH: What is it?
5   PT: I liked you better in the suit.
6   TH: The suit?
7   PT: The suit you were wearing.
8   TH: Mrs. Bidderlee, I haven't worn a suit in a long time.
9   PT: You looked rather like poor Dr. Ferguson, I must say. Very distinguished.
10   [PAUSE]
11   TH: Yes. Poor Dr. Ferguson. Mrs. Bidderlee, last time we were talking about -
12   PT: Before you begin Dr. Marsh...
13   TH: Yes?
14   PT: I have a complaint to make.
15   TH: All right.
16   PT: The maintenance here is atrocious. The cleaning staff. Derelicts. In their duties.
17   TH: What's the matter?
18   PT: Well just look around. This place is filthy.
19   TH: It looks fairly clean to me, Mrs. Bidderlee. But of course we can have someone
20   come by later and -
21   PT: I would prefer now.
22   TH: Mrs. Bidderlee, the cleaning staff doesn't even arrive until -
23   PT: Please Dr. Marsh. The spiders are everywhere.
24   TH: There are no spiders here, Mrs. Bidderlee.
25   PT: Really?
26   TH: Yes. Really.
27   PT: Then how do you explain this?
28   [PAUSE]
29   PT: Spider bites, you see. They must be in the bedding, I shouldn't doubt it's infest-
30   ed with them. I always react poorly to spider bites. You know many of them
31   are quite dangerous and I don't believe at all this nonsense about them killing
32   insects really they are insects why would they kill their own kind.

SESSION TEXT (CONTINUED)

33 [PAUSE]
34 TH: Mrs. Bidderlee - when did this happen?
35 PT: The spider bites?
36 TH: Yes.
37 PT: Oh. Sometime during the night I think. I believe so.
38 TH: While you were sleeping?
39 PT: I expect. Why?
40 TH: How did you sleep last night?
41 PT: Like a log. Like a rock.
42 TH: No problems with the - uh - shadow you were seeing before?
43 PT: The shadow. No. I...
44 [PAUSE]
45 PT: I shouldn't like to think about that right now, Dr. Marsh. I really want this room
46 cleaned. And another shower. I'll want one tonight as well. Perhaps you can
47 see to that for me doctor Marsh. You know I take a great deal of pride in my
48 appearance. And I would like to do something about this rash as well perhaps
49 you can have that Korean fellow come down and take a look at it. I've never
50 seen anything quite like it before have you probably an exotic breed of snow
51 spider unique to this area. I would think.
52 [PAUSE]
53 PT: Dr. Marsh?

2-10-05
2:10 a.m.   What we know: the facts.

Fact #1 - The markings are the same

Fact #2 - The sense of anger is same

Fact #3 - The physical symptoms
associated with the communion
is revelatory of the same coalesced
essence

So... it is Hansen. Again. Still. Why???
Kari is with him. What are his
motives?? Relationship between
Hansen and Rasmussen? Hansen and
Bidderlee? Unlikely, but....

ne wanted - Kari is with him

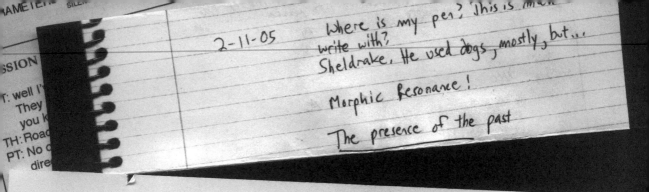

2-11-05   Where is my pen? This is [men?]
           write with?
           Sheldrake. He used dogs, mostly, but...

           Morphic Resonance!

           The presence of the past

KRIEGMOOR
PSYCHIATRIC INSTITUTE

INTERNAL CORRESPONDENCE - NOT FOR EXTERNAL USE OR DISSEMINATION

TO: c_marsh@kriegmoor-psychiatric.org

FROM: don_gilder@kriegmoor-psychiatric.org

DATE: 2/10/05

RE: BID-03

We'll check in on tonight as events and the schedule permit, though off the top of my head I can't recall any prior instances of this patient experiencing interrupted sleep or associated problems.

If I didn't say this before, thanks for the gift certificate, doctor. Totally unnecessary, but much appreciated.

KRIEGMOOR
PSYCHIATRIC INSTITUTE

INTERNAL CORRESPONDENCE - NOT FOR EXTERNAL USE OR DISSEMINATION

TO: c_marsh@kriegmoor-psychiatric.org

FROM: don_gilder@kriegmoor-psychiatric.org

DATE: 2/11/05

RE: BID-03

Well...

You called that one, doctor.

MEDLOG 1.2

MEDLOG AUTOMATED TRANSCRIPTION SERVICES
SESSION INFORMATION

CLIENT: KRIEGMOOR PSYCHIATRIC
PATIENT (PT): RONA BIDDERLEE
THERAPIST (TH): DR. CHARLES MARSH
DATE OF SESSION: 2/11/05
SYSTEM PARAMETERS: LANGUAGE DETECT/ENGLISH LINE RETURN DELAY/3 SECONDS
SILENCE THRESHOLD: -5.4 DB FILE FORMAT: MS WORD

SESSION TEXT (CONTINUED)

1	PT: well I've seen them of course. They're all over the place. Just like the roaches.
2	They may be giant roaches for all I know who knows how big roaches can get
3	you know they can live in space doctor they don't need air.
4	TH: Roaches don't need air.
5	PT: No of course not. They're bugs. They can survive a nuclear attack you know. A
6	direct hit. Why most scientists believe they're likely to outlive us.
7	TH: Really?
8	PT: Oh yes. By us I mean people in general of course not just you and I.
9	[PAUSE]
10	TH: Could we talk a little more about what happened last night, Mrs. Bidderlee?
11	About the shadow?
12	PT: I suppose.
13	TH: You were asleep...
14	PT: Yes.
15	TH: And then...
16	PT: I opened my eyes and I saw it. A black cloud hanging over me.
17	TH: Go on.
18	PT: That's all.
19	TH: Nothing else happened?
20	PT: I didn't sense anything unusual, if that's what you mean.
21	TH: Well...
22	PT: Pictures in my mind things that I'd never seen before in my life places I'd never
23	been. No Mexicans.
24	TH: What?
25	PT: No images of you dressed to the nines giving them what for. Oh Dr. Marsh. My
26	heart fluttered.
27	TH: Excuse me?
28	TH: Mrs. Bidderlee?
29	PT: Please. Call me Rona.
30	[PAUSE]
31	TH: All right. Rona. Now if we could - what are you doing?
32	PT: It's so hot in here. Don't you think.

DLOG 1.2

MEDLOG AUTOMATED TRANSCRIPTION SERVICES
SESSION INFORMATION

CLIENT: KRIEGMOOR PSYCHIATRIC
PATIENT (PT): DARRELL COVEY / DANNY RASMUSSEN
THERAPIST (TH): DR. CHARLES MARSH
DATE OF SESSION: 2/11/05
SYSTEM PARAMETERS: LANGUAGE DETECT/ENGLISH LINE RETURN DELAY/3 SECONDS
SILENCE THRESHOLD: -5.4 DB FILE FORMAT: MS WORD

SESSION TEXT (CONTINUED)

1 PT: well then let me go.
2 TH: Danny. You're not ready –
3 PT: I'm ready. Believe me I'm ready. I want out.
4 [PAUSE]
5 PT: It's either that or my lawyer files the papers.
6 [PAUSE]
7 TH: I've talked with the director, and we don't feel it would be responsible –
8 PT: I think I'm done talking.

CLIENT: KRIEGMOOR ~~PSYCHIATRIC~~
PATIENT (PT): NATHANIEL BARRON
THERAPIST (TH): DR. CHARLES MARSH
DATE OF SESSION: 2/11/05
SYSTEM PARAMETERS: LANGUAGE DETECT/ENGLISH LINE RETURN DELAY/3 SECONDS
SILENCE THRESHOLD: -5.4 DB FILE FORMAT: MS WORD

SESSION TEXT (CONTINUED)

1 TH: Good afternoon Nathan.
2 [PAUSE]
3 TH: Nathan. I know you can hear me.
4 [PAUSE]
5 [PAUSE]
6 TH: Nathan. Are you –
7 PT: Hello Dr. Marsh. I'm ready. Are you ready yet?
8 [PAUSE]

...at a later date to provide more.

2/12/05   4:12 A.M.
  Completed my review of reports received via
Internet investigative service. Hansen was in junior
high Waukesha Wisconsin 1969-1971. A theory suggests
itself: suppose the young Hansen had a girlfriend. Suppose
the girlfriend was enamored of Danny Rasmussen. Perhaps
she was always comparing him — Hansen — to Rasmussen.
Comparing unfavorably. That would explain his hostility. But
Bidderlee? No apparent connection. Her own history very
colorful: 3 marriages, 3 divorces, 7 children, 2 careers →

2-13-05   4:41 a.m.
  Completed extensive review of all relevant
patient files, examination of possible links
  between my patients and Charles Hansen....
none found. No links.

Why is he haunting them?

What have they done to him?

Unknown. Motive for Hansen's continued
presence at asylum unclear.

He has what he wanted — Kari is with him
now.

Isn't she??

MEDLOG AUTOMATED TRANSCRIPTION SERVICES
SESSION INFORMATION

CLIENT: KRIEGMOOR PSYCHIATRIC
PATIENT (PT): DARRELL COVEY / DANNY RASMUSSEN
THERAPIST (TH): DR. CHARLES MARSH
DATE OF SESSION: 2/13/05
SYSTEM PARAMETERS: LANGUAGE DETECT/ENGLISH LINE RETURN DELAY/8 SEC ONDS
SILENCE THRESHOLD: -5.4 DB FILE FORMAT: MS WORD

SESSION TEXT

1	TH: Hello Danny.
2	PT: Hello Dr. Marsh. It's Sunday.
3	TH: That's right.
4	PT: Why are you here on Sunday?
5	TH: Well you're leaving tomorrow. I'm not sure I'll have time to say goodbye then,
6	so I thought...
7	PT: Oh. Well that was nice. Goodbye Dr. Marsh.
8	TH: Goodbye Danny. Good luck.
9	PT: Thank you.
10	TH: Oh Danny - before I forget?
11	PT: Yes.
12	TH: I was going over transcripts of some of our sessions. I wasn't sure but ah - did
13	you know a patient here named Kari Hansen?
14	PT: Ummm..I don't think so.
15	TH: This is her picture.
16	PT: Nope. Never saw her.
17	TH: Never ran into her at all?
18	PT: No.
19	TH: Had a fight with her, or exchanged words, or -
	PT: No. What does this have to do with my transcripts?

MEDLOG 1.2

MEDLOG AUTOMATED TRANSCRIPTION SERVICES
SESSION INFORMATION

CLIENT: KRIEGMOOR PSYCHIATRIC
PATIENT (PT): RIONA BIDDERLEE
THERAPIST (TH): DR. CHARLES MARSH
DATE OF SESSION: 2/13/05
SYSTEM PARAMETERS: LANGUAGE DETECT/ENGLISH LINE RETURN DELAY/8 S
SILENCE THRESHOLD: -5.4 DB FILE FORMAT

MEDLOG AUTOMATED TRANSCRIPTION SERVICES
SESSION INFORMATION

CLIENT: KRIEGMOOR PSYCHIATRIC
PATIENT (PT): RIONA BIDDERLEE
THERAPIST (TH): DR. CHARLES MARSH
DATE OF SESSION: 2/13/05
SYSTEM PARAMETERS: LANGUAGE DETECT/ENGLISH LINE RETURN DELAY/3 SE
SILENCE THRESHOLD: -5.4 DB FILE FORMAT: MS WORD ONDS

SESSION TEXT (CONTINUED)

1 TH: A young girl. Early twenties -
2 PT: Oh no. Most definitely not. Early twenties, no. I don't associate with any of
3 them for one thing older women are a lot more - how shall I say it? - matur
4 Substantive. The girls today... well I don't know how to put it tactfully so I w
5 say anything at all mother always said best to remain quiet if you can't find
6 nice word.
7 TH: I understand.
8 PT: Whores.
9 [PAUSE]
10 TH: Goodbye Mrs. Bidderlee.
11 PT: Oh Dr. Marsh?
12 TH: Yes?
13 PT: I hope you stopping by today is not in lieu of our regular session tomorrow.
14 TH: No. I'll be here at eleven, same as always.
15 PT: Good. I'm looking forward to it. Because...ah. You know, tomorrow is a speci
16 day.
17 TH: Your birthday?
18 PT: No, no.
19 TH: Then...
20 PT: Dr. Marsh. I'm surprised. Disappointed. You don't know what tomorrow is?
21 TH: Well. It's February - ah. Valentine's Day.
22 PT: That's right doctor. Valentine's Day.
23 [PAUSE]
24 PT: I'll see you tomorrow, Dr. Marsh
25 [PAUSE]

KRIEGMOOR
PSYCHIATRIC INSTITUTE

KRIEGMOOR
PSYCHIATRIC INSTITUTE

Red Cliff Parkway
Bayfield, WI 48544

This is Dr. Charles Marsh. It is 2:14 a.m. February 14, 2005. I am at the bedside of patient BID-03 who has recently displayed symptoms - nocturnal hallucinations, visions of an amorphous shadow - remarkably similar to that experienced by previous patients HA-09 and HE-31. I am whispering so I hope the tape machine picks up my voice. I believe this shadow may be in fact the coalesced essence of HA-09.

Note to self: reconsider use of the word ghost. Carries much baggage, but...

2:41 a.m. Decision. Write as such, leave to editor's discretion.

2:45 a.m. I have brought a Valentine's day card for Kari. If there has been a misunderstanding...on the other hand, or rather I should say in the other hand, I have the modified degausser so no matter how this goes...

Whoops. One moment.

I'd better plug it in.

It is 4:14 a.m. Still sitting at Mrs. Bidderlee's bedside.

Note to self: remove name designation from final transcript. Always refer to patients by codes - good habit to get into for final article. Names will not be allowed. Review previous papers, make sure this is the case.

4:30 a.m. I have come a long way, I realize, in the few months that I have been at Kriegmoor. The thrill of discovery once more after my errors with the calculus...science is a wonderful thing. A forgiving discipline. I feel at home within its strictures once more. At last, the past is behind me.

It is 6:30 a.m. I may have dozed. I do not sense anything unusual in the room. Of course I could not bring my instruments so I may be missing something but - Shit. Dr. Marsh? Mrs. Bidderlee. What happened to your suit? Shh.

Go back to sleep. I'm sorry I was just oh is that for me that card? well yes I oh oh it's my dream come true Dr. Marsh my dream come true Kari who's Kari mmmffffff

MEDLOG 1.2

MEDLOG AUTOMATED TRANSCRIPTION SERVICES
SESSION INFORMATION

CLIENT: KRIEGMOOR PSYCHIATRIC
OTHER (O): MR. ANTHONY BIDDERLEE IN RE: PATIENT BID-O3
THERAPIST (TH): DR. CHARLES MARSH
DATE OF SESSION: 2/14/05

...ANCE DETECT/ENGLISH LINE RETURN DELAY/3 SECONDS
...DB FILE FORMAT: MS WORD

KRIEGMOOR
PSYCHIATRIC INSTITUTE

Red Cliff Parkway
Bayfield, WI 18544

MEDICAL WA

INCIDENT REPORT

DATE OF INCIDENT: 2/14/05
DATE OF REPORT: 2/14/05
REPORTING PHYSICIAN: G. YANAGISAWA
PATIENT: RONA BIDDERLEE

Details of Incident: Mrs. Bidderlee was found comatose in her bed 7:25 a.m. by Nurse Francisco. She was rushed to medical ward; examination reveals episode of severe oxygen deprivation/respiratory difficulties occurred sometime early a.m., resulting in cessation of upper brain functions. EEG is flat.

Treatment: None possible.

Commentary: Patient is in remarkably good health for a woman her age. Vital organs show minimal deterioration. Recommendation: obtain next-of-kin signature for possible organ harvest.

G. Yanagisawa 2/14/05

SION INFORMATIC

ENT: KRIEGMOOR PSYCHIATRIC
HER (O): MR. ANTHONY BIDDERLEE IN RE: PATIENT BID-03
RAPIST (TH): DR. CHARLES MARSH
E OF SESSION: 2/14/05
STEM PARAMETERS: LANGUAGE DETECT/ENGLISH LINE RETURN DELAY/8 SECONDS
SILENCE THRESHOLD: -5.4 DB FILE FORMAT: MS WORD

SESSION TEXT (CONTINUED)

TH: I know this is all very upsetting.

O: I just don't understand what happened. She's never had any problems like this before, doctor.

TH: I know that.

O: Healthy as a horse her whole life. And now...

[PAUSE]

O: Oh god this is terrible. This is all so terrible.

TH: I agree. It should never have happened.

[PAUSE]

TH: Can I ask you something Mr. Bidderlee?

O: Of course.

TH: The night before last - the first night your mother had breathing difficulties - I was asking her about what triggered those difficulties and she said -

O: Oh the giant roach.

TH: Well, she also used the word shadow.

O: Yes, well, she used a lot of words. As I'm sure you noticed.

TH: She seemed to imply that she'd had a dream of some sort that night. She didn't seem comfortable talking to me about it.

O: Ah.

TH: You don't sound surprised about that.

O: No.

TH: Why not?

O: She told me about the dream.

TH: Really?

O: Yes, and uh - well, to be frank doctor, she was embarrassed.

TH: Why?

O: It was a dream about you.

TH: Go on.

O: Uh. Forgive me for saying this doctor but my mother's dreams don't really seem very important right now.

TH: Oh I wouldn't say that. They may turn out to be very important. You'd be sur-prised at how things turn out - what sort of connections there turn out to be.

SESSION TEXT (CONTINUED)

33 TH: Any details you can provide may prove very helpful. The devil is in the details,
34   as they say.
35 [PAUSE]
36 O: Dr. Marsh?
37 TH: What?
38 O: Are you all right?
39 TH: I'm fine. I suppose I didn't have much sleep last night, but other than that...I'm
40   fine. Go ahead. Any details you can provide.
41 [PAUSE]
42 O: About her dream?
43 TH: Yes.
44 O: Well. Like I said you were in it. You had on a suit. She thought you looked very
45   handsome. Very distinguished.
46 TH: She told me that. That's interesting.
47 O: Why?
48 TH: I haven't worn a suit in...well, a long time.
49 O: Well this was just a dream, obviously. You were a lawyer in the dream.
50 TH: Really?
51 O: Yes. A good lawyer, she said. Very impressive. You sounded very sure of your
52   facts while you were testifying.
53 [PAUSE]
54 O: Hmm. I think she meant to say you were a witness. Lawyers don't testify, do
55   they?
56 [PAUSE]
57 O: Dr. Marsh?
58 [PAUSE]
59 O: Is something the matter?
60 [PAUSE]
61 TH: No. Everything's fine. Just fine. I'm sorry about your mother, Mr. Bidderlee. Very
62   sorry indeed. Goodbye. I'm sure we'll be speaking soon.
63 O: Dr. Marsh!
64 [PAUSE]
65 O: Dr. Marsh. Where are you going?

SPEAKING FOR THE TRUTH: DR. CHARLES MARSH

by Shane Barton

The statue in front of the courthouse bears witness to the old saw: Justice is blind. Everyone is equal under the law. To make certain of that equality, the legislature has recently mandated specific penalties for specific crimes, and taken away discretionary sentencing from individual judges, to eliminate any variations in punishment. Yet in a country where there are hundreds of killings each year, which criminals receive the ultimate punishment has always seemed a matter as much of politics and - to the consternation of many - race. How to eliminate the subjectivity in deciding whether or not to seek the death penalty?

Enter Charles Marsh, M.D., and the Behavioral Predictives Calculus.

Dr. Marsh was hired by Lucius McCormick, director of the Mental Health Board

charge: find a way to quantify the concept known as 'future dangerousness' - a factor the state is legally mandated to use in determining whether or not to apply the death penalty. He came up with the calculus after several months of research, but only recently have prosecutors decided to use it. Exactly what is this test? Marsh smiled when the question was put to him. "It's proprietary information," he told us. "But I can say it's not multiple choice. Prosecutors won't need to depend on gut instinct, or suspect testimony. There are no right or wrong answers, just - tendencies we look for."

"So it's subjective," I put to him.

Marsh shook his head. "No. We deal with objective realities. Psychiatry is a science, and (see TEST OF INTENTIONS, p. A15)

KRIEGMOOR
PSYCHIATRIC INSTITUTE

Red Cliff Parkway
Bayfield, WI 48544

This is Dr. Charles Marsh the time is 11:04 a.m. The phone is ringing,
it has been ringing for some time now. Most likely it is the director
calling, looking for me. Wondering where I am, why I missed sessions
with my last two patients. Dr. Padma came by before; I heard her
outside my office, calling my name. No doubt there re multiple e-mails
in my inbox, people, the same people, other people looking for me as
well. I won't open them; as even the most inexperienced computer user
knows, oftentimes the mere act of opening an e-mail will trigger an
automatic return receipt being sent, letting the sender know his/her
message has been read. In this case, it would also let the director, or
the other doctors know that I am in my office. I do not want that. That
is why the lights are out now. That is why I have locked the door. I
need to think.

11:30 a.m. The problem is, Mrs. Bidderlee's dream. The suit. I often
wore a suit in Austin, when I worked for the Mental Health Board. When
I testified. I did not like testifying; the hostility I often sensed
from the defense attorneys whose clients I spoke out against was
palpable. From the attorneys, and their clients. Unpleasant sensations.
There are implications.

I don't wish to think about this at the moment.

11:42 a.m. Returning to Mrs. Bidderlee's dream. Not a dream, obviously.
An encounter. The vengeance-seeker. What does it want? Why does it
torment some and not others? Why Kari and Jake and Nathan and Danny and
Mrs. Bidderlee? What do these patients have in common? I must examine
the transcripts.

12:14 p.m. Hmmm. Having spread the files out on my desk, I see something
I had previously missed. An immediate, obvious connection between Kari
and Jake and Nathan and Danny and Mrs. Bidderlee, a thing they all
have in common, unrelated to any parent or girlfriend or book or Native
American legend.

Me.

Possibly a coincidence. Possibly not relevant at all. Further review
necessary.

12:38 p.m. Fuck.

ON IN
T: KRI
NT (PT
APIST
OF S
EM PA

SESS

PT

TH
P

T
F
!

MEDLOG AUTOMATE
SESSION INFORMATI

CLIENT: KRIEGMOOR P
PATIENT (PT): MS. ING
THERAPIST (TH): DR.
DATE OF SESSION: 1
SYSTEM PARAMETE

SESSION T

1   O: that j
2   adhe
3   TH: I un
4   O: She
5   TH: Ye
6   O: I'v
7   to
8   TH: V
9   i
10
11 O:
12 TH
13 O:
14 T
15 C
16
17
18
19
20 O: I wa
21   condition.
22 TH: Mrs. Hansen, I don't think my
23   responsible for the deterioration in her con
24 O: Then what is?
25 TH: That's what we're trying to figure out. It may simply be the natural p
26   of her condition.
27 O: But it's only been since you started seeing her that this has happened. Doctor,
28   you'll forgive me for speaking bluntly, but I am a cause and effect person. It's
29   what I do every day of the week with my business. It's what allows me to accu-
30   rately analyze and forecast trends for my customers. And right here, right now,
31   I see a definite cause and effect. You bring up these ridiculous stories again,
32   which my daughter has spent two years trying not to think about, and she gets

---

MEDLOG AUTOMATED TRANSCRIPTION SERVICES
SESSION INFORMATION

CLIENT: KRIEGMOOR PSYCHIATRIC
PATIENT (PT): KARI HANSEN
THERAPIST (TH): DR. CHARLES MARSH
DATE OF SESSION: 9/12/04
SYSTEM PARAMETERS: LANGUAGE DETECT/ENGLISH LINE RETURN DELAY/8 SECONDS
SILENCE THRESHOLD: -5.4 DB FILE FORMAT: MS WORD

SESSION TEXT

1   TH: Hello. Are you Kari?
2   TH: Hi, Kari. I'm Dr. Marsh. Can I come in for a minute?
3   TH: I'm just going to sit down right here, okay? Move this tray out of the way
        so we can talk for a minute...there. I take it you didn't care for the meat loaf.
4   TH: I can have them bring you something else if you want - some toast, maybe
        some soup...
5   TH: No? Okay. Well, I'm sorry to get here so late. I've just - I'm new here at
        Kriegmoor and I've been making rounds all day, saying hi to all the patients
        here and you, unfortunately, are at the end of the list. Normally I'll be coming
        in the morning to talk to you, but tonight I -
6   PT: Oh my god.
7   TH: Kari?
8   PT: There's one now. Right there - can't you see? On the wall. It must have -
        it followed you in. Oh my god. Help me, somebody please, help me!
9   TH: Kari, there's no one here but you and me. Please take it easy. Kari!
10 TH: Nurse!

---

25   11 TH:
26   12 O2: Sometimes I think
27   13 O1: John!
28   14 O2: Well it's true. You go on the Internet you rea   who take out the wrong
29   15   prescribe the wrong drugs, doctors who take out the wrong   mistakes and
30   16   all night working and take drugs themselves and then make
31   17 O1: John! That's enough.
32   18 O2: I don't understand. He was fine up until he came here. Until you started seeing
         him.
     19 O1: John...
     20 O2: Fuck it.
     21 [PAUSE]
     22 O1: I'm so sorry.
     23 TH: That's all right Mrs. Hellinger.
     24 O1: It's just - Jake was very special to John.
     25   don't need to apologize.   have two children from my first marriage but Jake

KRIEGMOOR
PSYCHIATRIC INSTITUTE

Red Cliff Parkway
Bayfield, WI 48544

1:24 p.m. E-mailed apologies to director and Padma, relevant patients, staff. Splitting headache, I said. A migraine. Felt as if my head was going to burst open which it will had to lie down awhile but I'm all right now. Further review of papers reveals where I went wrong, when I went wrong, who I wronged. Facts dictate action, assumption of responsibilities: Barron rescheduled to 2:00 o'clock. But first: fresh coffee in my mug, a ream of paper in the printer, a few last detai~~~~~ to get in order.

KRIEGMO~~~~
PSYCHIATRIC INSTITU~~~

Red Cliff Parkway
Bayfield, WI 48544

Dear Luci~~~

I wish to
you last
you know
Mental
Which d
profou
from t
they
reorg
tapi~~
shou

I a
alu

S:

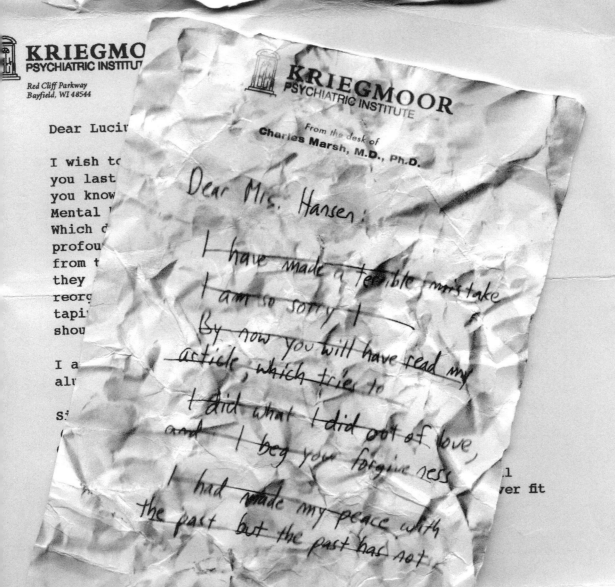

KRIEGMOOR
PSYCHIATRIC INSTITUTE

From the desk of
Charles Marsh, M.D., Ph.D.

Dear Mrs. Hansen:

I have made a terrible mistake

I am so sorry I

By now you will have read my article, which tries to

I did what I did out of love, and I beg your forgiveness

I had made my peace with the past but the past has not

KRIEGMOOR
PSYCHIATRIC INSTITUTE

Red Cliff Parkway
Bayfield, WI 48544

Dear Lucius:

I wish to apologize for my conduct while I was staying with you last month: I was under a lot of stress a lot of strain you know I have not felt entirely right since leaving the Mental health Board. My own mental health, as it were. Which does not invalidate in any way my discoveries, the profoundly revolutionary nature of which will be clear from the enclosed papers. I apologize for the disorder they are now in; recent events have necessitated a radical reorganization of some of these papers. Much ripping, and taping of ripped pieces was involved, as you can see. I should have used glue. Glue is neater.

I am also taking the liberty of enclosing two rolls of aluminum foil. Use them wisely.

Sincerely,

Charles

Charles

P.S. - It's 1:49. I wish I had more time to explain all this. I have so much to tell you. More than I could ever fit into a letter. A whole lot more.

P.P.S. - That's a joke, by the way.

51 PT: I think so. He's down the hall very far away I can barely hear him. He's arguing
52   with someone, I think. He wants more from them. A lot more.

SESSION INFORM...

CLIENT: KRIEGMOOR PSYCHIATRIC
PATIENT (PT): NATHANIEL BARRON
THERAPIST (TH): DR. CHARLES MARSH
DATE OF SESSION: 1/13/05
SYSTEM PARAMETERS: LANGUAGE DETECT/ENGLISH LINE RETU
                   SILENCE THRESHOLD: -5.4 DB FILE FO...

11 TH: Nothing more.
12 PT: Oh I feel a lot more, Dr. Marsh. I feel lot more all the time
13 TH Go on
14 PT: You would have me speak of the God within?
15 TH: The voice within you – yes.
16 PT: I speak to you now, Dr. Marsh. In his name. Set me free. Let me have you. Let
17   me ease your pain as well.
18 TH: I don't think that would be a very smart thing to do now, would it?
19

December 14 2004, 12:3...
Computer is not...
Hence forth...
this...

LATTIMORE
DEA...

John Gutsche, Staff...

At 10:12 a.m., this...
convicted killer...
death by l...
panel of...
th...

...stand how so pri...
...supposed to and...
...is three lat...
...lon. I...
...his veins problem...
...among...

KRIEGMOOR
PSYCHIATRIC INSTITUTE

From the desk of
Charles Marsh, M.D., Ph.D.

Lucius –

I wrote my letter to you and sealed the package and then I sat and thought and realized I may have rushed and it is critically important I get this right, so...

Just to be clear about that joke I mentioned in my letter, it's on me now, whereas before – well, this is perhaps putting it a bit harshly, but before, the joke was on Lattimore, Richard Lattimore, who I am sure you remember and perhaps even think of from time to time,

That, by the way, is not a good sign.

JURY TO LATTIMORE: DROP DEAD

The Gods. Laughable. Not science at all. And y...

The man is a tireless researcher. Unafraid to que... accepted wisdom. Admirable. Of particular interest: evidence he gathered suggesting presenc... of "super-intelligent" life form on Earth thous... of years ago. An alien intelligence. Spec mentio... Wandjina - the mouthless, shapeless creatures wh... haunt aboriginal desert.

Wandjina → Windigo. Coincidence?

6:32 a.m. An awful dream. Nightmare involvi... incident from my own past, a memory I wish to forg... The foreman's face, when verdict in Lattimore trial announced. Grim satisfaction. Job well done.

Fool.

John Gutsche, Staff Reporter - Austin.

At 10:12 a.m. this morning, a jury of his peers sentenced convicted killer Richard Dale Lattimore of Belva Plain to death by lethal injection. The four-man, eight-woman panel deliberated for less than three hours before imposing the ultimate penalty on Lattimore for his crimes. Lattimore, who had been accused of murdering Texas State Trooper Ray Granger after a routine traffic stop, was convicted last Thursday of that crime after only four days of trial proceedings. The penalty phase of the trial subsequently lasted only a single day.

The killer's sister, Wendy Lattimore of East Beulah, began cursing out the jury immediately, and had to be forcefully removed from the courtroom. Lattimore, who has steadfastly maintained his innocence throughout the trail, broke down as Judge Jackson Peck pronounced the jury's verdict.

Also present in the courtroom was the family of Trooper Granger. His widow Natalie praised the job done by Prosecutor Lewis Slyke, and also expressed her gratitude to Dr. Charles Marsh, whose testimony regarding Lattimore's "future dangerousness" - the likelihood that the murderer would kill again - was apparently a key factor in the jury's decision. Marsh relied on a proprietary series of tests he developed for the Texas Mental Health Board (the Behavioral Predictives Calculus) in assessing Richard Lattimore's predilection towards violence.

Lattimore's attorney, Rosemary Sackett, immediately announced plans to appeal, stating again that there was no direct evidence linking her client (see JURY FIXES DEATH PENALTY, p. A15)

now.

hurting me a l...

32

DEATH ROW FIASCO

Killer's Last Words: "I Can't Breathe"

by Denton Odegard
Staff Reporter

AUSTIN – A gruesome scene unfolded last night in the execution chamber at Los Verdes State Penitentiary, when an inadvertent kink in a line of plastic tubing resulted in an excruciatingly painful last few minutes of life for convicted killer Richard Dale Lattimore.

According to Bo Salley, State Supervisor of Executions, the kink prevented the sedative agent intended to render Mr. Lattimore unconscious from reaching his veins in sufficient concentration.

"You have to understand how these executions are supposed to work," Salley said. "There's three drugs: sodium thiopental, pavulon, potassium chloride. They get injected in that order. The first knocks him out, the second paralyzes the diaphragm so he can't breathe, the third gives him a heart attack. Now - what appears to have happened here - is that the first drug failed to do it's job, so that Mr. Lattimore was at least partially aware of what was happening to him while the second was delivered. Which is not at all what is supposed to happen."

The problem became evident only a few seconds into the execution, when the supposedly-paralyzed Lattimore began gasping for air. According to sources who asked to remain anonymous, this particular problem has been noticed before among some death row inmates, and so prison officials were slow to react, and by the time they did, it was too late. The pavulon was in Mr. Lattimore's system, and the damage was done.

Lattimore's obvious distress caused several witness to pale visibly, and one had to be helped from the room, in obvious physical distress of her own.

Natalie Granger, the widow of Lattimore's victim, State Trooper Ray Granger, expressed little remorse over the execution mishap. "I don't think my husband's last few moments on this earth were entirely pleasant ones either. Like the Bible says - as ye reap, so shall ye sow. And I can't help but think Mr. Lattimore got exactly what he deserved."

Warden James Eggers, visibly shaken by what occurred, apologized profusely for the malfunction to all present. "Nobody wanted this to happen. It's a terrible, terrible tragedy, and on behalf of the entire Texas penal system, I apologize to the Lattimore family, and will do everything in my power to help them to put the events of this morning behind them."

I CAN.

It was them. They lived here once. They congregate here; the magnetite is key: the magnetite accelerates the bonding process
and allows them to coalesce. Places of power - this is one right ██
here. The surveys show it. When they brush against me when they
touch me I see pictures in my mind their memories their lives the
things they did this place not as it is now but as it was then
hundreds maybe even thousands of years ago. Some mean us no harm

DATE OF SESSION: 12/8/04

SYSTEM PARAMETERS: LANGUAGE DETECT/ENGLISH LINE RETURN DELIMS SE...
SILENCE THRESHOLD: -5.4 DB FILE FORMAT: MS WORD

SESSION TEXT (CONTINUED)

1 PT: it covered me like a blanket and right away I couldn't breathe.
2 TH: Okay.
3 PT: It was the weirdest most awful feeling not the kind of I can't breathe when
4   you're swimming underwater and you run out of air but like –
5 TH: Easy Karl.
6 PT: It felt like my whole body was just shutting down like all of a sudden my veins
7   were getting thinner and thinner they were too tight to let the blood go through
8   it hurt oh god it hurt so much. And then I couldn't breathe like I was taking in air
9   and gasping but it didn't matter. I still couldn't breathe!
10
11 TH: Did this feel ...
12 PT: I don't know. It's hard to remember.
13 TH: Give yourself a minute.
14 [PAUSE]
15 PT: I don't think so.
16 TH: Why not?
17 PT: The asthma was...I couldn't catch my breath. This was more like - there was no
18   air. I couldn't breath even though I tried and tried.
19 TH: Okay. I understand.
20 TH: Jake why do you think the monster wanted to hurt you?
21 PT: I don't know. It kept saying it was my friend.
22 TH: What exactly did it say?
23 PT: Martian is friends. Martian is friends. Over and over. But it's not my friend. It's
24   hurting me Dr. Marsh.
25 TH: I know.
26 PT: It's hurting me a lot.

Questions in Lattimore Execution

State officials were scrambling for cover yesterday as rumors began to swirl around the capitol regarding last summer's execution of Richard Dale Lattimore. Details remain unclear as of press time, but apparently a key prosecution witness has recanted his identification of Lattimore as the shooter of Trooper Ray Granger. Though no one would go on record as saying so, multiple sources within the district attorney's office confirmed the charges at the heart of the new information. That they prosecuted - and killed - the wrong man.

"It's an unbelievable screw-up. You'll pardon the expression, but heads are definitely going to roll," said one obviously exasperated prosecutor, who blamed an overzealous, inexperienced trial attorney (assistant D.A. Lewis Slyke, who was handling his first capital case) and once more suggested that Texas, as one of the only two states in the union to consider "future dangerousness" as a factor in death penalty cases had to reevaluate their reliance on such criteria.

"It's not science, no matter what anyone says. We just spent two million dollars on a test that was supposed to be foolproof, and look what happened."

Lattimore's sister Wendy, who had steadfastly insisted on her brother's innocence all last year, has already announced plans to sue the state and everyone involved, in particular Mental Health Board officials. "You were wrong, Texas," she declared. "And you are going to pay. Doctor Marsh and his friends (see Lattimore, p. 160)

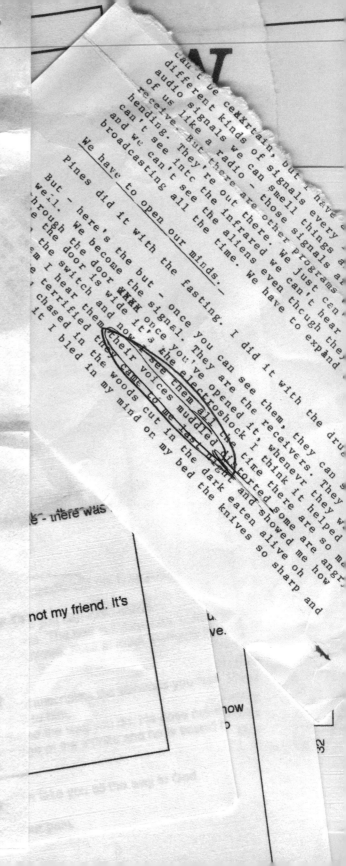

air. I couldn't breath even though I tried and tried. This was m[e]

19
20 TH: Okay. I understand.
21 TH: Jake why do you think the monster wa[n]ted to hurt you?
22 PT: I don't know. It kept saying it was ... [a]s my friend.
23 TH: What exactly did it say?
24 PT: Martian is friends. Martian is friends. Over and over. But it's n[o]
25 hurting me Dr. Marsh.
26 TH: I know.
27 PT: Dr. Marsh?
28 TH: Yes?
29 PT: Are there drugs you can give me? To help me sleep?
30 [PAUSE]
1 TH: Drugs.
2 PT: Yes.
TH: I don't know that drugs are such a good idea, Jake.

MEDLOG TRANSCRIPTION SERVICES
"Partners in Your Business, Partners in Your Patients' Health"
188 University Plaza D[u]luth MN 08953-0989

[T]H: Hello Na[than]
PT: I'm fine.
[T]H: Ready for us to take the tube ou[t ...]e
PT: That won't be necessary. God is with m[e].
[T]H: Really?
PT: Yes. He is with me all the time now.
TH: And he's talking to you still?
PT: That's right.
[T]H: And what does he say?
PT: He wants you. You and your friends.
[T]H: Really?
PT: Oh yes. That's what he said. Marsh and his friends. Let me take you to
doctor.
TH: I don't think so. I don't think in your condition you can even stand.
PT: I would manage. I've been thinking about this. The bed rail detaches. I[t]
be a simple matter. A handful of good solid blows. Four at most. Perha[ps]
Six to be sure.
[PAUSE]

1	O: she has something she wants to say to you doctor. Go ahead mother.
2	PT: Well I really don't think it's my place.
3	O: Of course it's your place. Speak your mind. Isn't that what you always told me
4	speak your mind?
5	PT: Yes but I really don't feel comfortable doing this.
6	O: Mother -
7	PT: I'm sorry dear.
8	O: Mother -
9	TH: Excuse me - Mr. Bidderlee?
10	O: Yes?
11	TH: I'm sorry. I have a very short amount of time to spend with your mother today
12	and I don't think this is the best use of that time.
13	O: Which is exactly the problem.
14	TH: Excuse me?
15	O: You haven't spent more than ten minutes with my mother during any single ses-
16	sion all week. I don't think that's right.
17	TH: Well it is a very busy time here as I'm sure you know, and -
18	O: I understand that to be the case. But what I also know is that I'm paying a
19	good deal of money for specialized treatment here, and I'm not getting it. That
20	doesn't make me happy.
21	TH: Well -
22	O: Frankly doctor, I feel you should have a greater sense of duty to your patients.
23	Responsibility.
24	TH: Responsibility?
25	O: That's what I said.
26	TH: To my patients?
27	O: Yes.
28	[PAUSE]
29	TH: I see.
30	[PAUSE]
31	TH: Perhaps

DR. CHARLES MARSH
KRIEG-SR55479-P44

KRIEGMOOR
PSYCHIATRIC INSTITUTE

Red Cliff Parkway
Bayfield, WI 48544

2:03 p.m. Running a little late. I had intended to clean the office, clear away my papers, but...c'est la vie. I have places to go. People to see.

A little rhyme of my own there. For old times' sake. For Danny.

CLIENT: KRIEGMOOR PSYCHIATRIC
PATIENT (PT): NATHANIEL BARRON
THERAPIST (TH): DR. CHARLES MARSH
DATE OF SESSION: 2/14/05
SYSTEM PARAMETERS: LANGUAGE DETECT/ENGLISH LINE RETURN DELAY/8 SECONDS
SILENCE THRESHOLD: -5.4 DB FILE FORMAT: MS WORD

SESSION TEXT (CONTINUED)

1	TH: Good afternoon Nathan.
2	PT: Dr. Marsh. You're late.
3	TH: Yes I'm sorry. You know why I'm here.
4	PT: Of course.
5	[PAUSE]
6	[PAUSE]
7	PT: Thank you. It feels good to stand. Let me just get the circulation going again
8	[PAUSE]
9	PT: There. Are you ready?
10	TH: I am. Please make it quick.
11	[PAUSE]
12	PT: Quick? Better to get it right than to rush, wouldn't you agree Dr. Marsh?
13	Wouldn't you agree?
14	[UNINTELLIGIBLE]
15	PT: One.
16	[UNINTELLIGIBLE]
17	PT: Two.
18	[UNINTELLIGIBLE]
19	PT: Dr. Marsh?
20	[PAUSE]
21	PT: Dr. Marsh?
22	[PAUSE]
23	[PAUSE]
24	[PAUSE]
25	[PAUSE]
26	[PAUSE]
27	[PAUSE]
28	[PAUSE]
29	[PAUSE]
30	[PAUSE]
31	[PAUSE]
32	[PAUSE]

ACKNOWLEDGMENTS

There are no words that can properly convey my gratitude and appreciation to Emmis Books publisher Richard Hunt for his efforts on behalf of this project. Richard and I share much history—from the food drawer to the flying bag of flour, from the Piggy Park to the eighth dimension, from the silky feel of Lindy's nightgown to the sofa bed on the subway ... and now, this book. I have studied the Oxford English dictionary for several long sleepless nights on end in my office, door locked, lights out, searching for a suitable word or a phrase, but in the end, came up empty. Therefore, I shall draw from the Ojibwe, and say simply:

Migwetch.

The legend of the Windigo is also drawn from the Ojibwe, though I have twisted it somewhat to the needs of this particular story.

With a few additional, obvious exceptions (the material in quotes, photocopies of public domain documents) every other word of this book is fiction.

The Kriegmoor Psychiatric Institute does not exist. There was indeed a Hermit of Hermit Island, but his name was actually Wilson, and he lived a good seventy-five years after the fictitious Pierce in this book.

The industrialist Herman Kriegmoor is similarly modeled on the nineteenth-century industrialist Frederick Prentice, who did indeed build a house of cedar for his wife on Hermit Island that she hated, though as far as I know it never drove her crazy.

The part of Danny Rasmussen was played by Greg O'Brien, to whom I owe thanks for providing pictures not just of his checkered past but of the band Ananda, who stepped forward to become the Paisley Diamonds. To Henry Fisher, Anthony Ianni, and Michael Vigilante, thanks as well.

Those pictures—and the other documents in this book—took on the illusion of reality because of designer Matthew DeRhodes, whose good-natured willingness to revise, rip-up, revise, wait, restart, and revise again cannot be acknowledged too many times.

My gratitude also to everyone at Emmis Books—Howard Cohen, Sarah Crabtree, Amy Fogelson, Jessi Grieser, Jack Heffron (for the eggs, the tip to Wisconsin, and reminders regarding the conventions of the genre), Andrea Kupper, Carie Reeves, Mary Schuetz, Jessica Yerega (no, I don't mind doing that again), and Meg Cannon, who I have deliberately placed out of alphabetical order.

Thanks as well to Tom Kovar and Claudia Rutherford for advice/assistance with forms psychological/psychiatric (all errors of fact and/or fiction are mine), to Bob Mackreth and Jeff Roenicke for help in imagining the Apostles/Hermit Island, to Pete Nelson, Pokemon master, for critical feedback and information regarding bugs and beer, to Leanna and Darnell for the ectoplasm and the encouragement, and to my parents for providing the template for many old forms, old books, and, of course, old me.

I found continual inspiration for this project in the works of H.P. Lovecraft and Del Amitri, both of whom write of the horrors lurking beneath the seemingly placid surface of everyday life.

This one is for Jill, who helped with the editing, the writing, the waking up, the sleeping, and, of course, a lot more. A lot, lot more.

For further information:
http://more.at/dastern